FOUR-CORNER SPREAD

NASH RUNNING BEAR MYSTERY
BOOK FOUR

BAER CHARLTON

MORDANT MEDIA ™©®
A Division of Charlton Productions

Copyright ©2023 Baer Charlton
Four-corner Spread
By Baer Charlton

All rights reserved.

Cover design by Roslyn McFarland, Far Lands Publishing

Sketch artist Kelly Eamon

Rogena Mitchell-Jones, Literary Editor
RMJ Manuscript Service, www.rogenamitchell.com

Published by Mordant Media, Portland, Oregon

ISBN: 978-1-949316-36-0 [paperback]
ISBN: 978-1-949316-37-7 [ebook]

10 9 8 7 6 5 4 3 2 1

CONTENTS

Powder

BODY DUMP

CAPTAIN KANI FORESTER flicked at his turn signal. More than half the time, it worked. And not for the first time, he softly cursed at the reservation bean counters who had him driving a twelve-year-old Explorer. It wasn't even a four-wheel drive. For any investigations up the canyons or out into the sand, he had to catch a ride with a more active trooper or borrow a four-by-four from someone else. The mocking of his compatriots never ended.

He knew it was supposed to be in a playful camaraderie, but the barbs hit him where he was defenseless. In the army, at almost seven feet, they took his nickname from his Scandinavian name for rabbit and the cartoon movie of their youth. His size and ability to finish any bar fight his army buddies got him involved in had cinched the name. The name followed him home.

The old man stood in the middle of the road; his body stiffened into an unnatural shape. His hands jammed hard down into the pockets of his weathered work coat. The elbows turned almost backward into his gaunt ribs. A pale plume of breath hung in the air —caught in the glow of the yellowish headlights of the older Ford Explorer.

With his window down, Thumper coasted the faded tribal police

SUV quietly up next to the man. The brakes only whined the last six feet. "Jesus, Cooter, I almost hit you. Stop acting like a defendant and get out of the street."

The wet, rheumy eyes were more from age than the few tastes of alcohol the man might have taken during his shift at the bar. "Well, hell, Thumper. You didn't." The man's hands had snuck out to his hips.

Kani put the Explorer in reverse. "Well, hell, Cooter. Let me back up here and I'll just try harder this time."

The older man rolled his eyes. "Then you'd have two bodies to explain to the council. And the one would be especially sketchy— explaining it to our wives and all."

Kani closed his eyes and wiped the early morning sleep from his face. "Okay, we'll talk about the mother-daughter team of our perdition later. Why are you out here in the street?" His head vibrated his forehead into a frown. "What body?"

The man waved his hand across the street in a sweeping gesture and pointed into the early morning gray. "Feller came in last night. Said he'd seen a body dumped on the monument. I ran out there when I shut the bar. It's there. I didn't recognize anyone. But I also wasn't going to do something stupid in the night, like checking for a pulse. That's your job."

Kani closed his eyes and slumped in the seat. "Uff da! I need coffee..."

Cooter nodded. "Yup. Breakfast too. How's your fuel?"

"I top it off every morning. The reservation is big."

The old man pointed across the hood of the truck. "I'll just get our supplies." He walked through the headlights to the passenger side. Bending by the side of the road, he lifted a large bag.

He opened the door and slid the bag to the middle between the seats. The bag dropped to the floor with the thump of something heavy. Kani smiled at the dull clinking of metal thermoses.

"Put your seat belt on."

The old man gave him a scowling look. And then slowly reached behind him to grab the seat belt. "Nitpicker."

Kani burped a small laugh. "Scofflaw."

The drive became the usual quiet as each examined their mornings. The two had spent many years riding around or going hunting. Sitting on the side of a small valley, watching the other side, was an excuse for spending time together in the quiet of nature. It wasn't always about throwing meat into the freezer but more about their therapy from the day-to-day of the reservation.

Kani finished the coffee in his cup. Thinking, he swung the empty red plastic cup out to Cooter. Cooter twisted off the top of the thermos and poured more coffee. He placed the cup back into the still outstretched hand. Kani hesitated momentarily, unsure if this was what he wanted—or needed.

The heap of dark clothes was obvious from the parking lot. It could be someone's spilled laundry bag, but he could sense it was something more ominous. Kani studied the early morning sky—not yet bright enough to bring out the tourists, but they would be here soon enough. It's still too early, even for the vultures. But he knew other birds would gather in the distance. He thought about leaving but instead prepared himself for what the morning light might reveal. Kani looked over at the old man. Cooter held his two hands out at the body.

Kani paused twenty steps away from the Explorer and then turned back to its rear hatch. His hand rested at the hatch latch, dreading what he knew he had to do next. He reached for the heavy plastic body bag inside the left side compartment. His fingers traced along the zipper with a sense of heaviness. Wondering again why they sewed in a well-made zipper even when they knew it was only meant for single use. Walking across the gravel, he stepped onto the pinkish-gray concrete. The exhibit building cast a shadow across the entrance. Kani studied the body as he approached. He didn't like the way the right foot twisted in. The left being toe-down to the concrete with the body on its back was also disconcerting.

He stood over the body and pulled his phone out. He took a picture of the body. The left arm reached into Utah. The head and right arm were in Colorado. The left hip and leg were squarely in Arizona, and the rest tried to run away to New Mexico.

Kani looked at the camera app and switched to video mode. Touching the red dot, he began filming as he slowly walked around the body.

"This is Southern Ute Reservation Police Chief Kani Forester. I'm at the Four Corners Monument. They reported the body to a citizen during the night. It is now daylight, and I'm here on the scene. There's no evidence of a struggle. The body appears to be posed. There's no sign of blood, so it is my first supposition to suspect someone killed them elsewhere and then placed the body here." He moved the camera closer to the face. "The deceased appears to be a male in his forties or early fifties. White, with a close-cropped hair and shaved."

He stopped filming and slipped his phone into his pocket. He knelt near the head. Reaching out with his left gloved hand, he felt for a pulse. The head shifted as he felt the neck. Frowning, he applied pressure and stood suddenly as the head rolled away from the body.

He stood silently studying the cut neck. The cut was clean and smooth. The lack of blood was disconcerting and disturbing at the same time.

As he returned to the Explorer, a chill ran down his spine. He tried not to think about the repercussions of a white man getting beheaded on a reservation, but the vivid images of Custer's Last Stand haunted him. He watched the news and followed news feeds and bombastic responses on the internet and social media. None of it sat well with the coffee in his gut. He liked his life and the quiet of the dull, boring desert.

He opened the door. "Cooter, I think I'm going to need your help here." He winced. "Before I call the Bureau of Indian Affairs and the FBI."

1

OUT COLD

"Nash, honey?"

Nash raised the aluminum snow shovel and stabbed it into the end of the tunnel. The tunnel had been the last three days of work. Fill the bathtub with the snow for half an hour, then rest for an hour while the radiant floor heat melts the snow. Then repeat. Meanwhile, at a quarter a game, she owed the man more than just the twenty dollars.

She looked back down the snow tunnel at the man waving the flashlight and the dog dancing on the door tread. "Yeah, Connie?"

"Come back this way a bit."

She squinted as the man turned off his light but pointed with his finger.

Stepping back toward the octogenarian, Nash turned to look at the end of the tunnel and the shovel. The snow was waving in an eerie dance of dark and yellow. And then she felt as much as heard the rumbling of the avalanche... except it was getting louder.

As fast as the yellow glowing snow and shovel turned dark, it was all replaced by the slab of orange metal. And then the large tires with chains. And the undercarriage of the enormous truck growling in the night. More tires and chains. And then open air.

Nash blinked at the missing snow and shovel. There had been no banging or clashing as the snowplow ate the shovel and the ten feet of snow.

She stepped the few steps out into the freedom gone missing in the overnight snowfall four days before. Somewhere in the snow was a black SUV with federal license plates parked in Constantine de' Amor's driveway. She backed it in, and the garage door just cleared the back. Just before the six-inch snowfall, the news had been predicting for the previous seven hours. Nobody ever expected it to dump those six inches every hour for the next seventeen hours.

The elderly man shuffled out through the tunnel as he laughed. "You won't find that shovel again. Ol' Elmer done gobbled it up, and the tiny pieces are all over my roof. But at least Powder can do her business like she wants to." He pointed at the dog squatting in the middle of the street.

Nash rolled her eyes. "I'll go get a bag…"

The man laughed and waved his hand. "Leave it. We can blame it on at least a dozen other dogs in the neighborhood." He looked at the strobing yellow lights on the back of the snowplow a block away. "Heck, if I wasn't such a gentleman, I'd also mark my territory on the side over here."

Nash snorted. "How high up?"

He held up his finger and thumb, separated by a couple of inches. "Enough… for a man in his eighties."

Nash watched the strobing yellow lights veer and then turn right. "How does he know where to plow?"

Constantine pushed on the small of his back. "They follow the power lines."

Nash looked up.

The man laughed. "Nope. They're under your feet. The power, phone, and cable run next to the water. The sewer lines are three feet deeper and over on this side of the street. They have a sensor in the truck. It follows the power line, so the plow is down the middle of the road in case someone parked on the side." He looked at the warm glow coming from the tunnel and the light over his porch. "That's why we all have power, and therefore heat, can cook, and take a shower. It's why most of us bought houses here. We have power and trees, birds, and sky over our heads."

Nash waved at someone a block away. "Jeez. Connie. It's cold out here." She snapped her fingers at Powder to heel.

The man slowly shook his steel gray military flattop. He wiped his hands down his T-shirt and stuck them in his pants. "Says the woman in the Arctic parka." He shivered and shuffled his fuzzy slippers behind her.

"Just ballistic. The Arctic version comes with a hood and is trimmed with fake fur. I'll take Powder's fur instead."

"I'll take jerky and bean soup."

Nash turned around at the door. Her one eye was almost closed. "Now you're just talking dirty."

He smirked and laughed at the commonality the two had found in the last two weeks. The man had grown up on the Pine Ridge Lakota reservation in South Dakota. His mother was Oglala Lakota, and his father was Hopi. They had met at a re-indoctrinating school and ran away together when she became pregnant. Hunting and living from the land was in Constantine's and Nash's cultures, and roadkill wasn't off the table.

As Nash pulled the heavy coat off, the man shuffled to the ringing phone on the counter. "Connie."

"Yeah. She's still here. She wasn't leaving without a helicopter, and they don't fly in bad weather."

"Of course. I was just going to pull out some soup, but biscuits and gravy sounds better. I don't have any eggs left..." He nodded and waved his finger at Nash's coat. "Sure. I'll send her over to come fetch you and the grub. Does she need to bring a shovel? Because the snowplow just took mine."

He smiled at Nash's rolling eyes. "Sure. She's only Paiute, but I think she's Indian enough to find you." He rolled his eyes and rolled his finger in the air—over and over. "Yes, dear. Fourth house down on the left. I'll tell her." He returned the handset to the phone.

"Marie Antonetti." He pointed to the left. "Fourth house down. She says she has the path cleared. I don't doubt it. Her son is next door and an agitated insomniac. He's got Downs Syndrome and was probably shoveling the sidewalks the whole storm. Anyway, she wants your steady arm and help to bring breakfast."

Nash looked at her orange-faced diving watch. "It's only five-ten...? Does she always call this early?"

His chest jumped with his harrumph. "We're old. What do you expect? After sex disappears, then the memory and sleep. I forget what else." He waved his finger toward the door. "Let me make some fresh coffee. I wouldn't be surprised if her son and a few others join in."

Nash looked down at Powder splayed out on the warm cork floor. "Hey girl. We're off for an adventure in the snow. Doesn't that sound fun?" She waved her hand to sweep the dog toward the door with her stage enthusiasm.

Powder rolled over with her back toward Nash and the door and groaned.

Connie harrumphed and turned toward the kitchen. "Army up, Marine. Be an army of one. Marie probably already had her clothes on and was standing by the door when she dialed. You're already ten behind and pushing a demerit with the old schoolmarm."

Nash rumbled at Powder's back. "I'm going. I'm going."

***

"So, what do we do with these ganefs?" The older woman leaned back and scratched Powder's belly.

Nash laughed. "Marie, if I didn't live in Washington D.C., I wouldn't know you just asked about the crooks. Even my wife has used the term ganef a few times, and she is Taiwanese and Irish."

The woman narrowed her one eye and pointed at Nash. "Keep her. She comes with two of the better cookbooks in the world."

Nash chuckled. "If it was her cooking, I would have kicked her to the curb the first morning after. The only thing she knows how to make is reservations. I kind of cook, but I don't bake. And I'm on the road half the time or more. So our hearts are set for maximum fondness, anyway."

Connie glanced at Marie's son Petra and the almond eyes, marking those with Down's syndrome. "And the crooks?"

Nash rolled her head over and smiled at the man. She understood where his focus was. "The local thugs who showed up in the neighborhood, we're still tracing. But the original phone calls came from India and were routed through Canada. My team tracked them down, and Interpol's shutting down their operation. But it's the local angle bringing me up here. Physical contact is almost unheard of."

"So now what?"

Nash turned to Petra. The man hadn't spoken a dozen words in the two weeks Nash had been there. But he was always listening. "Well, my showing up seems to have scared them off…"

He smiled and waved his hand at the snow-darkened window. "Yeah, but you also brought a lot of snow."

Nash smiled with her lips pulled hard over her teeth. "So, I guess the next job is to check in with all the neighbors. Connie says they all should have electricity and heat, but do they have food? Need medicine? Or maybe just to hear your friendly voice?"

Connie raked his fingers through what little hair he had. Spreading his arms, he stretched. "Big job. The police and fire will do it where the rich people live. But I doubt if the governor would call out the National Guard."

Nash thought about the truth of what the man was saying. The meeting just before the snow had brought out mostly a mix of people Nash usually heard lumped together as people of color. Except she knew the colors of the neighborhood ran from Slavic pink to white European, to varying degrees of black, brown, and red.

She rolled to one side and pulled out her phone.

She thumbed open the landing page and then held down the phone icon. Her left hand dropped near the floor and snapped her fingers once. "Come talk to Mama."

Powder was at her side and put her front paws on Nash's legs to look at the phone. The screen cleared to an Asian woman with a soft stubble of hair. The *woof* was soft.

"Good morning, sweet cheeks. How's my best daughter? Are you having fun in the snow? I saw you have a lot."

Nash pulled the phone up. "I dug a tunnel out to the street. This morning I screwed up, and the snowplow took my shovel. But at least we have a narrow street. Connie tells me they won't be back to plow more until they can see the parked cars. I guess chewing up cars and spitting them all over the houses is forbidden. Or at least frowned on. How's the condo?"

"The boys have the sidewalks cleared. God knows where they hid the piles, and the city plowed the street. So if I wanted to get out, it's there. But we can also get supplies in. How about you?"

Nash showed the phone around so her wife could see everyone. "That's what we were just talking about. With the street plowed, we need to reach out to the neighbors. The local thought is this area is not on the priority list... police, fire, or even the kids in the green pickle suits." She smirked an evil smile and side-eye. "Any ideas?"

The table could hear the woman's growl. "Let me get some coffee and make some phone calls."

Nash smiled. Her wife's energy flow was coming back. Today was a good day. "Love ya." The screen turned black. A text bubble from the text message center appeared. She returned the three purple hearts.

Nash looked up. "Wife's up and on it." She stood as she grabbed the coffee carafe. "I need more coffee."

Constantine stood watching Nash. He then turned to Maria wryly, holding up a thin spiral-bound notepad. Maria giggled, and then Petra joined in. "She doesn't know."

Nash turned from the coffeemaker. "Know what?"

Constantine flipped open the notepad. The pages were cross marked into quarters. Marked down the left side of each quarter were initials. Next was the time Connie had talked to them, and then a brief note of anything to notice, such as food, health, or occasion. "Last night, it was Bob and Doreen's forty-seventh anniversary. And Petra..." He nodded at the man. "Is down to his last twenty-four pack of toilet paper." He closed his eyes as he thought. "Which, with his bidet, means he'll run out of paper sometime in July."

"August." He leaned back with his hands fluttering on his chest. "I go to camp for three weeks in June."

Nash leaned against the counter. "Which means you already have this handled."

Marie smiled warmly. "Don't feel bad, dear. We've been doing this since you were still in diapers. We have four parties every year. Then, there are the barbecues. Almost every front door key is the same on this block. Since the eighties, we have made it a habit to talk to everyone else every day. In a way, we're all living together. Just in our own homes. And for some of us, we are here instead of in some institution or group home." She reached over and patted her fifty-year-old son's hand. "And mental health-wise, we all thrive better."

"So the phone scammers?"

Constantine scrunched the left side of his face. "Phone scammers don't stand a chance. But when they showed up on your doorstep, we knew we needed help." He held his hands out. "We just didn't know it came in such a pretty package."

Nash lowered her head and watched him through the tops of her eyes as she growled. "Ease up on the bullshit. I left my boots at the door." She twitched and pulled her phone out of her pocket.

Glancing at the name, she frowned at the time zone difference. "What's up, Muna?"

"Home office wants to know how soon you can wrap up Pennsylvania."

Nash snorted softly. "And big Tony is afraid to call me direct?"

"No. He just mentioned it in passing when we talked an hour ago."

Nash glanced at her watch and counted backward to the San Francisco time zone. "Muna, did you go to bed last night?"

"No time. They need you in the desert."

2

NOT RIGHT NOW

NASH STOOD as she rolled her eyes for the rest of the table. "But I need to work on my tan more. Lying around soaking up the sun is all there is here in sunny Pennsylvania. Even you ought to come on out and work on that pale skin of yours."

Muna squealed in all-nighter intoxication. "Who do you think you're talking to? Alex? Even Mike has a better shade of pink. Besides, I've checked the news. Are you getting around?"

Nash winked at Constantine. "Sure. Connie and I just had some neighbors over for an old-fashioned feed bag. Biscuits, gravy, eggs, bacon, a little salad from the garden, and fresh dandelion tops sprinkled over everything. A regular Ramadan feast."

Muna growled softly. "I'll stick with the eggs and biscuits, thank you very much. NOAA says you're buried seventeen feet deep."

"They lied by three or four… inches. We dug a tunnel out into the street. It's about seven feet tall. Mina could wear her Welch, Wang, and Choo war armor and still not touch."

"Requisition says you checked out a Suburban."

Nash snorted. "Yeah. The snow in the driveway is still hiding the Beltway golf cart. I only dug out the sidewalk."

"So it's not one of the four-wheel-drive units…"

Nash spoofed a mock shock. "D.C. has four-by-fours? When? Do they know how to drive them?"

The small voice tinkled with laughter. "They use them for getting out of the deep bullshit coming from Pennsylvania. How soon can you get to Pueblo?"

"Why Pueblo?"

Muna hummed, and Nash knew she was looking at something on the computer. "Because they have four units with serious snow accessories. One's a Hummer."

"DOD or a civilian wannabe?"

"Can't tell. It just says Hummer."

Nash closed one eye. "What's the serial number start with?"

"Seven three nine November… Oh never mind… It's a golf cart. Says so in the registration number."

Nash laughed. "Sure. I'll take it. November Golf is a National Guard. Good for at least forty-eight miles an hour before it shakes itself to pieces. But why Pueblo over… where am I going?"

"Autopsy is in Pueblo unless they kick it over to here. But you'll be ending up in the Southern Ute Reservation."

Nash laughed. "I hope they aren't still mad about my destroying the Hell Cat on their land."

Muna giggled. "I thought you crashed it on white man's land."

"The sheriff took it because he was close by. But eventually, it got kicked back to tribal. I don't think they got over a few hundred for the scrap heap. You have a contact yet?"

"Yeah. A Captain Kani Forester. Southern Ute Indian Police out of Ignacio, Colorado."

"Okay. Dump the information in my inbox. I'll get it when I can let Washington know if I can put chains on. If the pig even has chains. Meanwhile… get some sleep. And do it before you have thoughts about going down to the shooting range."

"Jeez. You're no fun anymore. Stay safe. I'll talk to you when you thaw out."

Nash thumbed her phone off and slipped it into her pocket.

Petra stood. "I'll go get us some shovels…"

Nash gave him a hard eye. "You do, and you're fired. And don't you dare go near my truck while I'm taking a nap."

"But you just told that person…"

"That I would call when I got around to digging out. Do you see me digging?"

"No."

Nash smiled and pointed at him. "Smart man. Now, excuse me. I need to take my dog for a walk before we take some naps to let this breakfast digest."

Petra had brought over a couple of shovels when he and Maria showed up later for lunch. The fresh loaves of bread had only added to Nash's guilt for not digging out the Suburban. With the third slice smeared with homemade strawberry freezer jam, she had promised to go dig out the backend to check for chains.

The top of the door was less than the height of the tunnel in the snow. But it was only the driver's door. The back half of the truck hid behind the wall of white.

She looked to the front, where Petra was clearing the driveway to the street. Even with another neighbor and his snowblower, the job was becoming an all-afternoon project. But she hadn't promised results to be quick.

Breathily, she leaned the shovel against the wall of snow and pulled her glove off to answer her phone. "Hey princess. How's the gridlock?"

Mina laughed. "I'm looking at three dogs tearing up the snow on the street. Nobody cares about leashes, so the kids are running wild. The husky dog is sweet on the little bulldog. I've seen her run a lot faster than she is right now. And she might let him catch her. How's the deep snow? You sound winded."

"Yeah, this white fluffy stuff isn't so light, but I'm looking at the door to the SUV. But I'm still in the tunnel. Who has a bulldog?"

"I think it's the two guys from the building across the street. It's young and small. I think he would fit under our daughter and still not touch. And you know how puppies have that awkward run and then fall on their face…?"

Nash looked out at the street where the man with the snow blower was blowing the snow up and over into another yard. She turned and walked deeper into the tunnel.

"It sounds like you're near one of those snow-clearing things."

Nash snorted. "Yeah, it belongs to a neighbor. But you must get the snow down to less than four feet for it to work. So we've been digging out the SUV and throwing the snow out into the street. He mows it from there and throws it up and over into the yard across the street. Digging out is a process."

"But you'll have the SUV dug out today?"

Nash glanced back down the tunnel toward the street and the branch off to the truck. "I'm not counting on it. I think today will be an accomplishment if I can figure out if the truck has chains."

"And if it doesn't?"

Nash growled. "The National Guard can come get me."

Mina growled. "I'm working on it. It seems the people in the pleasant state of Pennsylvania don't care how things get done in Washington. Even their senator has an acute case of I don't care."

Nash peeked down the street to see where Powder was. Nash stepped out to get a better line of sight. "I need to get video of this. Our daughter is really an undercover puppy." She adjusted the camera and timed the next shovel full of snow to come flying out of someone's tunnel. Powder stood waiting. The snow flew, and the dog caught a mouthful of snow in midair, like it was an Olympic event.

Nash stopped the video and sent it as a text.

She could hear the moan on the other end. "What?"

Mina laughed. "Where do I get a trophy for something like that?"

Nash laughed. "Right?" She could hear her wife moving around and guessed it was the call box next to the front door. She listened as the fixer in the family called the doorman.

"Clarence. I need a trophy of Powder catching snow like it was a Frisbee."

"How soon?"

"No hurry. Next week is okay."

"We're on it."

Nash was laughing as Mina came back on the phone. "He said he's on it. When are you really coming home?"

Nash growled. "I don't know. Tony mentioned a desert and an Indian reservation to Muna. So now I have her poking me with the same question."

Mina sharply tongued a swear word in Mandarin. "He's just afraid you'll haul his ass back out and give him more knife-probing lessons. I don't care which desert it is. It's all as cold as a well digger's instep right now. Tell them to move the crime scene to the beach in Barbados."

Nash leaned back into the wall of snow. "Yeah. That sounds perfect right now." She noticed the man with the snowblower coming back. "Oops. I've got to shovel. My daughter is standing in the street giving me the stink eye for goldbricking."

"Give my daughter a hug for me."

The phone turned black and then replaced by the text of three purple hearts. Nash sent back a heart, a kiss, and a cartoon dog hugging.

Slipping the phone in her pocket, she grabbed her glove and the shovel. She attacked the wall of white, hiding the back of the black SUV. Carrying the shovelful to the street, she pitched it to the closest snowblower tracks. Heading back for the next shovelful, she glanced down the road. The dog stood ready as she watched where Nash knew there was another tunnel.

Chuckling, Nash turned back to the tunnel. *Powder will sleep the sleep of the dead tonight.*

As the light waned, the tunnel was wide enough to get the back doors open. Petra stood watching Nash process the bags of preparedness the FBI always deemed to fill their units with. Nash looked in the one waterproof bag. She wondered where the SCUBA tank was to go with the mismatched buoyancy compensator, mask, and a single left fin with a broken heel strap. Thinking about all the sets of fins she had used and destroyed—none were ancient enough, or cheap enough, to have a strap.

Dropping the bag behind her, she thought about leaving it. Maybe someone could use the good waterproof bag after they trashed the Korean War-era equipment.

Lifting the floor hatch, she closed one eye and looked with scorn at the tiny donut wheel and tire someone insisted passed for a spare. *Do not drive further than twenty miles or faster than thirty.* Not for the first time, Nash considered putting four of the clown-car tires on a Suburban and put it through the performance drills out at Quantico. She pictured the extra padding armor and helmet she would need.

Glancing at the man patiently watching her, she kicked the bag. "Petra, this bag is waterproof. If you can use it for something, just throw away the junk inside. We have more than enough junk and don't need more."

He picked it up and glanced inside. "I'll ask Mama." He looked up with childlike wonder. "Why did you pack a big bag of junk in the back of your truck?"

Nash stared down at the bag. "Someone cleaned a beach and just forgot to throw the garbage away. It happens."

"Sounds... sounds silly to me."

Nash harrumphed softly. "You're not alone there, champ. You're not alone." She bent into the back of the Suburban and pulled out a heavy cardboard box. The sealing tape was rusting at the edges but was still intact. She examined the box for the sizing dimensions.

Carrying the box to the back tire, she wiped the tire of snow. The chains fit tires two inches shorter and narrower. She thought about the treads. She knew enough about driving and skidding around a skid pad to know she could get going, and even make it all the way home. But the first time she needed to emergency break; it would be all over. She glanced at her watch and then thought about all the snow above her head and on top of the SUV. *Tomorrow would be a better day to start.*

3

GETTING BACK

Nash raised her legs to the level of her desk, and then remembered where she was. Lowering them back to the floor, she looked around the almost empty office. Only two other agents had seen their ways to brave the snow and come to work. One was still in his insulated bib overalls. She figured the young man wasn't going to be in the office long—day or career. The bibs were the trendy mustard ochre of those workers who did dirty manual labor, and the hipsters who didn't know what actual work looked like.

Her father hadn't been an engineer for the railroads, so his bibs weren't striped ones. His were the least expensive farmers and poorly paid workers bought. She remembered the extravagant stacks of bibs in the feed store in the fall around harvest. Her mother would grab four pairs of bibs and pray she wouldn't have to sew in too many patches during the year.

Those on salaries like the division of highways usually wore the yellow ochre bibs. Mostly from the belief of the yellow color increased their visibility. But it was probably the hipsters who gained the advantage. Except, the always new and stiff look was the more visible. And having them dry cleaned was even more offensive.

Nash raised her feet to the top of her desk and continued with Muna.

"Suburban wouldn't budge. Even with the driveway cleared, the passenger-side and top remained welded to the snow." She grabbed her mug of coffee and took a sip. "Until the National Guard came along with their deuce and a half. They had a winch on the front, and we popped the cork out of the snow. Of course, there was still four feet of snow on top of the pig."

Muna giggled. "Yeah, I got the photo. I kept chuckling throughout breakfast. I was at the Cliff House after walking through a soft drizzle and feeling put-upon by the weather. But when it popped up on my phone, I scared Erin as he was pouring my coffee. Now we're all worried about you and severe weather."

Nash raised her one eyebrow. "Yeah? Have you seen the weather report for Pueblo, Colorado? Evidently, there is this thing called the Albuquerque Effect. When the temperature in ABQ dips under fifty, the upper regions of Colorado disappear under snow."

"So now what?"

"I'll milk it for a few days. Clean up the office stuff, and then see how the weather is. I'll reach out later to the Pueblo office and find out what their SUVs are like. But if I need to, I'll fly into Salt Lake and rent what is logical for the weather. Do you have any updates on the body?"

Muna looked at one of her other monitors. "It says they left Pueblo last night and should get delivered here later this morning. Someone got fancy. They are coming in chill boxes via FedUp."

Nash's eyebrows rose in honest surprise. "Wow, not just standard air freight. But I thought there was just a single body...?"

Muna turned, looked at the monitor, and shrugged. "Curious. But yes, it says multiple. More of a mystery than we thought."

Nash put her feet on the floor as the deputy director entered the bullpen. "Maybe I'll be flying to SFO instead of STL."

"Don't tease me with that."

Nash snorted. "Oil your guns, girl. I haven't had any range time for three weeks. I need to pound the hand before it turns into some kind of desk jockey putty. Big T is here. Gotta go."

"Say hi to the deputy director for me." She waved as the connection dissolved.

"That sounded like Muna."

Nash looked up at the deputy director. "Yes. It's drizzling out there."

His eyes closed as his face feigned rapture. "Ahh, to only be shoveling rain…" His eyes opened as he leaned against the next desk. "Any updates on your body in Colorado?"

Nash raised an eyebrow. "So all the updates on my cases now go through her instead of you?"

He harrumphed. "Yeah, like I'm in control?"

They held each other's stare, with the truth hovering between them.

Nash cleared her throat. "There seems to be a bit of confusion about whether it was one body or more. Pueblo, Colorado shipped something out last night and San Francisco is expecting it this afternoon. I'll let you know when I hear and know where I'm going."

The deputy director nodded slowly in resolve and then started looking around. Nash chuckled. "Snow. The minute I pulled the tactical coat on, she ran to the window, took one look, and ran to the bedroom and snuggled under the covers with her other mother. I think I ended up with a weather wuss for a daughter. At least with snow."

"And if you have to go to Colorado?"

"She'll change her mind when I put the tactical harness on her. She knows if there's an airplane involved, there are bound to be treats."

He looked around the empty office as he stood to leave. "Hmm, I wish all the agents were so treat driven."

Nash rolled her eyes to the left. "And then we would all be wasting away waifs blowing in the strong breeze of the world. Offer the treats and see if there are any takers. Not all of us are bound by duty."

He patted her shoulder as he passed. "Trust me. I'm grateful for those of you who recognize duty and persevere in its pursuit."

Nash grumbled mutely. "Pay bumps work wonders where the talk is but whispers of the wind." She watched him turn into his office and the door shut. "Hind wind at that."

She turned and closed out her official log and opened her personal account. First check was the nanny cam in her living room. She groaned at the image of her wife and daughter snuggled under a blanket, watching something on the TV. I should have been more of a weather wuss myself instead of calling the Uber with the big four-by-four truck.

She checked the weather in Pueblo, Colorado, and shuddered. The little clouds were nothing. It was all the snowflakes surrounding the clouds for the next three days. She clicked on one of her favorites. It looked like the drizzle continued until the evening and then cleared for the next five days. Nash smiled. She captured the report and enlarged it to a full page and printed it out.

Pulling out her phone, she thumbed through the important numbers and pushed the green icon.

"This is Rick..." His voice stuttered and he must have just looked at his screen. "Oh, good morning, super-agent."

"Hello, Magic Rick."

"Where are we going to?"

Nash thought a second. "Let's start with D.C. to SFO tomorrow."

She could hear his clicking and humming. "Well, I have James in the air at eight forty in the evening. You'll get in just in time for some late chow mein in the south city. Is it just you and the wonder dog?"

"If I can drag her out through the snow."

"Hmm... says here the snow stopped an hour ago. Are you in a basement or a bomb shelter?"

Nash snorted. "Might as well be. Headquarters." She stood and looked out the window. "Yup. Clear air. And we're clear for tomorrow?"

"NOAA says you're good until Thursday night."

"As long as Noah and Moses are on the same page, let's get us out of here. The wife can shove people around on the phone just as easily as she can in person. In fact, many prefer the separation."

"Done. I'll send the documents to your phone, and loop James in as well. Have a great flight, and happy hunting."

"Thanks Rick. As always, you're the best."

"That's what my husband says. Tata for now." Her phone clinked and went dead.

Nash laid her phone on the desk and shuffled through the thin stack of paperwork with her left hand. Her right hand dropped to pet the fur that wasn't there. Glancing down, she remembered and thought about snuggling under a warm blanket, watching some trashy movie on demand.

She shuffled through the papers but wasn't seeing anything. Her mind ran through the condition of her clothes in her go-bag. With a groan, she remembered she had pulled it all apart. The work had stopped there when a certain arm had circled her naked middle, reminding her of the duty of taking the dog for a walk.

The doorman had gladly overseen the walk. They had delivered dinner. And then the three had snuggled under blankets and watched some swashbuckling trashy movie from the fifties. The pile of funky clothes still lay on top of the washer. Waiting for Nash to remember.

The small white square appeared on the upper right of her computer screen. She clicked on the block, and it grew to fill her screen. Muna lay stretched to one side but had her left hand and index finger up. Nash waited.

The photograph looked like a bad photo collage a child had done trying to make a single person out of her whole family except the dog.

"This answered our question about the term of multiple bodies and just one body bag. The guys in Colorado got most of the clothing cut away and then bagged it back up and sent it here on the first flight."

Nash moved her cursor and enlarged the image. "It looks like there's no blood. Is this after the washing?"

"Mike called them. They said someone totally exsanguinated the parts before they got them. The clothes also showed no blood. Oz says it's the most bizarre case he's ever seen."

Nash's mouth pulled back on one side. "Which would explain why I get the case."

"What explains why you get it?"

Nash looked up at the approaching deputy director. She held her hand out toward the computer screen. "Just a simple case of a jigsaw puzzle, sir."

Tony turned and looked at the screen. He reached forward to enlarge the image.

Nash laughed. "Seriously? This monitor isn't even a true flat screen. It got hammered together with rocks and sacrifices to the smoke spirits." She reached over and clicked on the enlargement symbol. The image filled the screen.

Tony frowned. "What is this trying to be?"

Nash leaned in. "This is the body they sent to San Francisco in hopes Mike and Oz can make some kind of heads or tails of it all. No pun intended."

"It looks like they stitched together four different people."

"More like five, from what I can see. We'll see when they type match all the hands and feet to the body parts and head. But just for starters, I'd say this body and leg don't match the head."

He looked at her and then back to the grizzled image. "What makes you so sure?"

She ran her finger along the body and down the leg. "This guy is Japanese. Those full-body tattoos are Yakuza. The head is a white guy."

Tony snorted. "With tattoos these days, how do you know this guy is Japanese Yakuza and not an over-inked millennial?"

Nash rolled her eyes. "Mostly because of the haiku poem running down his spine. It's an old haiku from the north end of Honshu, the main island. A hipster wouldn't know better, and it will say something more like pig carts look half-priced on Tuesday if you wear pink shoes."

Tony rolled his eyes. "Another good reason not to get permanent ink where people can see." He stared at Nash for a moment, and when she didn't respond or add anything, he stood to go. "Don't you need to go refresh your go-bag before you fly?"

She closed her eyes and nodded. "I was just getting ready to leave. I need to call heavy-duty Uber. I'll need him for the airport tomorrow as well."

He ticked his chin up. "Remember to use the company card. What about San Francisco?"

"Muna taxi. I don't see me driving anywhere while I'm there."

"Not even to go see your sister?"

Nash gave him a hard look. "Please don't swear..."

He zipped his lip and left.

She watched him quietly close his office door as she thought about how different she and her sister always were. It was as if they were from two different parents. The side of her thumb worried in her teeth as she chewed. She thought about seeing things and wondered why they had stopped. In Pennsylvania, she had slept with no dreams. They had turned off.

She called up the Uber app and keyed in her needs. Grabbing her heavy tactical coat, she logged out of the system.

4

GO WEST

POWDER HAD SAT on the carpet looking at Nash and the two harnesses with a bored look on her face. She had only looked back at Momma Mina once. But when even Mina was pointing at the work gear, Powder laid down and looked with sad eyes at Nash.

Nash stood and turned to walk out. "Okay. I'll just tell James and Muna you didn't want to come anymore." At the door, she turned back to see Powder had scooted her nose into the heavier tactical harness with the FBI badge and ID. Two clicks of the buckles, and they were off to work.

Nash chuckled as Powder swayed her hips, walking down the jetway with her head held high. She stopped at the plane's door and looked at the flight attendant. Powder had never seen the slender Latina. The woman frowned at the unaccompanied dog in the tactical harness.

Another woman leaned forward from the door to the cockpit. "Oh. Yes. We have a body missing. Can you find James?"

The tiny gray stub of a tail wiggled. The game was on. In a shot, Powder stuck her head in the cockpit. A momentary sniff at the door to the toilet and a fast curve cleared the galley. She raced down the aisle toward the back.

James stepped up behind Nash in the jetway. "How long before she figures out I haven't been on board yet?"

Nash smirked and nodded her head toward the plane door. "You can't hear her, but she only bounced off the back wall. She's already… here." She pointed at the scowling face, showing the tip of one canine tooth. "I don't think she likes it when you cheat."

James swayed around Nash. "Well, it's not like I cheated on purpose." He looked back as he batted his eyelashes behind his Clark Kent's. "I found out they had forgotten to load the treats. And you think your girlfriend is mad now…? Imagine funcle James without treats." His hand dipped into the bag, pulling out a handful of small heart-shaped treats. They disappeared a split second before him, grabbing the fuzzy face and leaning in for a nuzzle and kiss.

He stood and turned to Nash. "Welcome aboard, agent. Nice of you to join my other favorite agent." He pointed at the front row to the right. "Your usual awaits."

Nash smiled at the glass with the double shot of scotch. "And here is to the start of another successful case."

"And I'll have your refill ready when you have completed your task. Only because I can't make you a cake." He turned his hand out toward the seat. In it was a metal coin the size of a poker chip.

As she sat, Nash took the chip and examined it. It stood for thirty years of sobriety. She raised one eyebrow and smiled. She returned it in a handshake. "I am so proud of you and to know you."

"That means a lot coming from you, agent. A lot." He glanced up at the passenger in the doorway, wondering why the aisle was blocked. After all, they were First Class. "Time to go to work." He danced away toward the back as the two women greeted the passengers.

Muna had flashed her ID to allow her past the security checkpoint. Softly bounced on the balls of her feet as she listened to the sounds from the jetway. She whistled a soft tune and was rewarded with the sound of claws on the thin carpet in the echoing tunnel.

She knelt as the gray streak burst from the tunnel. "How's my sister?" She leaned in to snuggle with the wiggling storm.

"If you spoil my daughter, I will never forgive you."

Muna looked up. "The barn door burned down in the tornado years ago."

The two hugged. "Chinese?"

Muna nodded. "I heard about this new place. Supposedly, the old head chef from Sam Wo's opened this when Sam's burned down or something. I don't know, but it's supposed to be authentic."

"In Chinatown?"

Muna ground her head back and forth. "Nope. Westside."

Nash laughed as they got to the car parked in a restricted area with an FBI placard on the dashboard. "Look at you. All local and stuff."

As they got on the freeway, Nash relaxed and hugged Powder as she scratched under the tactical harness. "Learned anything about the jigsaw yet?"

"Oz and Mike worked on blood matching. Nothing does. We have a blond white guy, a Japanese, what appears to be Latino, and maybe a First Nation." She glanced over and reached out for a quick scratch at the fur. "It's a real mixed bag. The shirt was a cheap flannel check from Target or similar. The pants are generic style jeans—no tag. The boot on one leg is a Redwing knock-off, the most common work boot. The Yakuza leg only had the white sock. Again, the cheapest and most common Target sells."

Nash frowned softly. "Not Walmart?"

"Nope. Mike was pretty certain about it. Target. He has the brand names and style numbers and all. One of the most sold socks in middle America."

Nash frowned. "Middle America? Yakuza?"

"Is it stranger than a dead Yakuza body showing up in Colorado?"

"No. And if I'm catching the case, it might be no stranger than the head being from a blond rabbi."

Muna's eyes grew large and showed white around her black irises in mock shock. Her head swiveled to look at Nash. "They have blonds?"

Nash groaned. "I'll take German Jews for a thousand, Alex?"

Muna frowned as she looked for a parking spot. "Alex is Jewish?"

"Alex Trebek, or our Alex?"

"Who's Alex Trebek?"

Nash pointed across the small street. "Park." She unlatched her belt and opened her door as Muna stopped to let her out. Powder looked around for the emergency, but she wouldn't be left behind.

As they walked across the street, a small blue car slowed and put his blinker on to say he would park in the spot. Nash whipped out her badge and ID and flashed it. The blinker stopped, and the California curiosity of the San Francisco hipster rolled down his window. Used to the privilege of being privy to seventeen forms of social information at a finger tap, Nash was nothing more than a walking, talking Siri.

"What's the police action, officer?"

Nash fumed inwardly. She didn't have to step any closer to smell what the man was smoking. Powder at once sat on the trigger. "Do you live here, sir? We're starting a neighborhood sweep of illegal drugs, ghost weapons, and a deviant sex trade of bunny huggers."

The man's eyes grew large as he tried to get his mind around anything after the drugs and a neighborhood sweep. His mouth gathered to a small *O* as he sped off.

Muna pulled up with her window down. "I saw that, agent."

"Did you see any other parking spaces in the last four blocks?"

Muna rolled up her window as she parallel parked in one smooth motion.

In the well-lit stockyard of flying chopsticks, clinking bowls, and conversations in many languages, Muna's chopsticks hovered over the dish of sweet and sour pork.

"Pork. Real pork." Nash's voice was cautionary, but her face was noncommittal.

The chopsticks moved to the General Tso's Chicken. "Just checking." Her eyes ticked a glance at the girl in the middle of the circle booth. Powder had delicately gobbled all the morsels the chefs had brought her. "So not a snow girl. Who would have guessed?"

"I called Uncle. Apparently, he hadn't thought about her spending the first winter almost hugging his little stove. Uncle figured the criminals wouldn't be out in Harkin if the snow flew. So they just stayed in and read or napped. But, in all fairness, growing up there, I never remembered snow any deeper than a foot or two."

Muna ticked her eyes right. "So a weather wuss."

Powder groaned a small whimpering protest and then curled up with her back to those ridiculing the pup. The two women, used to the canine commentary, chuckled, and returned to their dinner.

Nash put down her chopsticks and sipped on her tea as she thought. "Five totally disparate people."

Muna nodded as she chewed slowly on the General Tso Chicken. "Any look like they're female?"

Muna put down her chopsticks and pulled up her napkin. Nash watched the white napkin's starkness over the Iranian skin's blackness. The junior agent stopped patting her lips but stayed partially hidden behind the large flower of white cloth. "What?"

"Nothing really. I was just thinking about all the Arabs I ran into in the sandbox and around the world. But I don't remember any as dark as you and your mother."

The white fluff lowered as she felt safe with the direction of the conversation. "I think one of my great grandparents was a slave from…" She put up her hand. "Excuse me. An indentured house help. But they were from Sudan or Ethiopia. They would look at me today and wonder why I never grew up all the way to their full height. But they were what we refer to as blue-black."

Nash leaned back in the booth and slumped slightly. "Ah." Her eyes drooped.

Muna cocked her head. "And you never wondered about this before…"

Nash shrugged. "Mixing and matching never came up before."

"Which would explain Oz's quiet lately."

Nash raised an eyebrow. "He's the expert in the Body Farm. Has he said anything?"

"Not really. You know how he can get. He's got a large question, and he'll worry it to death until he has answers." She held her hands out and juggled the air. "With this, it's more like a giant jigsaw puzzle, and each piece is a puzzle of its own."

"It's worse. Any posed body is a message to someone. With more than one person, it becomes more about the intended receiver than the sender." Nash held up her hand. "Don't get me wrong, the sender is always important, but in this instance, we need to figure out the message and who it's being sent to."

"And with a large portion being Yakuza?"

"My question is more to the portion of the message. Is it proportional or directional?"

"How can we tell?"

Nash stared out across the restaurant. Her knowledge of the neighborhood was skewed anew—white millennials with high-paying tech jobs. Older residents leaned into the Greek background with infill of a few Asian cultures—but mostly Japanese.

The mixing hadn't come all at once. Some mixing started in the eighteen hundreds but sped up after the earthquake and fire of 1906. The humble stacks of homes lining the southern slopes of the Sunset District became a refuge. Wealthier city dwellers lost their plusher living in the marinas of the Tenderloin, Mission District, and up to Nob Hill snapped up the cheaper homes. One of the main reasons was that the west end was on separate water and sewage lines. The Army at the Presidio of San Francisco barraged the fire line with large packets of dynamite—extinguishing the raging fires.

Thus saving part of Nob Hill and Presidio Heights. But even with the Army's effort, almost a half-million people were displaced.

Nash brought her gaze back to her partner. She was sensitive to their ethnic blending, including a mixed-breed dog. And now, a puzzle mirroring so much of what their world was becoming. "Any guesses yet about the disparate mix of the new puzzle?"

Muna dabbed at her mouth. Laying her napkin on the table, she leaned back into the booth. She pulled her long braid from her back and gently stroked it to the side of her chest. She looked up as the tiniest tip of her tongue danced slowly along her lower lip. "Oz thinks it was a whirling dervish. The flying scimitars buzzed through a contingent of international conventioneers standing in front of an IHOP." She slowly blinked twice.

Nash lowered her eyelids to half-mast. "How clean were the cuts?" She watched for the shift in the smaller woman's body language.

"Mike says a finely honed scimitar or Samurai sword. Scalpel would leave multiple cut marks with stops and starts."

Nash glanced at her orange-faced dive watch. "Speaking of stops and starts... what time are you going downstairs in the morning to punch paper on the range?"

Muna twisted her wrist and looked up with one eye. "In about seven hours..."

Nash shifted, and Powder slid off the bench and stood ready in front of the table.

Muna chuckled. "Off to a more comfortable bed."

5

COUNTING COUP

THE NEW RANGE master glanced up from his paperwork and then looked again.

He frowned at the Hello Kitty pajamas over the O'Neil flip-flops. He was getting used to seeing them, with or without the tactical vest bristling with loaded clips for the agent's various pistols. The bare feet striding silently beneath the leather pants brought his right eyelid down.

The tattered olive-drab T-shirt stated Kill for Sam with a falling-apart depiction of SEALS rowing an inflatable at night. He had only seen the shirt twice before. His head fell, so his nose found his hand to be squeezed. He had learned to stay clear of any wearer of the T-shirt.

He raised his head in the silence. With matching black braids and black eyes, the two agents stood before him, waiting.

Nash's mouth softened on the left side. "Lanes?"

His eyes migrated from his daily dose of Muna to the taller. "What are you shooting?"

In one smooth flow, she pulled her weapon, removed the clip, and pulled the slide open while laying the weapon in front of the unknown range master. "Service issue. I'll need two hundred rounds… please."

He glanced over at his brief list of agents with range privileges. "Agent Bear?" He looked back at a darkening face.

"It's pronounced, Running Bear."

He blinked calmly, twice, as he slid the weapon and the clip back at her. Reaching behind him, he pulled a target off the back credenza. "You haven't qualified in the last month."

She glanced down at the extra-small sniper training target, not much larger than her spread hand. The red center was little more than a thumbprint and meant to represent a human heart at fifty yards.

She collected her weapon and target. "I'll be right back."

She turned right instead of left inside the sound-dampening door to the shooting alleys. She walked to the hundred-foot-long rifle alley and clipped the target onto the trolley. As the target retreated into the bowels of the basement, she slipped the clip into her weapon and pulled the slide to cock the gun.

The trolley was still running as she raised the weapon and took her stance. It was more marine than the FBI. It was more warrior than agent.

The trolley finally stopped at the end of its track between her third and fourth shot. She let the target settle, finished the star, and punched the center with the fifth round.

Slapping the recall button, she slowly withdrew the clip with seven rounds left. She ejected the thirteenth round from the barrel as the trolley stopped.

Collecting the weapon, clip, and lone round, she pulled the target from the clips. Turning, she glanced up at the cameras. She knew the master had watched it all.

She placed the round in the middle of the now missing red center dot.

"I didn't need the sixth round. You can keep it."

He silently pushed the racks of rounds across the counter. He had been a smartass by giving her a target half the size of a qualifying target. She hadn't flinched but shot in the range they created the target for. But while moving, they had erased the center mass. He would never question the barefoot, the T-shirt, or the agent again. He had learned his lesson. The tall Indian woman was everything they had warned him about... and more.

He stood at the large sound-suppressing window, watching the two shooters. There was no talking or coordinating between the two. But the flow of their motions was almost a mirror. Sections of the targets disappeared in tandem. If one started shooting the cross part in the lower right, the other would run their clip, marking the cross and then tearing the corner off fifteen yards away as the clips flowed from counter to empty.

Nash pushed over her racks of upturned and shortened shells. The master pushed back a cleaned, touched-up bluing, and refilled clip. "I believe you only pack it with thirteen instead of fifteen...?"

Nash winced as she slammed home the clip and cocked the one round into the barrel. Powder put her paws up on the counter as Nash holstered her weapon.

Muna rolled her eyes at the suffering face of the young master. "Next to the bottom drawer. The glass container. She gets three treats, or you might have to watch your back the rest of the day."

As they waited for the elevator, Muna leaned to play with Powder's ears. "I'll get him trained for the next time."

Nash sniffed as the door opened, and they stepped in. "He was okay. He just didn't know me. He'll be better tomorrow."

"Yeah. Maybe. But that was still crappy, giving you one of those minidots to qualify with. What the hell was with that kind of attitude, anyway?"

"This is one of my double months. I forgot to get to the Q to qualify on the sniper range. He might not have known the target was for rifles, so I just punched all the checkboxes at the same time. My fault, really... but now he knows. Has he ever given you crap?"

"Didn't know? He's a range master, for gosh sake. He should know the difference between a sixteen-thirty and a sniper's twelve-one-fifty. The first day Loomis was here, I didn't know Fritz had transferred. He told me I couldn't shoot in my PJs. So I came back in full tactical gear with Mike and Oz in their short scrubs and flip-flops. Clarence came down in his running shorts and a tank top with bare feet. Loomis got the point: San Francisco didn't give a rip how they did things in Boston or Austin. We don't look good to shoot; we shoot to look good. I watched him qualify to shoot his second week. So we made some blindfolds out of black cambric cloth. Five of us lined up, pulled on our blindfolds, fumbled at loading our guns, and sent our targets out. Targeting on the sound."

Nash had to sit down. "And he was probably watching the whole thing."

Muna smirked as she shook her braid around her head and back. "Recorded it." She turned to the computer, typed in an access code, and enlarged the video. The Oz barked a start, and all five drained their clips and hit the returns before taking off their masks and sticking them in their left pockets. Loomis comes out, glances at the targets, and asks to see Mike's mask. He pulls a mask out of his right pocket and leaves it with the range master. They made the sacrificial one from three layers of tight weave blackout cloth. The cambric is the loose woven cloth used for the underside of furniture—easy to see through.

Nash smiled. The man would either learn to relax and take a joke or get transferred to somewhere in Alaska. She looked at her Mini version and wondered if Dutch Harbor had an FBI office.

An hour later, at the sound of the elevator, Muna glanced back from her massive computer desk. The wall of forty-inch screens was three wide and two high. Long-running algorithms took most of the upper displays—searches for faces or other searches took days or months scrubbing the internet.

She stood as she glanced at her dive watch. Exactly an hour. The sound of the claws on the granite floor drew a soft smile. Muna noisily pulled open her top side drawer and rattled the lid of the glass candy jar. The gray streak rounding the corner immediately followed the rapid scrabbling of the claws.

Powder slid the last eight feet with her rump as a slide or brake. Muna's legs worked better. Maintenance had polished the floors since the dog had last tried her slide.

The two were still laughing and wiggling as Nash rounded the corner. "Two sisters roughhousing in the office. Treats must have been involved."

The toss of white hair and beard stepped out of the archway from the laboratory. "Ah, you're both in attendance. Fortuitous."

Nash smiled at her favorite instructor. "Good morning, Oz. With the sunshine, I would have thought you would still be out on the water."

His face lit up as he rolled his eyes. "The temptation was great to take her out for a dawn sail. But the air was dead, and I couldn't stand burning fuel if I didn't get a reward. So I settled for avocado toast with a poached egg as I watched the sunrise from the cockpit."

Nash smirked at the predictable man. "And how was the sunrise this morning?"

He closed his eyes as they rolled dramatically. "Meh. It got light. But no color. Speaking of color, are you ready to look at your fresh case?"

She waved her finger to include Muna and Powder. "We just shot and got cleaned up for breakfast..."

His shoulders slumped. "Well... maybe when you have time..."

Nash glanced in askance at Muna. The woman rolled her head, meaning *okay, but make it snappy*. Turning to the older forensic specialist, she smiled. "Maybe a few minutes to get the juices flowing."

Muna rolled her eyes.

Oz smiled broadly as his chest puffed slightly. "Oh, with this one, there were no juices to flow."

THE SUN WAS HIGH OVERHEAD AS THEY PULLED OUT THE chairs. The ocean in the distance had colored to the blue of midday. As Oz had described, the breeze was no more than created by the few starlings dancing in the morning light.

Nash pushed out the seat with its back to the window, and Powder jumped up and circled into her place. Nash's toe hooked on the leg and drew in the chair.

She gave Muna a hard eye. "You could have given me a warning. Cough or kicked the back of my pants or something."

Muna softly smirked as she repeated the phrase both had heard often from the same elder agent and medical expert. "The revealing of a corpse is in the elegance of time and knowledge and must be neither truncated nor accelerated."

"And the tattoos…?"

Muna rolled her eyes. "Well… to be fair, I warned you, the body and one leg were possibly Yakuza."

Nash leaned forward on her crossed arms with a groan. "Should we run away this afternoon and start him fresh in the morning…?"

Muna groaned. "We'll order takeaway Chinese from Fat before midnight. Maybe. But did you catch the teaser about the blue one arm not showing the pigments usually found on a Latino's palms, but rather that of First Nations?"

Nash grimaced her mouth into hard rolls. "I was hoping he had misspoken… but then I remembered how they had found the collection arranged on the Four Corners Monument. Which is buried deep in the Southern Ute Tribe's land."

Muna snorted softly. "By a couple of hundred miles. What are you going to rent this time, a Ferrari Four-by-four?"

"I've been looking at the map. It's a mixed bag between the Pueblo office and Salt Lake City. The city might not have snow capabilities, but what condition is Pueblo? It's going to require some talking to the agents in the hinterlands. And lending out their equipment is something they usually get touchy about."

"What do you want to do about Oz and the Yakuza?"

Powder looked up. Nash turned her head, and the three looked at their favorite waiter.

Nash glanced at her orange dive watch. "Ouch. What part of the grill is your lovely wife using at this hour?"

He swept his hand around at the one other patron. From the dishes, he languished over whatever was on his phone and resisted his departure. "Right now... anything you want. In twenty minutes... it will be lunch or get out."

Nash felt devilish and teased. "Strawberry waffle with extra strawberry compo and two eggs over easy."

"She mixed the berries. It's more straw, blue, and raspberries. And you want the eggs just thrown on top?"

Muna snickered. "I want mine just placed on top. I'm not into egg cruelty."

The waiter wrote. "Two pampered princesses, just how we like 'em, and a western omelet chopped in a bowl. Two large coffees and a large bowl of water." He spun on his heel. "Good to have you back in civilization, Nash."

6

OLD BLOOD

NASH GLANCED BACK along the length of the floating pier. The size of the pier was a real boundary marker between the wealth of Tiburon and a level even few of them could imagine. A capital tee at the end was wide and closer to the length of a football field. The boat rigging was for a few boats at a time, but the depth of the water spoke of a single deep-water yacht.

A pavé of the tiny yellow lights of San Francisco was more of a shaky banana scribble cutting the muddy black night from the chilling reflective water. None of it was warm or comforting.

"And you know this person from where?"

Oz turned. His hands were comfortable in his pants pockets. His cashmere suit draped as if sewn by Armani himself. Oz rarely, if ever, showed any size of his place in the world. Nash had only heard rumors the man had never needed to work and only did so at what interested him. Even for a standard career agent, he could have retired long ago.

"I was young. He was younger. And death was close. I chose between the laws of man and the humanity of God. Neither one of us had any business being where we were. And in the end, it was long and difficult. But lifelong friends rarely come easy." He looked back out to the bay. "At least in my lifetime, it has seemed so." He glanced back. His voice was a whisper. "They're here. Are you hiding any weapons? I need to know now."

"You made me promise."

He nodded. Only his white beard and hair seemed to move in the moonlight. "They will search you."

"And you?"

"Especially."

The skiff was more like a thirty-six-foot power launch or a stripped-down World War II PT boat. Black, silent, and deadly. Nash guessed at either all-electric or heavily muffled engines. Both were as deadly as the other stood for.

The two men stepped from the ends of the boat. There were no tie-up lines. Just business. From both sides, they approached Nash.

Powder's low growl brought a soft snap of fingers and a fingertip to the top of her arched ear.

The taller of the two Asians stopped. "No dogs."

Nash growled neutrally. "Nothing was said about dogs, only about no weapons. I have complied. Where I go, she goes."

The man held her gaze for three heartbeats. "Arms."

They were now on familiar grounds for Nash. Her arms were loose but fully extended and ready if necessary. The man hesitated at her full chest and height.

"Turn around." His accent wasn't as much Tokyo as it was San Francisco.

She turned. He didn't want to pat her down while staring into her chest. She had chosen white silk instead of her more neutral cotton. His hands were delicate but professional. But he was taking his time with her chest and armpits.

Oz shifted on his cane. "Hiza. I'm the muscle here. She's only the guest."

The man's head snapped at the Japanese word for him to heel like a dog.

A soft ember in the deep dark of the boat flared. Nash recognized the Japanese accent as pure Tokyo, which was easy to follow. "They're all fine. Let them onboard. Time is late."

The man stepped to the side and held out his arm in case they didn't understand.

Nash smirked softly at the man now standing neutralized. She glanced down. "Hiza." Powder responded to her finger at her thigh. The man twitched at the second time of the command being used in his language.

Oz and Nash settled into comfortable armchairs as the boat silently surged from the dock. The guards were like mist and dissolved into the dark.

The discrete lights of Tiburon retreated as the boat swung out into the middle of the bay. With a last surge, the vessel rose on hydrofoil legs, and the silence was almost complete. The ride was smoother, and Nash could only guess at the speed.

She turned toward the moon-reflecting hair and beard. "What do you think?"

The dark swallowed up the shrug. "In situations like this, I try not to. Based on the speed, we're heading somewhere off Treasure Island but not too deep into the south bay. If he's on his ship, the number of other ships waiting off Candlestick Park would be the best camouflage for it. A containership is a containership."

Nash harrumphed softly. "Less obvious than a mega-yacht. But where to hide the swimming pool and drape the sweetmeats?"

"When that is not your business, why waste real estate?" The man could have passed for a fine waiter in any city. The tray in his hand held two drinks. "I believe you like your fifty-year-old scotch without ice?"

Nash hesitated and then realized if they knew her choice of drink, they wouldn't waste good scotch with something as droll as poison. "Thank you." As she took the drink, she smirked. "Can I ask how fast we are going?"

"The bay is exceptionally smooth tonight. My guess would be

around forty or forty-five. But if you really want to know the exact, I'll ask the captain."

Nash sniffed at the scotch. It smelled like they had burglarized her cabinet at home. "Just curious."

He straightened, stepped, and presented the glass of sparkling water to Oz. "West side of the valley, sir. The east has been punky these last few months."

Oz took the glass. "Some tectonic shifts of last year. The west side will now be preferred for a few years."

"We trust your expertise, sir. I'll pass the word." He straightened and shook his left wrist. Looking at the watch, he turned to Nash. "The captain says we are enjoying forty-seven knots, miss."

Nash nodded. "A fortuitous speed."

"Yes, miss." The man dissolved back into the dark of the boat.

Powder was a lighter shadow as she hopped up and curled her backside into the corner of the lounge chair between Nash and Oz. Oz chuckled. Nash tried not to laugh.

"Did you have fun, Powder?"

The dog pumped her front feet as she looked at the movement in the deep shadow.

"Did you find weapons?" The dog danced her feet. "Were there drugs?" She lay down with her head on her crossed front paws.

The young man was back. "Your dog searched our boat?"

Nash drained the last of her scotch before commenting. "Are you asking me or telling me?"

The man cleared his throat. To admit innocence would be to admit a massive slip in security. To insist he knew would be at the risk of being caught lying.

Oz chuckled. "It's okay, Niko. It's the job she does without our knowledge. She is our security." He frowned. "It is Niko, yes?"

The man turned. "Hi. Yes, but if I interpreted her response…"

Nash shifted in her chair. "The weapons were a given. The dance is just too many to count. As for the drugs…? Yes. She found drugs.

But I'm guessing only one or two. And from what I knew of your organization in Japan, there was zero tolerance."

Niko bowed. "Same here. Would she show me where she found drugs?"

Nash shrugged and pushed her lip out. "Sure." She turned to Powder. "Show the nice man where the drugs are, please."

"Just like that?"

Oz chuckled. "Just like that."

Nash added. "You don't need me snooping around your boat. She will sit next to the person with the drugs. If she sits next to a cabinet, just ask her where the drugs are. She'll guide you." She pointed back into the boat's cabin. "Better keep up. She's already on it."

The man looked around and then muttered something in Japanese. Nash and Oz held their chuckling at the young man's expense until after he was gone.

"What do you think?"

Oz sipped on his water. "If you're asking if we'll hear a body being dumped in the bay…? My answer is no. They would not sully the bay where he makes money. My guess would be Nagasaki or Yokohama, wherever he is from. They will use it as a learning experience for his close and working family. They frown on drug abuse of any kind. Even excessive alcohol is not looked kindly on."

"And yet… both are stock in trade."

"Days of running rum are long over. Bars with brothels, on the other hand, are only part of the trade. The world is changing, and those who used to be experts at thuggery are using the internet more than fists and guns these days. Muna is a splendid example. In some viewpoints, she can be a thug or an information trafficker. A saint or a demon."

The small bottle and tiny glassine envelope fell onto Nash's lap.

Powder jumped back into her chair and settled smugly against the back. Nash softly chuckled as she turned to the man. She held up the two packets as a tiny red light shone from his hand.

"It appears our new first mate is struggling with allergies here in America." The light hovered on the small bottle of antihistamines. "The other, we are indebted to your dog."

Nash shook the small clear package of white flakes. "Her name is Powder. The same as black powder, this powder, or powdered sugar. We prefer the sweeter side of her, but when we are shooting, she stays on the other side of the sound wall. It's where the treats are."

She looked up at the looming wall of the container ship. Even in the dark of night, workers with lights on their heads were touching up the paint.

Niko looked up at the men. "Yes. Twenty-four, seven. The sea works to consume the ship, and we work to save it for another day."

"Quality means doing it right when no one is looking."

Niko smiled. "Yes. One would think your Mister Henry Ford had chipped some paint in the middle of the night in his youth." He held his hand out toward the descending gangway. "I believe our dinner awaits."

Oz stood. "Ah, good. It will be a family affair. Can I expect your mother as well?"

Niko shied his head. "Sadly, no. Her sister, Sophia, is in hospice care in Italy. She sent her regards and hopes she can be a guest for breakfast on your boat someday."

"She is welcome anytime. Sadly, I understand your father's position and why we will never have our times again without..." He waved his hand at the wall of the ship.

Niko held his hand toward the two men, helping Nash onto the small deck at the bottom of the gangway. "Who knows? You can talk to him about a few places he is interested in seeing or at least seeing again. How is your Swahili these days?"

Oz raised a brow as he smiled. "Tanzania and Victoria Falls are beautiful this time of year." He pointed at Nash and Powder climbing the stairs. "Her command of Arabic and Farsi would give her a better command of the slave trade language than I ever had. The response to my ordering dinner could result in something edible or being shown the way to the toilets. It was always a crapshoot. Your father was much better at it."

7

OLD EYES, FRESH BLOOD

THE GANGWAY ENDED at a smaller hatch. Nash bent and followed Powder. The dog was sitting in the small metal lobby the size of a child's bedroom. The older gentleman in the greasy white jumpsuit stood, wiping his hands on a large red rag.

Nash glanced down at the beaten, cracked, and slashed leather boots. She wasn't sure why the worker was greeting them, but here he was. The eyes crinkled softly below the toss of white hair.

The English was faultlessly San Francisco. "I'm sorry for this greeting, but time just got away from me." He glanced at the door behind Nash. "I do hope Oz made it up the ramp okay…"

Nash glanced back and saw the hand on the rail. "Right here." He paused and then stepped over the low wall through the hatchway. "Just not used to scampering up a forty-foot gangway anymore." He stuck his hand out. "Eko old friend."

The man held up his greasy hand. "I was playing with a new toy. Sorry, but Niko can entertain you while I clean up. I'll join you for dinner. I'm assuming you brought photos to look at?"

Oz patted the thin leather case. "I brought a pad so we can look at the detail."

Eko pointed at his son. "Niko is the better man for that. I lost track of all the technical stuff decades ago. Even the tattoos are now something else. It's a young person's world, Oz." He indicated his son.

Nash softly cleared her throat.

The older man smiled as his eyes narrowed. "No, Mrs. Running Bear, I did not forget you, nor am I a misogynist. But, as your wife can explain when you visit her parents, there are still protocols of age." He looked behind her. "Niko, please look after them. I'll meet you in the library. It probably has more of the tools you will need to identify the person they have in their possession. I'll be up in about thirty minutes. Grease from a century ago has a stickiness."

Niko bowed and opened a hatchway to their right. "This way, please."

The passageway was anything but nautical. Along the lower walls was rich mahogany wainscotting. The upper granite walls curved into the ceiling. Only the floor was utility carpeted in a deep billiard table green. Nash gently rode her fingers along the stone as she glanced back at the middle-aged Asian.

"A company in Germany uses a proprietary water laser to slice the granite. The stone is thinner than two-hundredths of an inch thick. The company bonds it to a linen backing. Many modern buildings with massive stones in their interiors use this system now. The stone in this hallway doesn't weigh more than a hundred kilograms. Probably two men glued it up and sealed it. It's very affordable, interesting, and sound-absorbing as well. The door on the right, please. Place your hand near the black diamond, and the door will open."

The door slid back to reveal an elevator.

The library would fit any castle, manor, or men's club. Dark-toned wood, fine-cut glass protecting light sources, and the smell of print on old paper and leather. As Nash stood looking at the wall of some of the greatest books ever printed, Niko passed by with the pad already booted.

"Not everything is as it seems. Or is the saying, Don't believe everything you see?" He plugged in the pad as the impressive wall of books silently slid into the ceiling. The large monitor was a single screen more than double Muna's array.

"I know an agent who would fall in lust with this terminal."

Niko glanced back with a smile. "I would give her one, but your government frowns on such gifts." The autopsy photos filled the wall in larger-than-living color.

The arm spread from left to right for over five feet. Niko stepped back as he pulled on a set of gloves. He held out a set to Nash. "You or the good doctor?"

Oz held up his hand. "Those are a young person's game. I still believe in sharpening my own scalpels." He turned and took a seat.

Niko gave Nash a brief lesson on using the gloves. "We adapted them from the technology of the game Wi. You can hold both hands up and spread the view like you do on your phone. Waving right or left will give you the same as swiping. Hold a single hand in the middle of an expanded image, and you can move it around."

He pointed his index finger at the large image of the arm. A small red dot appeared. "This arm isn't one of ours. But there is more here than is showing." Holding the dot on the meat of the forearm, he reached over with his left hand and expanded the image. "This photo was taken..." He looked back at Oz. "Your lab? And you use thirty-seven hundred kelvin lights?"

Oz burped a smile. "Standard lab unless you need the five thousand."

Niko turned back to the desk and ran his hands over the keyboard. "If I adjust the light..."

The arm turned dark, but several tattoos appeared. "Your man has a past to be proud of but has worked hard to hide it."

Oz leaned forward. "What is the light?"

"It's a mix of ultraviolet, xenon, and some filters. I'll send the specs to your email. It's very easy to replicate, but if you have any problems, just reach out. I believe I'm on loan, as it were, until we settle this mystery."

He waved at the large screen until the torso and leg appeared. Bracketing the image with his hands, he turned the image to spread the length of the wall. "This is ours. But how old?" He studied several sections as he zoomed in and out and moved around.

Focusing on the upper torso, he turned the image and spread it until it filled the wall with skin art. A few taps on the keyboard, and most of the tattoos disappeared as new ones became apparent. "He has been here for a while. It's probably the East Coast, but maybe in the Midwest. I will have to study a few more things and reach out."

Reducing the image, he focused on the cut edges. He turned back to Oz with a raised eyebrow.

The older man smiled in a small mew as he tipped his head. "And that is the question. Single blade. Single cut. One movement. If there had been some micro shattering on the spinal column or the pelvis, I would have said something heavy and fast, like a powerful man and a Samurai sword. But... no fractures. No micro-abrasions like you would find from a surgical bone saw. Flat out... I'm stumped. But I can tell you the bodies were power exsanguinated before they were flash frozen."

"And before they were..."

Oz shifted. "I'm not sure. I have never had any reason to drain all the blood from a body, power flush it, and then freeze-dry it. Even at the Body Farm, where we thought of many things, this process wasn't on the list of things to do to humans or animals."

They all turned at the soft sound of a section of the library reducing into the wall. The mechanic wore a soft, red sweater over a button-down shirt. The soft draping slacks, Nash recognized as Armani. The shoes were as much slippers as they were shoes.

"Niko has kept you entertained, I hope."

Niko reached his gloved hand out and grabbed the air. In a motion simulating throwing something, the screen cleared. Eko glanced back at the large, empty screen. "Maybe you can find some early photos of my new toy."

The dutiful son played over the keyboard, and a slow-moving montage appeared. The jungle vines and plants all but obscured the walls and benches. The elder man was bent over a mound of plants and rust, but his face was of an excited child on Christmas day.

Nash squinted. "It looks like an old motorcycle."

The man smiled a similar smile as in the photo. "Not just any motorcycle, but a 1923 messenger motorcycle by the Harley-Davidson motorcycle company. The first Harley-Davidson brought by the United States Army to the Philippines by a young Douglas MacArthur."

Nash watched the series of photos as the vines and foliage were surgically removed to reveal the squat heap of rust. "Is anything salvageable?"

"More than I had even hoped for. The grease and dry section of the islands helped in the preservation. But, alas, there will also be a lot of machining of parts and forming structural frame sections. But the motorcycle exhibit isn't for another three years."

Oz looked smug. "Where's the exhibit being held?"

"Hiroshima. The first one hundred years of motorcycles in Asia. Toda is secretly working on four units dating back to eighteen eighty-seven. Three Japanese and one from China. One was a racer I sold him. A hundred and ten cubic centimeters producing almost eighteen brake horsepower. I'd like to see it get done. But too much would need to be reproduced from original blueprints, yet so much adapted over the years."

Oz laughed. "Adapted…? Like the weird little scooter we stole in Laos?"

"You stole. I was beyond helping with anything."

"Well…" Oz squinted one eye as he sagged his head to one side. "I was tired."

Niko chuckled. "Was that the cart you stole after you carried my father on your shoulders for thirty miles?"

Nash shot a quizzical eye at her old mentor. "I never heard this story."

Oz groaned. "Because it's still classified."

"By whom?"

Oz pointed at his old friend. "Besides, it was kilometers, not miles. And mostly flat walking."

Eko laughed and slid Nash's hand into the crook of his arm. His other hand rose and dropped, describing a jagged terrain of steep mountains. "Yup, extremely flat. But the worst was his bony shoulder digging into the bullet wounds in my stomach." He held his hand out at a door opening at the end of the library.

"Well, at least you're still alive. So I guess I did something right."

Eko softly laughed as he leaned toward Nash's shoulder. "He plugged holes with stalks of rice grass. I haven't looked at a bowl of rice the same way since then. I even swore never to raise my children on rice. Lucky for Niko, his mother is an amazing cook, and we enjoyed a more Mediterranean diet." He glanced back at his son walking with Oz. "Hence, I have an athlete but not a Sumo wrestler."

"May I ask what you were doing in Laos? I'm sure Oz wasn't supposed to be there either."

As they turned into the dining room with a large table and a view of the north San Francisco Bay, the man patted her hand and guided her toward one end of the table. "In those days, the areas bordering Vietnam were more like your wild west in the eighteen-eighties. Anything and everything was being bought and sold. I was there to establish avenues of commerce important to our family. Some involving metal, some with more valuable metal, and of course, as was the day, flesh and drugs."

"But you intimated you're out of the slave trade…"

"I found it repulsive then and even more so today." He pushed her seat in. Holding his hand out toward the seat at the head of the table, he kissed his lips. "Powder?"

Nash looked behind him. Powder was looking at her. "Don't

look at me. It's the man's house... err... ship. He calls the shots as to who sits where."

The dog delicately stepped up into the chair and circled to sit. Eko pushed her chair in as he leaned forward. "I hope you enjoy what the chef has prepared for you. The elk isn't roadkill, but it was roaming free only a few months ago."

Nash glanced at Oz.

Eko smiled. "No, my dear. I fully anticipated my old friend's pescatarian pallet. You, on the other hand, can enjoy surf, turf, or both. We have the elk steaks and golden shrimp from my friends in Louisiana."

8

REACHING OUT

Niko and Nash stood on the prow of the boat. The captain had told them they could have their privacy. He would keep the vessel at a leisurely twenty-eight knots and not up on the hydrofoils. Powder lingered there for a few minutes but then returned to the shelter of the cabin with Oz to get away from the breeze.

Niko glanced back. "She's an amazingly trained dog."

Nash kept her eyes focused on the open water of the bay. "When you were two, you had received more training to do what you do than she has ever received. She does what she does because she wants to. I only ask her to do something for me or try to figure out how to ask. If anyone got any training, it was me."

"But she sniffed out…"

"And if I asked her to find dog treats on the boat, I don't think she would have moved off the seat."

"There aren't any…"

Nash ground her head around. "And you didn't think there were any drugs, either."

The man's eyes turned to tiny pencil lines.

Nash barked a small laugh. "Don't even try the look with me. My wife found out it didn't work on me. It's the Chinese Mother's look for insolent children. A Jewish mother from Queens is next up the scale toward nuclear arms. It's a tougher neighborhood than Brooklyn. As you work your way up the threat level, you finally come to a Paiute mother. Just her look can knock you back into last year."

The man laughed. "So I'm to believe she just knows what you're talking about?"

Nash looked back across the black water. "Anyone on board who has a sweet tooth?" She turned. "Hidden candy?"

"There are a few who might…"

Nash turned toward the rear of the boat. "Do you want to ask her, or should I?"

He held up his hands. "No. I trust you. So drugs and candy?"

"Bombs, dead bodies, skeletons in a river, treats, yeah… there's an entire list. And I don't think we've covered half of what she can do."

"And no training."

"No training. Just an Indian reservation dog who chose the right people."

He snickered. "Like she just wandered in one day and said you're my new people…"

Nash shrugged. "Kind of like. She trained a man called Uncle, and a couple of years later, she trained me. I got her the badge, and we've been a team since then."

"Maybe she can tell you who the body is."

Nash shook her head. "That's not the way it works. But if we get close to who killed them, she'll know. I'm betting on it."

"Them?"

Nash thought for a moment. "Your man is only the torso and one leg. There were two arms, another leg, and a head."

"I wondered at the strange shape. I was hoping for at least the upper arms. That would have told us the family."

Nash squinted as she held her hand out to walk along the deck to the back of the boat. "When you made the crepes, you removed your coat and rolled up your sleeves."

"It's the traditional way. And the apron."

"But you don't have any tattoos…"

He stopped her at the door to the bridge. Opening the door, he ushered her in. Once inside, he removed his coat and handed it to a deckhand. "In here, we operate for night vision. I know with your military background, you're used to the red light. But we mix in some of the ultraviolet and a version of a French light." He rolled up his sleeve. The tattoos glowed a light green, the same as those on the short-sleeved deckhand and pilot. "Different processes of tattooing respond to different lights. We can now go unmarked and still show our credentials when needed. We find it less disturbing to the general public."

The pilot turned his head and muttered softly.

Niko nodded and thanked him. Turning to Nash, he pointed his hand toward the back door.

Nash smiled. "Yes. Five minutes."

As they stepped off the boat, a black car quietly idled on the dock. Two men in suits stood at a casual attention. The driver stood at his open door. Nash recognized the protective angle of the parking and the positions of the men.

She smirked softly. "Please tell me these are yours and not the IRS."

"For us. I can drop you at your car."

Oz growled in a soft, bearish way. "After that meal, I need to walk the hundred yards and more."

Nash turned with raised eyebrows and a twinkle in his eye. "If you prefer, we could always drop you a few miles up the road…"

Oz took a more avuncular tone. "I'll start with the hundred yards. I couldn't carry a half-dead Yakuza a few feet these days. Much less a few miles."

Niko shook his hand. "Good to see you again, sir. It has been too long since I've seen my father having such a fun evening."

"Son, it's always been way too long. But any or all of you are welcome on any barbecue night."

Niko bowed slightly. "Tomorrow, I will arrange a light system and then call. Maybe Thursday night dinner. The fresh fish come on Thursday morning. Do you have any preference as to the fish or crustaceans?"

Oz pursed his lips. "I think I'll leave it up to the expert at the market."

Niko leaned toward Nash and pointed at Powder. "How much of an expert is she at a fish market?"

Nash shook slightly with a chuckle. "I guess we'll find out together. And maybe we can tap into the little electro wizard, Muna. She is an expert at eating halal."

"Thursday. Is nine in the morning too early?"

"We'll be off the shooting range and ready for breakfast by seven if you care to join us for breakfast. I don't think I could get clearance for you on the shooting range."

He held his jacket open. "I'm not a United States citizen. I can't and don't carry a weapon." He shrugged. "I've never shot a gun before. But if we throw playing cards... I sat for my degrees at Oxford after Cambridge. Darts are good, too. I just never acquired a taste for beer."

"Seven for breakfast, it is then. Bring your Cambridge shoes; breakfast is a mile or more away." Nash folded her hand into Oz's elbow and turned him around the car.

The car drove by as the three stood to one side on the dark dock. The taillights flared for a split second and then turned left at the end.

Nash started them walking. "Now. That was an interesting evening." She turned to a glowing Oz. "What exactly were you doing in Laos?"

His grin became toothy. "Your clearance isn't high enough. Mine no longer goes there, either. Let's just call it dastardly deeds in a time of hell. Not our country or those of us who were there in service to the country is proud of the moment or deeds." He glanced back at the bay. "Except for one. Saving lives is always noble. No matter who they are."

———

"THE SHRIMP SOUNDED GOOD." MUNA SLAMMED THE next clip into the pistol. The .380 hardly twitched as the entire clip flowed through the pistol, and the upper right cross disappeared.

Nash slipped a high-capacity clip into her nine-millimeter and dotted the top of each crosshair in each corner. Then came the lower points, followed by left and right, right-left, left-right, and the last right-left, and a quick dot in the center of all four. "We're going to the fish market tomorrow, and you get to choose what fish you want. Nobody trusts my taste in fish."

"You like something other than raw fish?" The tips of the red star disappeared, and then the center. "We need some new targets."

Nash barked a laugh. "Go ask Loomis for some sniper targets and then shift lanes. It's amazing how relaxing the fresh challenge and distance is."

"Cease-fire on the range. Cease-fire on the range. Running Bear and Al-Faragi report to the lab. That is all. Resume firing." The three other lanes returned to their firing as Nash and Muna policed their brass and cleared their alleys.

Mike looked around the corner at the sound of the desk drawers. "Ah good." He pointed at the one screen on Muna's desk. "We got hits on the two hands."

Muna sat as Nash came over and passed on a chair. "What kind of Muskogee Indian name is Roberts?"

"At some time, a white man probably mixed into the family. What kind of first name?"

"Tab."

"Tab Return, or just Tab?"

Muna looked up with a sour face at the pun or joke. "Tab."

"Like Tab Hunter, but I don't think he was Muskogee."

The two looked at Mike. "Who?"

"An old actor from the middle of the last century. I think my mother was in love with him."

Nash looked back at the computer screen. "So, no more formal name?"

Muna enlarged the document. "Nope. Lives in Oklahoma City. Or did. Certified and bonded electrician. The company mostly does new construction of commercial properties."

Muna moved the other ID over to the left screen and enlarged it. "Bosun's mate Gary Webb." She turned. "What's a boatswain?"

"The Navy calls them boats or boson's mate. He's a first mate or chief petty officer. They're the lifeblood of a ship. The boats oversee everything sailorly and assign duties on a ship. What did he do?"

"Says here ship's security."

Nash and Mike looked at each other. "Naval Intelligence. Stationed out of where?"

"Um…" Muna scanned through a large document. "Norfolk. Navy Criminal Investigation."

Mike's lips furled. "So a guy from Oklahoma and a guy from the D.C. area." He looked at Nash. "What about last night?"

"They didn't think west coast. But Niko is bringing you a light for looking at the tattoos. Oh, and we must figure out how to barbecue some fish tomorrow."

Mike rolled his eyes. "What kind of trouble did you and Oz get us into?"

Muna spun in her chair. "Speaking of which, where is the wizard?"

"Sun's out until about three this afternoon."

Nash frowned with one eye closed. "Because of light winds?"

Mike snorted. "Not for Oz. He only goes out when they're twelve knots or more."

Nash rolled her eyes as her stomach felt like a large fish rolling over in the warm waters under the summer sun. She pointed back at the screen. "So we have a Navy detective and an electrician on the wrong reservation. Let's start building a graph and map this. There must be a connection between them and our unknown Yakuza."

Muna stood and pointed at the large surface of six old desks jammed together. Figurines and other toys stood guard under the wall of windows, lighting the polished oak surfaces. "Is that a big enough graph for you?"

Nash winced and looked at Mike with a wink. "You think Thomas the Tanker Truck works for a Yakuza or an electrician…"

Mike rolled his eyes as he turned. "Oh, lord save me. I have work to do. You two work out how you want to run this. I still am trying to figure out how they cut them up."

Muna turned to Nash with wide-faced excitement. "Maybe we need a pirate?"

Nash snorted. "I was thinking guillotine." Her stomach gurgled, and she looked down at Powder, sitting up, looking at the exit. "Yes… and breakfast."

Muna sat back, stroking her thumb and forefinger over her upper lip to her cheeks as she stared at the computer screen.

"What are you thinking?"

"I'm thinking pancakes in Daly City."

Nash stood. "I'm calling shotgun. I got lost the last time I tried to find your dolly place."

Muna leaned over and gave Powder's ears a scratching as she stood. "How many times do I have to explain it all to you? They're called action figures."

Nash hummed as she pulled on her tactical jacket. "Yup. Action figures who never move. Must be a Gen Z thing."

Muna flipped the key fob in the air. "Yeah…" She glanced back at the archway to the lab and dropped her voice as she walked past. "But it was Gen X who invented them. And you millennials who lined your bedroom walls with them."

9

LAYING IT OUT

Niko walked cautiously along the large cluster of desks. Along the top was a photo of the body part. The weight holding its position was a small figurine. He smiled tightly as he picked up the helmeted cartoon character with a strange cylinder for a hand.

Muna slowed as she walked out of the lab. Her squint was only momentary until she saw the small smile. "Memories?"

Niko turned. "It was a brief summer fling. The car accident had left me in a wheelchair. The kid down the hall was obsessed with this game. He taught me the game along with enough deaf sign language for us to talk to his mother when she would visit each night."

"Do you stay in touch?"

Half of his face winced. "Sadly, no. It was my fault. I thought I was being protective of them. But they went back to France, and I'm sure the kid just figured I blew him off as a kid. And when I was a kid, I know I hated the same thing."

Muna bobbed her head gently. "Try being the smallest person in your class, a different color, and a few years younger. At least you two had the connection for the summer while you recovered."

He put the figurine back on the photo of the arm. "At least I got to keep my legs. He wasn't so lucky." He glanced out the window. "Funny. I never thought about Rusty and what he must have been going through that summer." He looked at Muna. "Losing his legs and all. It must have been hard on him. He was about twelve or thirteen, and we were on a ward, mostly filled with older men. The kid should have been out running around with his friends... I can only imagine how it must have changed when he got home and was now in a wheelchair."

Muna rubbed behind her ear with her fingers. "Kids are resilient. Kind of like Electric Man. Get zapped and get back up for the next round."

Niko looked sadly at the photos of the arm, driver's license, and a family photo. "Unless you run out of lives. In the game, you just hit reset and start over... and then, there is reality."

"How did the kid lose his legs? Or did you know?"

Niko turned his head and closed his eyes as he tried to remember. "Something about a wading pool and electrical cable. They took them both off just below the knees. I remember him swinging his phantom legs as he played the game."

"This is when you were in England?"

"Same time. But no, it was summer break, and I was here in San Francisco. It was the same year we had a freighter capsize and sink a few hundred miles off the gate. Strange summer with freakish storms."

They turned at the sound of Nash's boots combined with the more rapid clicking beat of Powder's claws on the granite floor. "What do you think of the layout?"

Niko's neck slightly flushed as he glanced at Muna. "We kind of got distracted by a trip down memory lane." He swung back to the large layout. "Is this so you can see if there is any correlation between the victims?"

"Yes. If these two were, say, both in the Navy, then we would pin them and run a familial connection with, say, a yellow string from person to person. But if they both had business in Colorado, we would run a red line from each of them to the monument in the center. Somehow, they will all have the redline. But we must also figure out the yellow, blue, and black lines."

The man turned slowly in thought. "What are the other colors?"

Nash continued. "Hypothetically, we could use blue if they are in the same business. But I doubt your guy is an electrician or a detective for the Navy. So we're down to black and yellow..."

Muna rested her hands on the table and leaned in. Her tone was serious, but Nash could tell there was a bit of playfulness. "Black is mayhem. Yellow is for magic. And when we need it, green is for..." She looked around with wide, crazed eyes. "Well, green is always for dragons."

One of Niko's eyes slid shut. "Because mayhem was already taken... and there is always the possibility of dragons."

Muna squealed with glee as she clapped her hands. "You knew the line."

The man bowed slightly. "I might be from a different generation and definitely from a different culture, but those books have been around longer than I have."

"I just..."

"Yes. You assumed. But not all books wear the covers you think they should."

The small pennywhistle was soft but shrill. They all turned as Oz smiled and waved them back into the lab. "If you children are finished playing with your dollies..."

Muna leaned toward Niko. "Says the man behind the curtain."

Maintenance had rigged the new light from a movable work-light stand with a long, flexible arm. The light was over the autopsy table. The torso and leg lay on the table.

Oz handed the small controller to Niko. "I thought I'd let you do the honors." He reached behind them and turned off the standard lights.

Niko pushed the first button on the fob. The black light was the same as in every teenager's bedroom. The torso glowed with only a handful of tattoos.

"These are just general tattoos. Let's roll him over. The family crest will be over his heart."

"SIR. THE DIRECTOR IS ON LINE TWO."

The Deputy Director picked up the phone. "Of course he is. Neither one of us should still be here."

"And yet, Tony, here we are."

Tony softly closed his eyes as he pinched his nose at the bridge. "Please tell me you're calling to ask me to go kill a bottle of good scotch at the Blue before we do serious damage to a pair of steaks."

"Hmm… stick a pin in that thought while you explain to me why I have the Ambassador of Japan sitting in my office."

"You both like playing mah-jongg?"

"The game is Chinese and has nothing to do with his unofficial investigation into us holding a Japanese citizen."

Tony fell back into the comfort of his large chair. His eyes were wide, his forehead furrowed. "Did he explain who exactly is holding this person and where?"

The conversation was muted by the man's hand over the lower section of the phone.

"FBI in San Francisco."

Tony leaned his head into his hand as he pinched his nose. He was afraid he knew the answer. "Two divisions working out there. If the main office has taken this person in for questioning, you'll have to call them direct. I've been told enough times not to stick my nose in their backyard. The hard walls of compartmentalization aren't my preferences, but I'm willing to work with them. As for the white sedan towed out of the Castro district last week… it wasn't my people. My agent is a squint attached to the medical forensics lab out there."

"Just a minute. I think it's your people who are holding this man." This time, he didn't bother covering the phone as he asked for a name and details.

Niko bent in. "The house or family is Wakana. They are from the Chiba prefecture outside of Tokyo. An old and honorable family." His finger lightly tapped the upper chest as he switched the lights to the more obscure mix. Glowing in the skin was a finely detailed depiction of Mount Fujiyama that would make a woodblock master artist proud. Niko tapped the image. "This is your man."

The deputy director could hear the other man leaning forward and writing something. He looked at the dark windows and wondered if he would miss dinner. He had missed lunch. Even breakfast had only been a pancake wrapped around three pieces of bacon and his hydroflask full of coffee as he strode to the SUV and driver.

The director looked to one side of his computer and then back. "Sorry, I wanted to get the right pronunciation. The man's name is Fuji, like the mountain. His family name is Wakana. As in the third commander of the Pearl Harbor fleet."

Tony frowned. "American?"

"No. Sorry. The fleet who bombed Pearl. An auspicious family."

Tony glanced at his computer screen. "But no reason given why we would hold this person?"

"None."

Tony opened a dialog box through the interconnect. He thought about which agent and then reached into his pants pocket. He opened the screen and started a text. Sending the text, he turned the phone face down on the desk.

"I just reached out to our special agent who may have some…"

The phone pinged and then rattled softly on the leather writing surface.

Tony turned over the phone. He touched his thumb to the message. The screen filled with the overhead view of a tattooed torso and leg. He had seen mutilation before, but he wasn't sure which was more disturbing, the lack of head and limbs or the profuse tattooing. The former was a mystery, but the latter spoke volumes about the body or the person it had been.

He forwarded the image as he continued with the Director.

"San Francisco confirms they have Mr. Wakana. I'm assuming there are questions the embassy may not answer. I've texted you the photo of what we are dealing with. But I'm guessing the answers will be slow in coming. Can we ask about the nature of the ambassador's concern?"

The soft ping was audible over the phone, and Tony knew the other man was looking at the grisly image. The biggest question would be how much to share with the political envoy.

"Hmm. Sir, we have confirmation your citizen is indeed at our offices in San Francisco. But he's not being held as much as he can leave whenever he wants, but is unable. As you can see in this photo, he's just unable to. Can they share with us why the Japanese diplomatic corps is interceding on behalf of a member of the Yakuza?"

Tony could hear the translation getting heated.

The director moaned softly. "I'll let you go. I think I have a pressing meeting in about thirty minutes at the Blue. If you could make the arrangements?"

"My pleasure, sir. Enjoy your conversation. I look forward to the debrief in a half hour."

He moved his mouse and cursor to a new small picture box in

the upper corner of his computer screen. As he clicked, his smile grew, even though he knew it wasn't about joyful news.

He burped a small chuckle as Nash opened her mouth. "I see once again you've landed one of those easy-peasy open-and-shut cases you so love."

Nash pushed back slightly as Muna joined her and a middle-aged Asian wearing a worn sweatshirt extolling Cambridge University. "Deputy Director Tony, this is Niko, our consultant and expert in all things Yakuza."

"I saw the body. As did the director, who showed it to the Japanese Ambassador in his office, making an official inquiry into why we were holding one of their citizens." He blinked as the weight of his statement settled in. "Care to explain?"

Muna leaned forward and pulled up another image of all five body parts. "Last week, someone staged this collection on the Four Corners Monument. They placed the four extremities in the four states. The legs were south, and the arms north. The monument is located deep in the Southern Ute Tribal lands. Niko has helped us identify the Japanese national who, I might add, has no fingerprints."

"Naturally?"

Muna shook her head. "Surgical."

Niko held up his hands. "Fairly common."

Tony glanced at his watch as he groaned. "I have an appointment. Keep me posted."

The three bowed slightly. "Absolutely."

10

NAVY FIRST

JAMES'S EYE GREW LARGE. "When Magic Rick said a party of four, I thought he was joking. I just grabbed the manifest an hour ago. Muna, you'll be over here with mister... Be still my beating heart." He fluttered his hand against his chest. "You must be Niko." He held out his hand to shake. "James. Or anything you want to call me in the morning."

Nash leaned in as she maneuvered into her standard seats of 1A&C. "If he gets obnoxious, just tell him to go to his crate. Tilly can take over."

James gave her a hard side-eye as he shook the good-looking Asian's hand. "Stop, girl. Tilly's on maternity leave."

Nash's head snapped up. "Wait. What? She wasn't showing a few weeks ago."

James rolled his eyes. "Not her silly. Their grand champion, Chow Chow, dropped a litter the other night. Chows are delicate. So she took the month, and her wife will take the following month off."

Niko shut his overhead storage and settled in next to Muna. "How many?"

James stepped back to the galley. "She was still in labor when Tilly called. But at the time, there were already eight."

"Hmm. Large litter. Especially if it's the first time."

Powder curled up on her seat with her back to the conversation that wasn't about her.

Nash glanced at Powder and then over at Niko. "You have Chows?"

He shook his head. "A close friend raises them."

Muna looked up from her phone. "Show or guard?"

Niko smirked at the standard assumptions about big dogs. "Mostly emotional support, but I also would suspect having the many large dogs roaming the farm provides some sort of security. But mostly, the monks like the large dogs for their love of cuddling on a chilly night."

"Monks?"

Niko's right eyebrow raised at the harmony of the two women and James. "A truck farm for retired Shaolin priests."

Muna frowned. "Wouldn't it make them priests instead of monks?"

"Technically, yes. But these are all retired, and they considered the farm a monastery. There are a few Buddhists as well. And Brother John Paul was once a Franciscan. So they're multi or non-denominational. Whichever your leanings are."

Nash smiled as she watched James prepare for departure. "And your leanings?"

His eyes turned to slits as his cheeks grew from the smile. "I'm partial to the red ones instead of the black ones. But the long hair and maintenance of a large dog in the city... I'll stick to my goldfish."

"Koi?"

"Too much work. I only have an eighty-gallon tank. So, a handful of Lionhead and a single Black Moor a friend gave me for diversity. They're happy and follow me when I walk by, so I'm happy. It's a quiet home."

Nash's forehead dipped. "Then you don't live on the ship?"

"When it's moored and not moving, I'm fine. Otherwise, I like my feet on the ground. I like Tiburon, and it's close to the various wineries we have interests in throughout the region."

"Wine?"

He turned and looked at Muna. "And rice."

She closed one eye. "Saki?"

"Not as large a world market as vodka, scotch, and bourbon."

Nash frowned as the plane surged down the runway. "I thought bourbon had to be made in Kentucky and be out of corn and rye…"

He tossed his head. "And they must make scotch in Scotland… unless they're labeled as rice alternative whiskeys. It's all in what you call them. There's a nice bourbon-style whiskey made in Oregon. But it's made from winter wheat and oats or something. Russia tried to get a lock on vodka, but the number one selling vodka around the world is Polish. But a rice distillery in Japan is catching up."

Nash smiled. "And your degrees from Oxford and Cambridge…?"

"International business, philosophy, and international law. I'm not barred, but it helps me understand those who we hire. If necessary, I can sit in the second chair. But I'd rather not experience that kind of exposure. But the education helps me read complicated contracts."

NASH RECOGNIZED THE THICKNESS OF THE WINDOWS and the look of weight in the black SUV idling at the curb. A similar-looking one stood behind but wasn't armored. Muna was supervising the loading of their bags.

Niko held out his hand. "I'll talk to his family. But it might take a few days. Tradition will dictate some delicate meetings and a slow approach to the subject. I'll stay in touch and let you know when I'm back in town."

Nash nodded in understanding. She had talked to families in the Middle East and Japan. Family was family, and traditions were strong. "We've got a similar dance. It's bad enough with all the compartmentalizing within the bureau, but now we'll have to deal with the Navy. No department or bureau wants to talk to outsiders about one of their own."

His one eyebrow twitched. "Good luck with that. At least with us, it's family." He looked behind Nash and smiled. "Incoming on your six."

James slid up, and his hand and arm slid around Nash's arm. "Well, girlfriend, where are you taking a lonely sailor for dinner?"

Nash rolled her eyes at Niko. "Jeez. Twenty minutes on the ground, I'm already put to work."

Niko bowed slightly as he turned. "I'll leave this one to you. Nice meeting you, James."

"Enjoy your stay, Niko."

Nash looked at James and his bag. "Really? You're off?"

"Off and ready. What are we doing?"

Nash glanced at Muna standing beside the SUV, then pulled out her phone. "Let's find out. Muna won't be going up to see her family until tomorrow." She pushed the single icon and then the speaker.

"It's about time. Your flight landed an hour ago. Where's my daughter?"

James' eyes chased his rising eyebrows. "Ooh, a pushy woman. I like her."

Mina's voice was sharp, and her words ended crisp. "Who's the man?"

Nash laughed. "It's flyboy James, and he's out of the plane and lost on the tarmac. Muna is in the spare bedroom tonight as well. Have you got the evening for us all to go out?"

"Absolutely. As soon as I got your text, I canceled the senators and the president. I get my honey, my daughter, and new people. What more can a girl want?"

Nash laughed. "Nothing Vera Wang, just something casual. It's been a long day for all of us."

"I'll call the farm to see if we can get the last seating. Are you headed here now?"

Nash turned to James. "Are you riding with us?" He nodded. "We'll drop the driver where he needs to go, and then we have a Suburban to spread out in. Warn Chester. I don't know if this beast will fit in the garage."

"I've got it managed. He can park it out front. Just get home safe."

MIKE AND OZ STARED AT THE SINGLE LEG. THEY HAD cycled through the new lights, hoping to find anything to help.

Mike rested his hands on the edges of the stainless-steel table. "Just when you were really hoping for some kind of prosthetic part with a serial number..."

"Not even DNA can help us here. The freeze-drying even destroyed the marrow in the bones. At least with the others, we could reconstitute the fingerprints. But nobody ever thought we might need a comprehensive database for footprints."

"Does the Wizard of Oz have any new thoughts on how they cut the parts so cleanly?"

Oz reached over and flipped the leg over by turning the foot. "Nope. I'm still at an impasse. Even a knife honed to scalpel sharpness would still leave tool marks as it sawed back and forth through the meat. And the bone would also show some marks." He ran his gloved finger over the smooth half-ball of the joint.

"Would a laser..."

Oz looked up at Mike and smiled. "No, Mister Bond. I expect you to die." They both laughed at the movie they grew up with. "If a laser could cut this thick, it would take time and leave burn marks. Even at speed through something in surgery, the heat of a cold laser still sears the meat. It's the same smell as when you're burning a body or the burn pits of bodies in certain countries."

"So the laser is out because of the size of the cut and cooking the meat. And I'm going to assume a plasma torch would even be worse."

Oz snorted a couple of bubbles of snot out of his nose. "At forty thousand degrees Fahrenheit, it's four times the temperature of the sun's surface. So, even seconds would leave a very severe sunburn. Enough to turn this all to charcoal." He patted the cut.

"I watched the butcher the other night as he sliced lunch meat. The steak was so thin, he held it up, and you could see his eye through it…"

"At the Body Farm, we had a case. A butcher cut up the neighbor who was having an affair with the butcher's mentally disabled daughter. The meat was okay, but the toothless slicer left chatter marks on the bones. And those were only the hands and feet. I don't think the slicer could do anything with a radius, much less the humorous."

Mike hung his head and looked at the older man through the top of his eyes. "Oh, now I know you're just trying to make a joke."

Oz shrugged his head and face. "Maybe, but only distally."

Mike held up his hand. "I'm not as good at this as Muna. I'm going back to work."

Oz glanced at the clock, high on the wall. He nodded at the machine. "Not unless you plan to pull an all-nighter."

Mike looked around and up as the longhand clicked back and then onto midnight. His lips furled. "Dang. The girls aren't here, and we're still working Muna hours."

Oz rolled the leg back into the locker. "So I've noticed. My wife and I used to enjoy the sunsets on the back deck with a martini or even just mint tea. Now, she just grazes the food locker at home, and we do the same here."

Mike pulled out his phone and punched his way around. "Well, I'm not going to do it anymore. I'm setting an alarm to get out of here at a reasonable hour. I don't live upstairs."

Oz leaned over to look at the phone. "Ten at night is a reasonable hour?"

Mike pulled it back and edited the data. "Okay, maybe six is more like it."

Oz straightened. "When you were here alone… when did you go home?"

Mike tried to stare him down. His shoulders collapsed. "Saturday night. Maybe." He rolled his eyes closed. "Most of the time, I camped out in room six. It doesn't get the morning light, and the view is out to sea."

"And you were younger."

Mike shrugged.

"Go home Mike. Don't come in until noon tomorrow. Then we'll get breakfast."

Mike closed one eye. "What about you?"

"I'll be in room six. Now that I know the secret to the smaller room."

Mike blew out a slow snort. "And closer to the bathroom."

Oz pointed at the man. "An important thing to know."

11

HOW ABOUT WE PLAY NICE?

N ASH DROPPED her ID and badge out in front of the receptionist. "Special Agent Nash Running Bear. I'm here to talk with Gary Webb's supervisor."

The woman didn't even blink. "They're not here."

"Then I'll settle for the deputy director or the director."

The woman's face hardly moved. "They're not here."

Nash turned her eyes to black slits. "Who is the officer of the day?"

"They're not here."

"How about the head of maintenance?"

"They're not here."

"Any of the forensic team?"

"They—"

Nash felt the soft pressure against her leg and glanced down. "Yeah, yeah... I know. They're not here. Well, miss, my dog just returned from her reconnaissance of your offices. So wherever your director is, you might let them know a full search squad of DEA agents, as well as an ATF bomb squad, are at the other end of this phone." She pushed the single icon.

Mina answered.

Nash held the receptionist's stare. "This is Special Agent Nash Running Bear with Special Investigations. I'm putting you on tactical speakerphone." She touched the icon.

Mina's voice was as cold and mirthless as a southern senator's heart. "Teams are standing by at your call, agent."

"My K-9 reports multiple registrations of illicit drugs and suspect explosives. I advise take-down teams in three-by-five formation."

"Are we to assume a hostile response?"

"There has been zero cooperation to this point."

"Stand by agent Running Bear. Air support is coming online as we connect to the Pentagon."

The receptionist picked up her phone and punched a number. "Sir. We have a situation down here involving an FBI agent." She listened. "Yes, sir." And hung up.

Moments later, a young man in a gray suit and tie exited the elevator. He walked over to stand in front of Nash. He pointed at her phone. "You won't need it. The director would like to see you if you'd follow me." He turned and walked back into the elevator.

Two floors later, they were walking down a carpeted hallway. At a large door, he knocked twice and then opened it for Nash and Powder.

The man behind the desk was more at the end of his career than in the middle. What little hair he had left provided a narrow white collar around the lower part of his head. He glanced up and then resumed reading and signing a short stack of documents. "I'll be with you in a moment. Jake, please get agent Running Bear an extra-large coffee with two shots of creamer and two packets of pink death." He looked up at her for confirmation.

Nash turned to the suited underling. "Three shots of whatever you're using for white paint these days. Unless it's real half-and-half, then two is fine."

The man nodded and retreated.

Nash looked around the office, large enough to have a minimal conference table. The man had lined the walls with more historic events memorabilia than personal.

"I never served. I was born with only one foot. I can run the qualifying course, but service wasn't an option in my day." His hand never slowed down, and his eyes kept scanning the documents. "I've met your wife a few times at events. I recognized her voice on your phone downstairs. Does that little trick work very often?"

Nash leaned into the news clipping of the hostages being led out of the embassy in Tehran. "Never tried it before. Usually, when I work my way down to the janitorial staff, the person realizes I'm not going away." She turned. "But usually, there is at least some detente between departments and services, and I don't have to call for a battering ram."

The man signed the last document and leaned back into his chair as he screwed the cap on his pen. "We're more used to being confronted with explaining who we are than someone knowing one of our investigators."

He looked at the door as the underling returned with a tray of coffee. "Ah. Jake. This end of the conference table, if you would please." He stood and strode to the long table. As the door closed, he pulled up his pant leg to expose the short prosthetic.

Nash maintained his stare. "I trusted you. Only a fool would joke about such a thing."

The man looked down at Powder.

Nash snorted softly. "Short of using the elevator, she makes her rounds. We can avail you of her services, or you can bring in your own drug dogs. But you have a problem. My guess would be edible like gummies."

He thought for a moment. "I think it would be best to keep it in-house." Sticking his hand out. "Abner Grossmann."

They shook and sat. Nash ignored the coffee. "Gary Webb."

"He's not here."

Nash drew a breath through her nose and let it out slowly.

"He's out in the field. Colorado, I believe."

Nash slowly drew up both of her arms and pinned the elbows on the table. She gently brought her chin down to rest on the tops of her fists.

"What?"

Nash slow blinked. "I'm just waiting to see how far out this line of bullshit can go. It seems the entire building is based on bullshit and stonewalling."

The man frowned. "We can call him…"

Nash leaned back in the chair. "Please do. I'm dying to know what hand he answers his phone with." Her right hand slid into her pocket and her phone. Drawing out the phone, she found the photo. "Because we know it's not his right hand or arm."

The director leaned in. "What is this?"

"Gary Webb's right arm and hand… according to his fingerprints."

The man stood and stepped to his desk. He pushed a button on the desk phone.

"Yeah?"

"Is Yari in?"

"Should be. You want him there or in MTAC?"

The director looked at the back wall and thought. "Let's start here."

He stepped back to the table and carefully took his seat as he stared at Nash's phone. She swiped and then poked in her code. The image returned.

"A little over a week ago, this…" She swiped the screen. "Someone arranged this collection in clothing. Then they spread it over the Four Corners Monument on the Southern Ute Tribal reservation. The arms and legs extended into the four states." She swiped to the next image of the clothing removed.

The director leaned in. His hand, with the thumb and finger pinched, hovered over the phone. "May I?"

Nash nodded. "We've identified the two arms. The torso and leg are Yakuza and one of their own is tracking down the family as we speak. The other leg and head, we haven't gotten very far on… yet."

He looked up with a frown. "The Yakuza? The Japanese Mafia? Is cooperating?"

Nash relaxed back into her chair. "Yeah. Cooperation. What a concept. And all with a simple phone call, then dinner, a couple of hours deciphering the hidden tattoos, and a relaxing flight out here in First Class." Her face was pure Paiute stone.

She didn't flinch at the soft knock on the door.

"Come."

The large man stepped in. With a black leather jacket, he could pass for either Chechen or Russian mafia, or just a plain wrapped Eastern European thug. "You needed me, sir." His voice was softer than his appearance.

"Come in." The director waved at Nash. "This is Special Agent Nash Running Bear with the FBI. Nash, this is Yari Oh. He has a longer name, but it will break your jaw if I try to say it."

The man came over and leaned in with a crooked smile. "Yari always works."

She smiled. "Nash. We have a tech who everyone forgot his real name, so he is just Oz."

He burped a small chuckle. "There was an older instructor years ago down at the FBI's Body Farm. They just called him Oz or the Wizard. But he'd be long retired or dead by now. He was a nice fella."

Her eyes slid toward the director. "If you need his expertise or just want to ramble down memory lane with him, you can call the forensic lab out in San Francisco. He's far from retired. He bought a forty-seven-foot sailboat a couple of years ago. If you were close enough, I think it can sleep up to eight."

The director rolled his eyes slightly at the smile response to the information. "Yari is agent Webb's supervisor."

Nash picked up her phone. "Oh. Really. When did you last talk to him?"

The large man closed one eye and pulled out a seat. "He took some personal time about a month ago. We haven't heard from him since." He sank slowly into the chair. "I have a feeling you might have a line on his whereabouts."

She booted her phone and thumbed it to the photo, and then laid it on the table and pushed it over. "Partially. They found this in Colorado about a week ago. Did he have any next of kin?"

The man looked up as his shoulders slumped. "A younger sister. I think he went out there to locate her. We remembered him talking about her getting a job out there. But other than when she had arrived, he never heard from her again. He was worried."

Nash leaned in toward the large man. In the corps, she remembered some of the largest, toughest men were the ones who had the most delicate insides. "Did he ever call back and report on what he found?"

"Not really. He was talking to one of the squints in forensics and mentioned how many ways a licensed massage therapist could be employed. Nobody thought much about it at the time."

Nash glanced at the director but continued with the larger man. "When was the last time someone tried to reach out to him?"

The man gathered his arms crossed on the table in tighter as he glanced out of the side of his eye at the director. "About the time you were calling for a drug raid." His small smile was shy. "We monitor the front desk. We may be in the middle of a Navy base, but anything could walk through the front desk. You're lucky you didn't try to get physical with Midge. She's taken out sailors my size and hyped up on drugs."

Nash recognized the stick the man measured people on. She had seen it in basic, on North Island, and in the sandbox. Everything was physical or battle prowess with them. "I could take her."

The man's one eyebrow rose a notch as his mouth pulled back in a slow smirk. "I'd bet a Benjamin on Midge."

"I've bet my life on my dog. She hasn't let me down yet."

One eye narrowed. "That's cheating."

Nash pushed her finger out along the table. She tapped the nail twice on the wood. "So is the nine-millimeter she has strapped to the underside of the desk. As for the claymore glued to the front wall of the desk, well... we already covered the potential whack walking through the door."

"But on a mat in regulation gear?"

Nash glanced at the director, who was sitting back, sipping his coffee. It was obvious who was really in charge if not running the entire show. "Is that what it takes to get cooperation around here? A Navy Marine cat fight?"

Yari cocked his head. "I thought this was about FBI and NCIS? How do you get leathernecks squids?"

Nash waited for the fifth slow heartbeat. "Ooh rah. Same as you."

The director put his mug down. "If the pissing match is over. What kind of help do you need from us?"

Nash nodded at the director and turned back to the hulking man across from her. "Where was he when he called back?"

"Outside of Pueblo. He mentioned a prison."

Nash stood. "Cañon City." She glanced down at Powder, who had been staring at the man since he walked in. "My dog says you have something in your pocket, and it's not treats for her."

He leaned and pulled something from his pocket. He flipped the evidence bag inside of an evidence bag with a gummy bear in the middle. "Strange, an FBI agent would be partnered with such a highly trained drug dog. I would have expected it to be assigned more to a DEA agent."

"She lived with a DEA agent for a couple of years. And then she met me. If you think she's good about drugs, you should see how she is with skeletons in a river and buried bodies. And before you make another bad assumption, no, she's not. She's never had a day of training. But she is a Paiute Indian reservation dog. And she has run classes training trainers at Quantico. You can call down and ask. And if you ask nicely, they might even give you the information." She turned and nodded at the director. "I'll see my own way out. My dog remembers the way."

The director glared at the larger man. "I'll forward all the information we have on his family and last communications."

Nash paused and played with her phone. The director's phone pinged in his pocket. "There. Text it to me. We're in the field."

12

REGROUP

NASH'S EYES WERE BURNING. She closed them and rubbed them with her thumb and forefinger. It wasn't helping.

"A few rounds of sushi and a couple of sashimi helped better than rubbing the eyes. Also having multiple screens."

"Oh jeez. Now I'm even hallucinating her giving me advice instead of just kidnapping me at gunpoint and putting me out of my misery."

Muna dropped into the chair beside the desk and hugged the fur and tongue, taking over her lap. "I don't think the gunpoint would be a smart idea in this building... or city. How about I just tell you I have updates and I cannot disclose them in the confines of these walls?"

"Al-Faragi. They led me to believe you weren't coming in until tomorrow."

They both looked up at the deputy director. *Shit.*

Nash stood. "We were just leaving to go to a top priority situation update. But it's off-site."

Tony glanced at his watch. "If it has anything to do with a couple of fingers of scotch and decent food, I'm buying."

The two women stood unmoving. Nash finally closed one eye in a wince. "Saki."

Tony glanced at his watch again. "Oh goodness. Look at the time. I think I'm late for dinner with my wife... wherever she is or wants to be. See you in the morning."

They watched the man retreat to his office.

Muna stood and leaned close to Nash. "So it's true about the man and eating bait?"

Nash's eyes narrowed. "No..." And then she started chuckling. Nash pulled out her phone and thumbed up the camera. She switched to selfie mode and leaned closer, taking a picture of them smiling. "Now think about him coming with us to sushi and you sharing the intimate details about meeting with your family." She looked at the photo and laughed. Turning the phone around, she hummed.

The two laughed their way out of the building.

The man standing next to the limousine stared into his phone. "Niko."

He smiled as he looked up. "I was just going to call you."

"We were just going to go find some sushi." Nash looked to Muna for her okay.

The smaller woman laughed. "Sure. The intimate details weren't as intimate as you think. They're my parents, after all. But what about Mina? Is she working?"

Nash breathed a single laugh as she pulled out her phone. Typing the word sushi, she attached the second selfie. "Let's see if this gets her attention."

Three purple hearts pulsed on the screen.

Nash smiled at Niko. "At the risk of sounding stereotyping, do you know any good sushi places? And if so, where is she meeting us?"

Niko opened the back door of the limo. "She wouldn't find it. It's private. We'll pick her up."

A TRADITIONAL ROOM WHERE THEY SAT ON THIN MATS and their legs hung under the table was behind the sushi bar. The bar patrons faced them, and they could see them, as well as the chefs processing the fish. The public side was modern Yokohama with glass, chrome, and LED lights instead of neon. Niko had explained the traditional room was only for part owners. There were only seven such bars in the world, and none were in Japan or even Hawaii.

Muna smiled at Nash. "Fujisan."

The squat powerfully built man nodded a bow. "Hi, Munasan."

"It's Nash and Mina's anniversary. They need a special dish."

Nash's eyes narrowed at Muna. And then thought about the date and turned to squint an eye at her wife.

Mina pushed out both palms in a halting form. "I'm thinking, I'm thinking."

Both knew their wedding date was not public knowledge as they performed it quietly in Tanzania. Nash looked across the restaurant, but her sight was a small green valley at the base of a mountain filled with coffee bushes. She could feel the small hand of the little girl guiding her to the center of the village where her bride stood with the Masai chief. Her voice was soft and barely more than a mutter. "The season is right..."

Mina leaned in. "But we didn't file the paperwork until June."

Muna snorted at their confusion. Leaning over, she put her arm around Powder's neck. "Silly mommies. They can't even remember when they became a family."

Nash's eyes danced around the table, looking for the right answer. "Bone creek was..."

Muna fumbled with Powder's harness. "But she was only a reservation dog then." She unsnapped the badge holder and withdrew the metal badge. She spun it and slid it along the table.

Nash stopped the badge and picked it up. She studied the back of the metal and then pulled out her own. Her snort was soft and airy. She showed the small set of numbers—the issue-date—to Mina. She held her phone with the date up next to it.

Muna's laugh tinkled. "It's why I came back today instead of tomorrow."

Mina leaned forward and looked at her. "But why would you remember this specific date?"

The wet black eyes reflected the lights of the bar. "It was the day I finally got a sister."

Fuji placed the two fancy vegetable carvings staged with sweet shrimp and sashimi flowers in front of the two women. "Here is to happy life." The next bowl of carefully arranged bits of sashimi he placed in front of Powder and bowed.

The deep-fried ice creams were just smears in their bowls. Niko dabbed at his lips with his napkin as he formed the response to Nash's questions. "Yes, the family was grateful for information about their son. It wasn't the news they had ever wanted, but it also wasn't unexpected." He shrugged. "It is the life."

"When did he go missing?"

"He left for Colorado last fall. His niece had struggled for some years with drug addiction, but had cleaned up. She took classes at a school of eastern medicine and learned body working with healing herbs. The family was hopeful. Last summer, she and a girlfriend had planned a trip to California to camp and look for work. The last time they heard from her, she had found work in a massage clinic in Pueblo. Her letter said it was more Asian based than American and indicated it would be a good fit with her education."

Nash mussed. "Pueblo isn't far from Cañon City. And the massage parlor angle sounds too close for coincidence."

Muna winced as she studied a map on her phone. "Ouch. Half-hour or an hour with snow." She glanced up. "When did the Navy go missing?"

Nash's mouth hardened. "He dropped off the grid about two months ago. He had a month of personal time, so they didn't start looking for him until it was too late. His last credit card charge was at a small motor lodge there in Cañon City. But the postmark on the last letter from his sister was a small town named Westcliff." Nash turned her head to look at Muna.

Muna frowned, flustered. "Is that supposed to mean something to me?"

"No. That's your cue to do your magic and tell me how close it is."

Her voice was soft as she raised her phone. "Um... Oh. Close. But a small low pass between them. So forty-five miles, but well over an hour with snow. Two to four hours in the summer."

Niko cocked his head to the side. "Why so long in the summer?"

Muna placed the phone on the mat beside her. "Extrapolating from the information on the region popular for hiking, camping, fishing, hunting, and just general touristy stuff, as well as it being Colorado... the estimates could be right on or less than your experience."

"So just tourists?"

Nash leaned back with a laugh. She looked at the man and her wife. She held up two fingers. "Colorado is notorious for having two seasons. Snow and construction. The latter coincides with the tourist season. And if you have ever been stuck behind a bunch of retirees in their RVs pulling a car or boat... I don't have to explain the speed limits." She glanced over at Muna and smiled. "Unless it's a handful of man-children in a certain beat-up rust-bucket."

Muna choked and coughed. "And is good for at least a hundred and twenty on a Colorado open road."

Nash raised one eyebrow at Niko. "Probably faster."

"And this is one of those big bus kinds of RVs?"

Mina laughed and clapped her hands. "Not the one I saw. It looks like the one the brother had in the comedy movie about Christmas, and he pulls up and everyone wants to hide."

The man's face animates with surprise. "And it's that fast?"

Nash rolls her eyes and rocks her head back and forth slowly as she recites the litany. "And armor plated, smoke, rockets, fifty-caliber machine guns, oil slick, anti-personal mines, surface-to-air missiles, radar, two-thousand-horse-power engine, and a kick-ass satellite Wi-Fi umbrella."

Niko lowered one eye to a slit. "Are we talking about an old beater RV or James Bond's car?"

Muna grimaced. "See, that's where the men acting more like boys in a candy store starts to really blur the conversation."

Nash nodded. "One is a mechanical genius who can make a Volvo engine sing like a Ferrari. Then there's the kid who is the electronics wizard who got recruited right out of high school at fifteen for his skills."

"They didn't let him graduate?"

Mina snorted softly and rocked back. She placed her hand on his arm. "Oh, no. He graduated. At fifteen. They were just standing at the bottom of the stage and didn't let him walk back to his seat."

Niko's eyes became slits. "What was the hurry?"

"Samsung, Rocketdyne, Intel, and Apple were all sitting in the front row. If a kid could get a Nobel for a school science project... Felix would have one."

"What was the project?"

Mina leaned in. "Oh, who knows? I'm just a simple Asian girl trying to make a couple of bucks to survive in Washington."

Muna hugged Powder. "Don't walk over there. It's getting too deep to swim."

Nash rolled her eyes. "But back to Colorado..."

Mina glanced at Niko. "It sounds like someone needs to get a lot of massages. But how many massage parlors can there be in small towns?"

Muna looked up. "Evidently, illicit parlors are a problem. In a place called Colorado Springs, they're battling a few dozen of them. They're thought to be practicing prostitution, gambling, and money laundering. Even the conservative state legislature is making moves to shut them down and register the rest." She looked up from her phone. "And that's just a quick glance. I can get more for you tomorrow when I can access my real computer."

Niko snickered. "Why, I thought they cybernetically attached you to all your computers."

Nash gave him a hard look as she dipped sashimi into her soy sauce. "Don't give her any ideas. And I certainly forbid you from taking her out onto the ship. It's hard enough to keep her acquisitions and lust for technology in some kind of budget."

Muna poked Nash's shoulder. "What's he hiding out on a ship?"

Nash's head ground around. "Stinky, filthy, unkept, greasy men. Who eat a lot of bacon."

The smaller woman growled. "My sister eats bacon." As she side-hugged Powder.

Niko leaned forward and frowned down what had obviously become a family dinner. "What's wrong with bacon?"

Mina turned and tried to hide her laughing. "Muna keeps halal. Well... kind of. She keeps Muna style halal. Which is to say, she doesn't eat bacon, but wolfs down pork rinds cooked in thermal nuclear sauce." Mina glanced back at the junior agent. "Until this last year, she wore a hijab like her mother. Now... neither do. Their beliefs are in flux."

"Does her mother eat pork rinds?"

Mina peeked back. "I don't think so."

"So there are family issues." His face tossed a shrug sideways. "I can relate. Which is why I'm moving the family businesses into different avenues of income."

Mina blinked a few times as she thought. "Wasn't the Yakuza traditionally in human trafficking along with the drugs and such?"

His nod was slow. "Historically, it was part of the drug smuggling trade. But as product went from a few kilos to thousands of kilos, how things shipped also changed."

13

SOONER DIRT

THE FOUR STOOD LOOKING at the burned-out hulk of what used to be an electrical contractor's business. Smoke was only the smell. The heat was gone, but the eye burning stench of burned plastic, rubber, wood, and copper hung acrid in the air. The only structural members taller than Muna were twisted metal I-beams that had been the ribs of a metal building.

The man in the yellow helmet and almost white shirt stepped carefully through the rubble. He had waved a two-finger acknowledgment of their presence, but wasn't rushing to finish his work. The yellow plastic tape wasn't his, but might well have been. The only thing shinier than his belt buckle and helmet was the gold badge on his shirt.

At Quantico, Nash and Muna had learned about the compact box of a tool with its two long tubes for a nose. The sniffer searched for petrochemical accelerants when there had been a fire. The man deftly swept it around him as he traced a path they couldn't see.

Niko leaned toward Nash. His voice was hushed too only them. "What's the tool he's using..."

"It's called a sniffer. It sniffs the air and runs a fast, rudimentary analysis looking for what is called an accelerant. Usually gasoline, kerosine, diesel fuel, alcohol, or any benzine fuels. They use all of them to make a fire start or burn hotter and with more destruction. Like throwing a cup of rum into a hibachi." She pointed at the melted steel and tin building. "There was a lot of explosive used also, but this is about burning the building to the roots. Think of it as a metaphor for killing someone, and then their family to the last child in the cradle, five cousins distant."

He turned to look at her. "Scorched earth?"

Nash looked down and kicked at the dirt. "Yes. Kind of like it. But scorched earth is more about Hannibal burning everything to the dirt, and then sowing the land with salt so nothing would grow for a generation or three." She looked up. "This is a redneck version on a much more individual level."

"But this looks recent. And they killed the guy..."

Nash winced her one cheek. "It wasn't about him. He was looking for his niece, Sarah. So this was about his sister or brother. Family." She squinted at him. "All the way to the baby in the cradle. Biblical." She looked back at the approaching fireman. "We're in the buckle of the Bible Belt. Guns, bibles, and in this case, fire, but no brimstone."

Nash and Muna flipped open their ID wallets. "FBI. Special agents Al-Faragi and Running Bear."

He switched the sniffer to his left hand and stuck his right out. "Kutter Keaton. I'm what passes for the arson investigator in these parts."

Nash waved her finger at the sniffer. "Because you're the only one who knows how to run a sniffer, or the only one who could afford one?"

His smile was soft. "Obviously you understand how things work in rural America." The man scratched at the close-cropped hair on the back of his head. "What's the FBI's interest in this burn?"

Nash shook her head. "We're here about the death of Tab Roberts."

The man's face winced at the name. "We got a body. But that

wasn't the name." He pulled a small book out of his back pocket. Thumbing through, he found the page he was looking for. "Fella by the name of Chet Espinoza. Fifty-seven. He was the night watchman or something."

Muna looked up from her phone. "When did the fire start?"

The man's face changed to a scowl as he looked at the small black woman. "In the night."

She held up her phone. "According to The Oklahoman, the fire was first reported shortly after closing. Care to amend your *in the night*?"

Nash gave the man a hard look. "Who else was in the building at the time?"

The man's face darkened as he turned back into the aftermath of the burn. "Fuck you feds."

"We'll look forward to seeing your report tomorrow."

His one finger hung in the air as he continued to walk away.

Niko blinked his wide eyes as he looked from Muna to Nash. "Interesting. I've never experienced such blatant... um..."

Muna growled as she turned back toward the SUV. "Prejudice? Hatred? Ignorance? Lack of cooperation? We're the FBI. We get it all the time."

Nash grimaced. "She's right about the hatred by the local law enforcement toward what they see as the meddling by the federal government. But this was beyond fed and locals. This had a little cowboy and Indian mixed with black on white, and some Asian thrown in for good measure. Or he just hates dogs. Either way, this is where we always start, and then turn Muna loose with the computers." She looked at Muna as they opened the doors. "Whose jurisdiction is this?"

"It looks like tribal... but all I find is the local sheriff. Sending the address now."

Nash's phone pinged as she plugged it into the USB port. She touched the map and the maps app started routing.

A small squat building was obviously a sub-station. A sign

with eight-to-six hours posted on the door confirmed it being only a three-man show. The county wasn't going to spend much out in the hinterlands, especially if it was also tribal land. Not when campaign contributions usually came from a whiter community.

Nash checked her watch at the closed door. *Lunch*. She looked down the street. An auto-parts store was to the left. The gas station a block away looked empty or also closed for lunch. She pointed at the auto-parts. "I'll go ask. Muna, do your thing."

Muna studied her phone as her thumbs vibrated on the screen.

As Nash and Powder walked back across the street, Muna looked up. "The Bib and Tucker?"

Nash rolled her eyes and smiled crookedly. "Why do I even get up in the morning?"

The deputy wasn't what Nash had expected. Two darts at the shoulder placard starched into knife edges defined the back of his shirt. His haircut was almost military. She glanced at the boots. At least the point-toed cowboy boots fit her expectations. The slender man did not.

Nash turned the stool next to him and settled in. The man turned his face to her until a slim stretch lacking scars showed. She dropped open her ID wallet.

He looked. "I'm on my lunch."

Nash swung her knees in. "So are we." Muna and Niko sat on the other side.

"Hey!"

Nash looked at the bucktoothed waitress with Dutch braids.

"Dogs aren't allowed in here."

Nash turned and looked at Powder. She patted the empty seat next to her. "Show her your badge."

Powder hopped up on the seat and sat. Her attention was calm but threatening.

The woman took in the harness and badge. "Oh. That's different... I guess."

The deputy went back to stabbing his fork in the salad. "Drug sniffer?"

Nash reached across the Formica counter and pulled the single-sheet menu from the rack. "Active interdiction and multi-level investigations. Drugs to buried cadavers and any bombs along the way. What's good, or at least safe?"

"They're out of pulled pork, but the sloppy chicken is good. We slaughtered the chickens on Sunday. The replacements are in the chick coop now. I'd recommend the salad, but most people don't like poke salad, field greens, and chicory."

Nash closed one eye as she looked at Muna. "Sounds more nutritious than just lettuce."

He pointed the back of his fork at the waitress. "That's what the wife says."

Nash hummed. "The chicken is personally raised. I'm guessing the greens are hand-gathered, so I detect some ownership here?"

"It was supposed to be our retirement business."

Muna looked up. "Last time I checked, people retire from business, not to a business."

The man bobbled his head around and pointed his fork at his wife. "Ask her."

The woman with the name tag reading Chickee came to a slow stop in front of the deputy. "Are they bothering you?"

He shook his head softly. "Just unclear on how this is retirement."

She rolled her eyes into her closing eyelids. "Thirty-two years as a trauma nurse in a New York hospital and his thirty-seven in the Navy. Know what you want?"

Nash nodded. "Slowing down but not stopping. He says pulled chicken is good. I'll cut her's up." She nodded toward Powder. "But a bowl is easier."

"Two chicks." She looked at Muna and Niko.

They shrugged. "Same."

"Coffees?"

Nash held up three fingers. "Four."

Her head vibrated, and then she laughed. "A dog drinking coffee. I'd pay good money to watch."

Nash smiled. "She hasn't ordered it yet…"

As Chickee walked away, Nash turned slightly in the chair. "Which hospital?"

"Jamaica Queens. It got all the dregs of the city and the port to boot. When she got the job, she spoke English and Muskogee. Now, we can get in trouble in seventeen other countries we've never been to. The Navy only taught me French, Spanish, and swearing. You?"

"Marines. Mostly stuff useful in the sandbox. But I picked up enough to learn Swahili and Japanese."

"Throw some Russian in with the Swahili, and you can get a taxi for a discount in New York." He pushed the plate away and sipped his coffee. "So, what brings you to my territory?"

"Lunch."

"Lunch is over."

"Torched electrical contractors."

"Tab and his sister's place. What about it?"

Nash nodded as Chickee put the sandwiches down. "Chet Espinoza? Was he alone?"

The deputy squinted. "Who?"

Chickee blew out some air. "Cheut Eschowwe. That asshole Kutter must have written the fire report." She turned toward Nash. "The man is the biggest racist this side of the Proud Boys. Even his wife admits he's an asshole."

The deputy stuck his hand out. "David Robertson and this is my wife, Chickee. Don't ask. It's her real name. She's the Creek of the family. She grew up ten miles from here."

Nash smiled at Chickee as she shook the man's hand. "Nash, like the car they supposedly conceived me in. Running Bear, I'm a northern California Paiute. This is my partner, Powder. Pure reservation dog." She pointed at Muna and Niko. "Muna al-Faragi and our consultant, Niko. So, what can you tell me about the fire?"

"Four men busted into the shop and shot Cheut. They pistol-whipped Dot something bad, and then they threw gasoline all over the shop. On their way out, they threw a road flare back in the door."

Chickee held her hands to her mouth. David glanced up. "Yeah. She woke up this afternoon. We talked for a bit, but it was a strain for her. They have her jaw wired shut, but tomorrow, they're going to have to go back in to rebuild the jaw. She'll lose half her teeth."

"What did the guys want?"

"According to Dot, they said nothing. It was just a solid beat down and burn everything to the ground. They never counted on her being so tough and crawling out the back door. We found her a block away."

"Do you think we could talk to her?"

"Give it a few days. I know they were giving her a sedative when I left. It's amazing the woman's alive."

Nash winced. The strength of a woman in life-threatening circumstances never ceased to amaze her. "What can you tell us about, Tab?"

He looked at his wife. "You knew him better than I did."

She closed her eyes as her right hand found the back counter to lean against. "He went looking for Dot's daughter a couple of months ago. Business was slow, and they were worried. He never married or had kids of his own, but she was like his." Her eyes narrowed. "What do you know about him?"

Nash licked the edge of her lips. "He won't be coming back."

The two harmonized as their eyes locked. "*Shit*."

14

PUEBLO PROBLEMS

MUNA STOOD on the sidewalk in front of the black SUV. Her hand shaded her face as she gazed into the distance. A couple of milky wisps of clouds played tag in the distance. "I thought we were in the mountains." She turned as Nash and Niko walked over.

Niko laughed and pointed at the terminal. "You need to look this way to see mountains. Out there is just sky, air, clouds, and when the wind is exactly right—dust."

Muna snickered at Nash. "He thinks I'm just a silly city girl. I know the difference between mountains and airport terminals." She nodded toward the SUV and the agent waiting as she zipped up her tactical jacket. The reflection of Niko and Nash bounced around in the mirrored sunglasses like multi-colored Pachinko balls on a silver field.

The agent in a suit under his winter coat peeked over at Muna and the dog on the center console. "Welcome to the Great Plains."

Muna narrowed her eyes as she ground her head around. "Where did you hide the Rockies? This is Colorado, isn't it? My ticket said Colorado, home of the Rockies."

The man frowned and glanced to see if she was joking. "Coors

Field is in Denver. The mile-high city is a thousand feet lower in altitude than you are right now."

"Where do I get oysters?"

The man turned right and was silent for three blocks. He pulled up to the curb and pointed at the restaurant. Nash started laughing. "This I've got to see." She opened her door and looked at Niko. "Dinner?"

If his skin wasn't already pale, she would have sworn he had just blanched.

"Do they have anything else to eat?"

The agent looked back. "Sure. Snake, bison, whip lizard, ground-hog, and quail egg omelets."

Nash stepped out. "You had me at bison."

The interior was a tribute to every do-it-yourself Western motif decorator. The walls and ceiling looked like they had come in with their leftover decorations and nailed them up for the past eighty years.

Muna sipped on her water as she scanned the menu. She looked up at the waitress, who looked like she had been wearing out the linoleum behind the counter for the last forty years at least. "I don't see the oysters."

"Honey child. We don't put them on the menu anymore. We got 'em. But just not where they might offend some city folk and have them make a tacky talky for the internet."

Muna closed the menu and smiled. "I'm in the Rockies..." She glared to her left at the agent. "Or that's what he insists we are. So I want to try the oysters, please."

The waitress only hesitated for a moment to write in her little book. "Sheep, goat, or sweetbreads?"

Muna cocked her head as Nash smiled. "What's the difference?"

"Golf, duck eggs, and you'll have to share with the dog."

Powder kneaded her front feet on the stool as she looked at Muna. Whatever it was, she knew it was going to be good.

Nash leaned forward. "Goat is sweeter than lamb, but depending on how they cook the bull, it's what I'm having."

"Are we sharing bitesies?"

"If we can get them past Powder."

Muna leaned over and looked at the Asian. "Niko. Are you in?"

He pointed at the menu. "The bison brisket, Ruben, is more my speed."

She studied the agent. He held up his hands. "I'm just here for the coffee."

Muna peeked at the waitress, still holding her pencil over the little book. "Let's take the goat and bull on three plates, please. And coffee."

Later, as Powder licked the last of the three plates, Muna laughed as she looked at Nash. "We're here for how long?"

Nash pointed at the stacked plates. "At least for a few more runs at dinner. Now I definitely know I inherited my mother's lack of cooking acumen."

Ethel wandered down the back passage of the counter. "If I leave them plates for another couple of minutes, Dillon won't have anything left to wash." She looked at Muna. "Well? What did you think about your first go at balls?"

Muna laughed. "We'll be back."

"Did you leave room for fresh pie? I've got cherry and apple."

Ethel laughed at the waving hands. "Four more coffees it is, then."

As she left with the check and Nash's credit card, Nash looked down at the counter. "Hey, Max. Are you working on this investigation?"

He closed and squinted one eye. "Normally, I'm in finance only. But we don't have any interface with Special Operation and Investigations, so…"

Muna choked slightly on her coffee. "He drew the short straw."

The man's lower lip curled in hard against his teeth as his eyes glanced at the dark woman laughing at her joke. "It was more like I was ten minutes late to work that day. Why?"

Nash blinked a single slow time over her slight smile. She had been there too many times. "How much have they filled you in?"

"Someone dumped the entire file into my interconnect last night. I had just finished dinner, so the images..."

"Did it have the update on Sarah Richardson?"

He nodded. "The missing girl from Oklahoma? Yeah. I ran the name and all, but I didn't get any hits for Colorado. Well, this part, at least. There are three in Denver and one in Vail."

Muna turned the coffee mug with her thumb. "Two in the Denver area are over sixty. The one in Vail is married with two kids." She looked up. "I'm forty-seven fifty-nine Mike Alpha. I dumped it on you as soon as I knew who we'd get for local support. Sorry."

"No. We're good. I'd just never seen that kind of file and spent the evening reviewing it because you guys were heading this way. Usually, I get thin files dumped in my inbox, and I have a few days to get around to them at my desk."

Nash's head jerked. "You have an inbox?"

Muna growled. "Ignore her. She has a trash box on her desk with leftovers from nine administrations." She waved down the man's questioning face.

"There was also a Tina Webb. She'd gotten a job at a massage parlor in Cañon City...?"

The man held up two fingers. "Two establishments fit the bill, but no Tina Webb. Didn't find one here either. But if they never got new driver's licenses, then they have no regular reason to be in the system."

Muna frowned. "What about getting their massage license for Colorado?"

"With places like that, the..." His hands curled two fingers each to make air quotes. "Therapists work for a month or two and then move on. So they never bother to get their licenses updated. It's a health code thing. But the health department doesn't even have enough inspectors for restaurants. So hotels, motels, barbers, and massage parlors only get hit about once in their careers—if that."

Muna looked at where the plates cleaned by a dog had just sat. "So nobody cares if a restaurant is clean or there are no bedbugs in a hotel?"

Max's eyebrows shot up. "Oh, they do. So everyone knows how to keep things right, and if they don't, social media is a great controlling big brother. If I weren't here, how would you choose where to get dinner?"

Muna held up her phone.

"Exactly. And each of those apps you might use also provides a star rating right next to the restaurant's page. Did you think about looking up this restaurant?"

Nash shook her head. "We had you."

He looked at Muna, who shied away with a small smile.

He laughed. "And...?"

"It said you're part owner."

He laughed louder. "It didn't. But I might as well be. I've been eating her since my father brought me in, still wearing diapers. But that's not what we need to know about the case." He looked over at Nash. "Any thoughts on looking for the girls?"

"I guess kicking in the door and asking everyone where they are at gunpoint is out?"

Muna snickered.

Max closed one eye. "I take it you've done it?"

Nash held an evil eye on Muna. "Not here. Per se. But I spent some time in the sandbox. There, the boot was faster than days of handing out candy bars and making nice, nice with the locals."

Muna held her fist up to her mouth as she coughed. "Barbados."

He glanced at Muna and then looked at Nash. "What about Barbados?"

Nash glared at Muna. "She wasn't there. And the guy deserved a lot worse than he got."

Max rolled back on the stool. "So we're talking about going in and making nice, nice?"

"When was the last time you had a massage?"

He shook his head. "Sorry. I grew up here and live near Cañon City, up in the apple orchards. Everyone in Cañon knows me and what I do. Which is why I'll be sitting behind my desk on this one unless you need an introduction or something."

Nash rocked with understanding. Her eyes danced around the counter as she thought about new directions.

"My back has been acting up lately. I could use a few massages."

Nash smiled and looked over at the older Asian. "And what's your cover? I don't think there are many Asian orchard workers in their fifties."

His eyes opened round. "And why not? My gardener is in his eighties."

Nash raised her left eyebrow. "You have a Japanese gardener?"

"Noo…" He cocked his head to one side. "But he is Asian. He's Mongolian and Korean. I hired him at a bonsai competition and show. He was holding the gold and bronze medals. I provide anything he wants, and he takes care of my garden."

"How much garden can you have in San Francisco?"

He rocked with his soft snort. "None. But I have three acres in Tiburon at my house."

Nash softly smacked her forehead with the heel of her palm. *She had forgotten where he lived.*

Muna chuckled.

Nash glared at her.

Muna held up her phone. "Felix wants to know if he should bring Alex and maybe the sheriff?"

Nash thought about Thomas's torso with all the scar tissue. If anybody could use a few rubdowns, it would be Sheriff Thomas Brady. "How's the bus in snow?"

Muna bent to her phone with her flying thumbs. She sat up and waited. "He says it would be better if they brought the conventional truck and a trailer, but the bus will get by." She looked up with a smirk. "I think he believes in spring."

The agent next to her laughed as he pounded on the counter. "Where is this guy? In Los Angeles or something?"

Nash rocked with a soft smile. "Close... but closer to Mt. Shasta and about the same elevation as here. Just milder winters."

He snickered. "The best-kept secret is we're in Colorado. People think of deep snow and freezing. But we're in a kind of temperate banana belt here. It can get hot, but that's good for the peppers. But the winters aren't about deep snow as much as wind and chill. Just dress for the cold, and when it gets nasty, stay home."

Muna fluttered one eyelid. "What about when you have to go to work?"

He nodded with his upper teeth, gently biting his lower lip. "There's always the good news, bad news to it. The bad news is you must go to work. But the good news is most people stayed home, so the roads are clear—mostly. If you're here even half a winter, you've learned how to dress and what to carry in your vehicle. A bitter day at work eventually ends. If there's heat at home, you can warm up."

Nash leaned back with a memory of a chilly day. Five of them were sitting around the fire in heavy coats. And then the scrawny kid ran up in his tiny nylon running shorts and shoes. His chest was naked to the bone-biting chill.

"I don't think the boy knows what cold is. He carries a Thermo-nuclear heater inside him wherever he goes."

15

CAN I GET A MASSAGE?

THE RUST and battered truck with the weathered construction toolbox in the bed eased back into the crumbling parking bumper. The young man swung the door open and then paused to remove his aging, yellow, hard helmet. Most of the stickers were logos of tools he used in construction. One was all but scratched off, but the bear still danced. The light splitting through the triangle prism was the freshest and held a place of honor on the front of the helmet, worn backward.

Felix ran his fingers through his mop of curly black hair as he kneed the door closed. The large Chinese dragon logo on the painted-over window reflected darkly in his wraparound blackout glasses. The toothy smile slowly came as he thought about what was inside the establishment.

Chilled light spilled into the subdued interior as he opened the door. He looked around. Everything was black, and then he remembered the dark glasses. Sliding them up into his curls, the scanty decorations came into focus. The lobby wasn't where they spent money. A screw-together couch and chair braced the one wall. A few Asian-looking scrolls hung from random nails on the walls. The desk was little more than a fat podium he usually saw in a restaurant.

The young blonde woman standing behind the desk appeared more Midwest than Far Eastern. "Hello. May we help you?" Her smile appeared frozen somewhere between a date for the prom and with cousin Chester.

"I was wondering…" Felix started and then cleared his throat. "I wanted to find out…"

The young woman smirked. "A massage?" He nodded. "First time?"

"Yes, ma'am."

The laminated flyer appeared in her hand. "The basic massage is a hundred for forty-five minutes. We have several kinds of massages. Each one is a different price. Did you have anything specific in mind?"

Felix rocked his weight from foot to foot as he stared at the small menu. "Um…" His right hand found his curls.

The blonde gently chewed on her gum as she sized up the young construction worker. His jacket and pants weren't trendy baby poop yellow but worn dungaree. The knees on the insulated pants had patches of layered duct tape. His all-but pulled-out right pocket was the obvious hanging point of a heavy tape measure. The jacket had a few patches crudely sewn on with heavy thread or fishing line.

"What did you want to work on? Sore back? Arms? Legs? Let's start there."

He glanced up and hesitantly handed back the menu. "Um… I guess that hundred buck thing."

"Okay. A straight-up massage." She held her hand out.

He froze. Frowned. He then reached into his back pocket for the wallet that caused the white square in the denim.

She led him through the red curtains into the back. It could have been any storage area for any small business except for the two open doors. Felix guessed the rooms were the same. A narrow massage table stood in the middle of the tiny room. A full child's bed would have filled the room. There was a narrow corner shelving unit with a small boom box on the top shelf. Unlit candles lined the next shelf below. An elephant statue stood between the pink and yellow candles. The room smelled like something his mother or grandmother might have decorated the air in their houses with.

"Sandalwood and lavender."

"What?"

He waved his hand in the air. "The smell. Those candles remind me of my grandmother's house. She liked sandalwood and lavender. And never lit her candles, either. She was afraid of house fires." He put his hands on the massage table.

The blonde turned. "Easy sport. I'm going to leave and close the door. You get undressed and get under the sheet so there's no funny business. Okay?"

"Okay."

She dipped her head. "I'll be back in a few minutes." She pointed at him and then the table. "Naked, and then under the sheet. Leave your arms and head out. And on your back. We'll start there." She slipped out of the door.

"Okay."

Felix unbuckled his belt and slipped out of his work pants. He stumbled slightly, and as his hands landed on the massage table, the fingers of his right hand curled under the edge—depositing a bug.

He sat on the chair and untied his boots. Prying them off, he leaned to one side of the chair. His left hand slipped another bug on the inside of the chair's metal legs.

Finally pulling off his T-shirt, he pulled the sheet back and slid under. He crossed his hands behind his head. A moment later, there was a soft knock on the door.

"Come in."

A dark-haired young woman slipped into the room. He recognized her from the photos.

Felix frowned. "Where's..."

"Mary Beth runs the front. I'm Tina. I'll be your masseuse today. What are we working on?"

He pointed at his back. "I bought the hundred-dollar package."

She squirted lotion from the pump bottle in her hip holster. "General, overall it is. What brings you to Colorado?"

He took a small breath as her hands glided down his chest. "What makes you think I'm not from around here?"

She snickered shortly. "At this time of the year? Nobody's tan is beyond their face and neck. I'm guessing I'm going to find some tan lines down there at the top of your legs."

He rolled his eyes as they closed. "I ride motorcycles and run."

"Motorcycles only tan the face." She dug into his chest muscles. "What kind of running?"

"Usually five to ten every morning. I produce a lot of heat, so mostly only running shorts and shoes. What do you do when you're not working?"

She rolled her eyes as she pulled the sheet over his torso and started working on his right arm. "All I ever do is work."

"You gotta have some time off…"

She worked on his hand. "We're short-staffed." Her voice dropped to just a whisper. "Your clothes say construction, but our hands say desk jockey."

His eyes opened as he looked at her, massaging his hand. "Construction pays more than working at Walmart."

She held up the sheet. "Roll over." She laid the sheet back down along his back. "Construction is dangerous." She dug into his shoulder and leaned over near his ear. "Almost as dangerous as snooping where you shouldn't."

He turned his head and whispered. "I know your real name is Sarah Richardson from Oklahoma. I'm here to help."

She rubbed him in silence for a few minutes more. She pulled the sheet up. "Your time is up." She leaned down next to the barely covered earbud in his left ear. "I don't know who you are, and I don't care. But you best not come back if you know what's good for you… Or me."

Felix stopped at the podium front desk. His left hand slipped around the edge and under the top shelf. "I just wanted to…"

She glared at him. "Goodbye."

He held up his hands. "I'm going. I'm going."

She pointed at him as he turned at the door. Her voice was hard and strident. "And don't you ever try that with another woman. You hear?"

He pulled on his jacket. "Yeah. Got it."

The coffee on the bus was hot and sweet. He sipped as he stared into the four black eyes.

Nash cocked her head. "But didn't want to be saved?"

Muna added. "Or ask who you were."

He shook his head. "Nope. Just get out."

Uncle turned from the monitor. "But planted five bugs in under a half hour. That's got to be a record."

Alex snorted as he turned from the microwave. "Are you kidding? I watched him plant twenty trackers and bugs in under five minutes one day in Chico. The group of Pride Boys didn't know who had sold them out, but we rounded up over six hundred long guns and seven hundred pounds of reloaded ammo. Best damn gun show we ever went to. Nobody pays attention to the geeky kid with a Winchester T-shirt."

Felix laughed. "Fun day. I miss those days." He glanced at the scowling face of the sheriff. "Jeez, Brady, it's not like there haven't been any fun days with you around. But they were fun—not having to play fair."

The large blond man scowled harder. "Are you saying I'm no fun?"

Uncle growled as he pulled on his braid. "Well… if the bite in the ass fits…?"

"Bite me, teepee boy."

"Sit on it, Mr. Wigwam, with no toilet."

Nash frowned at the local sheriff-turned-pass-around federal consultant. "You still haven't fixed the toilet in your teepee? What's the holdup?"

"The county says I have to dig a pressure mound leach field before they'll sign off."

Nash glowered. "It's reservation land. Not county."

Uncle rumbled as he cleared his throat. "Nope. We surveyed it. It's twenty feet outside the reservation."

She raised one eyebrow at the old Indian. "Then make like a hunter and move the damn teepee. How hard could it be? Do I have to come home and do everything for you two?"

"He poured a concrete floor."

"Then pour another one and use the first one as a patio."

Muna looked up from her phone. "Alex? Are you getting this?"

The man adjusted his headphones. "Recording."

Felix frowned at Muna. She glanced up. "It looks like your visit stirred up some shit. Whoever the guy is, he doesn't like the fact you two had words and a shortened session."

Felix batted his eyelashes. "I'm willing to go back for more. It felt good."

Uncle barked a soft chuckle. "That's the main idea. It's why people pay big bucks and keep going back." He peered over at the silent Asian in the passenger seat.

Niko held up his hands. "No argument from me. I'm just a fly on the wall with you guys."

Nash leaned back. "Any thoughts, though?"

"Lots. But as to the girl? When does she go home, and where does she live? I'd approach her somewhere she feels safe or is a more neutral ground."

Felix frowned. "Explain neutral ground."

Niko uncrossed his legs and turned more on the seat. "In nego- tiations, if I come to your office, I'm at a disadvantage. It's your turf. Same goes for my office. But if we meet at your favorite restaurant, the same applies. So when you want to truly negotiate a fair deal, choose a place where nobody has the advantage."

Muna pointed at the seat. "Reach your right hand down on the side of the seat and push down on the lever."

Niko frowned as his hand did as directed. The seat released and swiveled around to face the others. His face lit up. "Cool feature."

Uncle snorted in a grump. "Yeah. Some of the old farts were thinking back to the middle of the last century. So, if you were getting ambushed, where would you want it?"

"Gas station. Pay for my gas, and I would be more likely to listen to what you had to say."

Muna looked back down at her phone as she muttered. "What if you don't drive?"

The Asian's eyes crinkled as the smirk pulled back on the left. "Public transport is even better. What's more neutral than a bus full of strangers as witnesses?"

Alex took his headphones off. "Shit." He looked up at everyone else looking at him. "We have a problem, Houston."

Muna glanced up from her phone, where she was reading the transcript from the bugs. "I'll say. I guess gas stations and public buses are out. They're moving her." She peered over at Alex. "How many places in Pueblo do you think they have?"

Alex rubbed his face with his hands. His eyes blinked and then widened as he thought. "Legit and public or the otherwise?"

Felix glanced back and forth at the two. "I don't understand."

Thomas bounced his hip back against the counter. "In the crude jargon of city law enforcement, it's called sluts and slots. If the establishment is running a whorehouse in the back or upstairs, they are usually also running some kind of gaming as well." He eyed Niko. The man nodded slowly.

16

ON THE MOVE

"I CAN TELL you broadly where the bug is. But it's not a tracker. Therefore, I know if they're moving the massage table from Cañon City to Pueblo, but not wherever it is in Pueblo."

Nash grimaced. "And if the table isn't her personal table…"

Niko finished. "They won't move it."

Felix slumped into the booth. "But at least I don't have to put replacement bugs in there."

Nash looked at Niko. "What about your Kathy?"

He shrugged softly. "Her family said the last time they heard from her; she was in Pueblo. So, I guess it means our searches have merged."

"Or they were the same search all along."

"There is that."

Uncle turned from stirring soup on the small stove. He leaned his hip against the counter.

Nash grunted softly. "I know that look. What are your thoughts, Indian?"

He grumped as he turned back to the soup. "Just that. Did you ever reach out to the tribal cop?"

"Not yet. It's not like there was any kind of secure crime scene to examine. I think they stuffed everything into garbage bags and shipped them off." She looked at Muna.

The smaller woman shrugged as she sipped on a mug. "Ask the boys. I didn't get roped in until they wanted my younger eyes or just to listen to more dad jokes."

Uncle rumbled from the stove. "Give the guys a little slack. Oz is going through a rough patch and might have to sell the sailboat. And Mike... well, he's Mike."

Nash scrunched the side of her face. "Sell the black hole in the water? Why?"

The man slurped at the wooden spoon of soup. He wagged his head back and forth and pushed his lower lip out. "I don't understand boats... but evidently, there's a boat called a Hans Christian Andersen, like the writer, a few docks over. It's about twenty feet longer, but it's rigged so a single person can sail it alone. He thinks they could just live on board." He looked up at Nash as he shook his head. "I don't think his wife is going to go for it."

Niko let out a soft whistle. "Tough call. Marriage or the boat. It has been the end of many a good marriage."

Nash grunted softly and looked back at Uncle. "Unless it's your teepee." She turned to look over at Felix, staring into his laptop. "Anything?"

He shook his head. "All I get is silence. I don't think they moved the table." He glanced at his watch. "But it's early for anyone getting a massage."

The door of the bathroom swung open. Thomas, still in his jogging sweats, stepped one foot into the hallway. He pulled the toothbrush from his mouth, the foam rimming his lips. "Unless they are expecting a happy ending to start the morning."

Nash and Uncle turned. Muna dropped her head onto her arms as Felix ducked his head.

"What? We are talking about a massage parlor, aren't we? How legit did you expect it to be in a cowboy town dominated by a federal prison?"

Muna rolled her head to look at Nash. "Invite frat boys to the house; get a frat party."

Thomas stuck his toothbrush back in his mouth and wound his way through the bus to the front door. "Okay. Okay. I'm taking my toothbrush and leaving. I need a shower."

Niko chuckled as he stood. "I need to get my bags out of the room. Nash, the keys to the SUV, please?"

She fished them out of her back pocket and tossed them. "Warm it up. Muna and I'll be out in a moment."

Alex snapped his fingers. "Oof. I forgot to get all those boxes of new Kevlar drapes and vests from the backseat."

Nash waved him down. "Chill. I moved all those boxes into the third row of seats yesterday. They're not in the way. We can unpack the boxes and move them into the bus tonight when Muna and I get back from Pueblo." She sniffed a few times and screwed up her face in disgust. "Meanwhile, someone needs to do laundry. It is getting a locker-room smell in here. And I don't mean in a homey, nostalgic way."

He saluted her with his two fingers.

Muna closed her laptop and slipped it into her bag. Picking up the small, hard-cased satchel, she turned to the door. "The trackers and bugs are all registered and set. I'll go help Niko stow his gear." She turned at the bus door and raised her chin toward Uncle. "Anything else on the shopping list while we're in town?"

He turned and opened the small refrigerator. He grimaced as he hummed. "Maybe another quart of half-and-half." He closed the door. "See what they have in the way of some fresh fruit like apples, bananas, or maybe apricots? Something healthier than your piggy rinds."

Muna rocked with a soft snort. "You just don't like how the napalm cleans by scorched earth on that delicate, elderly tummy of yours." She stepped down from the bus as he grabbed a wooden spoon to throw. Smiling at the sunshine, she muttered at the lack of actual heat. "No heat and no humidity." She smirked; it was a straighter hair day.

Niko started the SUV and set the heater on high. Getting out, he walked to the back. He toed his bag out of the way as he opened the back hatch. Powder sniffed at the larger bag. Niko laughed. "It's legal chocolate. Your mother bought them for my father. Let it go for once."

Muna chuckled. "Nothing gets past the super nose." She slid around behind Niko and Powder. She always insisted on having her equipment on the right side of the trunk.

Nash stepped out of the bus, holding a thin envelope. "Hey, Niko?"

Muna slipped the small black case into the back and turned. Niko straightened and lifted his bags into the space left. He looked over. "Yes?"

"Did you mean to leave this packet of information on the missing girl?"

Nash's left hand loosened on the envelope as her right hand moved back toward her holster.

An orange and red flame blossomed from under the front of the SUV. The open driver's door took a bow and then flew back past the shocked face of Niko as the explosion found its way into and around the large black SUV. The distinctive government license plate and front fender shredded into shrapnel. The explosive wave of fire and metal crossed the parking lot before Nash's hand touched her weapon.

As the back half of the SUV struck the three in the back, the wave slammed Nash back into the bus. The metal rattled against the armor; chipping paint more than the illusion created by the paint. Inside, Uncle and Alex were the target of the pan of soup as it threw Felix back into the bathroom.

The door to room nine slammed open. Thomas stood in horror at the scene. He pulled his cell phone out of his still-unbuttoned jeans. Barefoot, he ran across the parking lot.

"Nine-one-one. What's your emergency?"

He stopped between the SUV and the RV bus. It tore his mind both ways. "This is Sheriff Thomas Brady of Harkin, California. I'm at the Teton Motor Lodge in Cañon City. We just had a bomb go off. We need at least three ambulances and emergency medical."

"Sir, we only have one ambulance in Cañon City. And one at the prison..."

"Then we'll need a medivac."

"Sir, how many people are injured?"

He ran with a sense of urgency and dread, his heart racing as he closed in on the lifeless body by the bus. Dropping to his knees, he felt for Nash's pulse, desperate to find life still beating beneath his fingertips. His voice cracked as he spoke. "This is an act of terrorism against federal agents—I don't care how you get them, but I need every available resource here now. I want police, fire-fighters, sheriffs, National Guard, and even prison guards if you have to. Oh, God... there's one FBI agent down already, and her pulse is weak..."

Rising, he shouted toward the bus door with a mixture of fear and rage. "You all okay in there?!"

He ran across to the back of the burning SUV and the heaps on the ground.

Alex stumbled out of the bus like a broken doll, blood dripping from the gash on his forehead and smearing across his shirt. He kneeled beside Nash with trembling hands, willing her to still be alive. She was unconscious. He held her wrist for the pulse as he checked what was causing the bleeding. "It's okay, Nash. Help is on the way. Just stay with us."

He glanced at Thomas standing at the back of the burning SUV. The man bent and grabbed two legs from a dark heap. Dragging the body across the parking lot, he left it on the sidewalk in front of the rooms and ran back for the other one.

Kneeling, he picked up the small body and ran toward the build-ing. Halfway through, the burning gas tank exploded. The massive ball of orange flame swatted Thomas and Muna through the doorway of his room as the flames enveloped the entire parking area.

Alex huddled over Nash, shielding her as the flames ignited his shirt and scorched his hair.

Moments later, the shrapnel that had been the SUV returned—raining down a metallic hail on the otherwise silent parking lot. Two blocks away, a car alarm bleated inanely. The black smoke of what had been rubber, metal, and plastic merged into a single column of stench and hell.

17

GETTING OUT

AT LUNCHTIME IN THE BLUE, power ties range from the old school red to college rep to the perceived power of yellow and itty-bitty fishes. But when the genuine power finally gets together for lunch, nobody makes jokes about it being five o'clock somewhere. Nobody cares. Only the bottle from the top shelf matters.

A custom-cut Giorgio Armani pantsuit in old-bone silk charmeuse strode through the tables. The young hostess scrambled behind, trying to stop the woman but also afraid to even try. The woman's hair wasn't a wig and was short enough to be seen as a pure power cut with no fuss. Hard-lined makeup on the woman stressed the chillingly severe fix of her eyes.

She stopped at the almost hidden back table of five. "Hello, Peter."

He looked up with a smile that froze in horror. "Mina. What a surprise."

She turned her head slightly to the hostess. Her voice was laced with the potential of frostbite. "I'll require a chair."

The nod was small as the young woman retreated to perform what could be her last service at the Blue. Working at the notorious as well as famous watering hole of Washington power could either reward or destroy.

"Interesting ploy having your secretary slip about you being in a meeting in Arlington. Too bad she doesn't know you well enough to pull it off. You never wander west of the river… unless it is to visit your mistress in Alexandria." She cocked her head coyly. "How is little Bitsy these days? Why, she must be a sophomore now. How exciting for you."

The graying senator relaxed in his chair. His face was a passive smile, but his eyes were seething cauldrons of hatred. "Graduate school."

Mina didn't acknowledge the chair but simply sat. Patiently, she crossed her long legs and folded her hands in her lap. "My… how time has flown. Must have been the pandemic and all."

The younger man, in a shiny black silk suit, matching silk shirt, and chrome tie, held his fist to his mouth and cleared his throat. His cuff link reflected Mina in miniature.

Mina slowly blinked as her head ground around toward the man. "Vlad? Did you have something to say? Maybe something about a certain house on a certain island whose former owners used to enjoy the company of young girls? Or maybe you could entertain us with the stories of the money you can bring to bribe a certain vote to swing your way. I hear the Committee on Foreign Relations is going to have a remarkably interesting vote soon." She held her right hand out toward the senator. "Peter is on the committee. And if I remember correctly, it could have an enormous impact on how your county does or doesn't do business with the United States." She looked at the senator. "Or do I have it all wrong, Peter?"

The man was a statue of studied politics. "Why are you here, Ms. Lee?"

"Oh, Peter… Why would I ever interrupt such an important meeting between a powerful senator and an active agent of the Foreign Intelligence Service of the Russian Federation?" She glanced patronizingly at the Russian. "Yes, I know… he has a Belarus passport, but he was born and raised in Siberia and studied under Putin himself. He was an excellent student at researching the enemy and how to bribe them to betray their country… Except my people were better students."

Her eyes opened in surprise. Her right hand pointed behind her at a muffled commotion at the front of the restaurant. "Oh, did I mention the paparazzi, as well as three members of the ethics commission, wanted to have a brief word with you? Maybe about exchanging highly regulated NATO supplies with a known enemy? Or something about…? Well." She stood. "I'm sure you'll produce something good to explain dealing with an enemy of the state. And you holding that ultra-high security clearance and all. I'd like to say it was fun, Peter, but it wasn't. You've been a corrupt sleaze as long as I've known you. Enjoy your retirement… if they let you." She nodded at the other men, who were silently wishing they could be anywhere else. "Gentlemen."

She turned as the first three reporters walked up with their cameras already showing glowing red dots. She smiled. "Enjoy, gentlemen. And make sure you get the correct spelling of every-one's name. Those Russian names can be very confusing."

Her face was stone as she strode back out of the restaurant. She knew she wouldn't be welcome in the Blue for several months. But she considered it a small price to pay for rooting out evil at the highest levels of government. She made a note to think of an extra special reward for the researchers. They had dug up extensive and damning information she had already sent to every news service in D.C. Some days, it wasn't about getting a paycheck.

Her hand rested on the vibrating phone. The vibration was generic. There was only one ring vibration code she would stop everything for.

She handed the fifty to the valet for keeping her black Mustang at the curb.

He held her door. "Always a pleasure to see you, Ms. Lee."

She paused halfway through the door with a thought. Standing, she fished her slim wallet out of the inner jacket pocket. She fingered several hundred-dollar bills and pulled out the thin stack. "Stewart, after my stunt here this afternoon, I'm probably persona non-grata for several months or the next election cycle. Please spread this through you boys as my gratitude for all the years of your service. Hopefully, when the management calls to invite me back, you guys will still remember me."

He smiled with a small bow as she slipped into the sports car. "You will always be our favorite, Ms. Lee. And please give our regards to your lovely wife and daughter."

Smiling, she pushed the start button, pulled on her seat belt, and fished out her phone. The number wasn't a contact, but she recognized the first three numbers and the bureau they assigned the numbers to. Only one person in the building had her personal number other than her wife.

Scrolling through her contacts, she found the deputy director's personal cell number. She thumbed the green phone icon and dropped the phone in the cup holder. She could hear the phone ringing over her stereo system.

"Anthony."

"Tony, it's Mina."

"Are you home?"

Her eyes crunched closed. "No. I'm sitting in front of the Blue."

"How fast can you pack a bag and meet me at Dulles?"

She checked her mirror and fingered the turn signal. "I can buy anything I'd need in a bag. Even Dulles has supplies."

He snorted softly. "Not in the General Aviation terminal."

She watched the traffic as she waited at the curb. "Where are we going?"

"Colorado. It's still winter there."

She stomped on the accelerator and swerved into the small gap. The truck behind her blared his horn. "By seven."

"Perfect. And just so you know, they're still in surgery but not critical. So take your time and drive like a sane woman. We're the only ones on the plane… because this time, Mina… It's personal."

"The fucking plane better be ready when I get there, Tony." She thumbed the red phone on her steering wheel as she took a fast right through the red light.

THE WALL OF STAINLESS STEEL REFLECTED A BLURRY man. The black scrubs ended where the shiny legs began. Flames, reminiscent of a 1950s hot rod, laced their way up the leg with a single blinking light. He turned on his solid leg, transferred the body onto the tray, and pushed the drawer back into the cooler. He absently closed the door but hung on the large, levered handle.

Mike turned and looked through to the other part of the lab. The harder, more technical science parts of their work. He studied the white-haired man bent into the exhaust chamber as he portioned out samples into the array tray. Mike knew the process was tedious and exacting—he waited but glanced over at the computer terminal. The screen was still blank, except for the FBI logo in the center. For some reason, the blankness ate at his gut.

He glanced at his wristwatch. The time matched the school clock mounted high on the wall. Teasingly, the minute hand softly clicked back half a step and then forward another minute. The red arm swept past the one and continued.

Mike watched Oz insert the tray of samples into the heater and adjust the shaker. As he set the timer, he closed the door.

"Has Muna checked in with you today?"

Oz turned as his smarmy smile grew. "She's a grown-assed, full-blown woman, mommy. Let it go. The kids go out and play until the streetlights come on, and only then do they come home for dinner." He grabbed his large coffee mug with a green dragon circling it, forming the handle. "Damn." He slurped the last cold drop and looked across the room at the arch leading to the office room and the coffeemaker. The light beyond was dimming.

Mike shook his head. "I grabbed the last of the coffee about an hour ago." He glanced at the clock. "Didn't you two have a dinner date tonight?"

Oz put down his mug and leaned back against the autopsy table. "Had is the operative term here. She found the flyer this morning for the Hans Christian. She made me pull out the expense book on the Swan before I even had breakfast."

Mike burped a small chuckle. "How bad?"

"The haul-out was the lion's share. Although the dock fees would more than double, I pointed out it comes with a full hook-up of power, water, and sewer. Even more importantly, it's grandfathered in for full-time live aboard."

Mike pursed his lips. He could feel the punch line coming. "And… her response was…?"

"She patted me on the head as she told me it was a good thing. And then she pointed out that sleeping on the couch hurt my back. And I would have my own bathroom so she could leave out her makeup."

Mike raised an eyebrow as he pivoted on his mechanical leg. "Ouch."

Oz grimaced. "Yeah. Ouch." He glanced at the photo they had taken of the one severed arm. "Hey, have you had any more thoughts about how they cut the bodies up in the Colorado case?"

Mike glanced back over his shoulder. "I'm still going with a lightsaber. Disrupting the nuclear bond of the atoms is the cleanest I can think of. But did you pose the question back to the Body Farm? I'm sure they kept pushing research forward since you left."

"I talked to Leonatus last week. He's as stumped as we are."

Mike kept his face placid as he studied the folder. "So even with all their cutting-edge research, they still couldn't even lend us a hand."

"I argued they should have the answers to our questions, but he pointed out my argument didn't have a leg to stand on."

Mike moved to peek into the lower cadaver drawer. "The man just lost his head for the body of the case. I mean…" He straightened and turned with outstretched arms. "We're trying to get help so we can do our best job here, and all we get are bits and pieces."

Oz finally smirked a sad smile. "Some of our best work, and Muna isn't here to appreciate any of it."

Mike chuckled. "Maybe we should install some automated cameras in here and record this stuff for her."

Oz pulled on his jacket. "Let's not. We've both seen her shoot. And she just might not be in a forgiving mood some days. I think recordings might just exacerbate the situation."

"Yeah, maybe you're right."

Oz clicked his cheek as he tapped his thumb down on his finger gun aimed at Mike. "You know I am." He waved his finger around the lab. "Don't stay too late. There will always be more work in the morning. San Jose is bound to find some new bodies or something they need help with."

Mike looked up as the older man reached the office area. "Hey, Oz?"

The man turned back. "Yeah?"

"You don't think Muna would be giving us the cold shoulder from Colorado just because she doesn't like our jokes? Do you?"

The man turned toward the door, heading to the elevator. His voice boomed deeply in the hollow of the empty office room. "At that altitude, it's highly unlikely. Good night, Mike."

Mike turned back to his standing desk. His voice was barely more than a thought. "Good night, Oz. Enjoy the boat."

18

WHY DO DEER STEP SILENTLY

THE DEPUTY DIRECTOR and Mina stood waiting at the doors leading to the surgery. For the third time, the nurse showed her hand at the seats as she explained a surgeon would be out as soon as they could. Mina gazed around at the depressingly trivial pictures and worse framing lining the walls of the waiting room. She glanced at her wristwatch. The heavy gold dive watch had cost her fifty bucks on a backstreet of St. Thomas. She didn't wear it often but found when she did that it lent a sense of gravitas her thin womanly watches never did.

She looked back down the hall. "I need coffee." She looked at Tony. "They probably don't have anything stronger in a hospital…"

He held out his hand. "Let's start with the cafeteria and see where it goes from there." He stepped to the nurse's station. "Here's my card with my personal cell phone number. We're going down to the cafeteria for at least some coffee. Unless someone can offer us something stiffer to put in it."

The older nurse had heard it all. "The only stiff anything you can stick in the coffee is a plastic swizzle stick." She pulled the card toward her and glanced at the numbers. "I'll let the surgeon know where you are. They'll probably need some food or coffee themselves. They've been in there a long time."

Mina lowered her face to look out of the tops of her eyes. "Long enough for us to fly here from Washington, D.C."

Tony pinched the bridge of his nose. He had a sense of the power moves in Washington but didn't work on battle-weary nurses in the Rockies. He took Mina's arm and guided her away from the nurse. "We'll be in the cafeteria."

The small paper cups stood three deep on the table when the two surgeons walked into the cafeteria and looked around. Tony fished the wallet out of his left back pocket and held his badge and ID up.

The two in matching blue scrubs came over. Mina stood and held her hand out toward the other chairs. "Please. What can I get you? Coffee, food, scotch, and water, twenty hours of sleep?"

The woman collapsed into the chair as the man stood frowning at Mina.

Mina ran her hand over her short hair. "Sorry. I forgot to comb it this morning. Please. Sit. We'll start with coffee."

The man blinked and then sat. He looked at Tony. "Is she FBI?"

"No. Her wife is. The one you just worked on."

The woman swiped her cap off her short red hair. "I'm Katie Munson. This is Ted Cooper. So her wife is…" She closed her eyes and winced. Opening them, she blinked. "Al-Fara…?"

Tony vibrated his head. "No. That's my other agent. Muna al-Faragi. I was told she was out of surgery several hours ago."

"Her right lung collapsed. We had to go back in. There was a piece of shrapnel lodged around the side. It hadn't bled during the first surgery, so we missed it. But in recovery, her O2 saturation dropped, and then she was having trouble breathing. The team shot an X-ray this time to see if there was any more shrapnel. We're pretty sure we got it all. She'll stay intubated overnight and see where she's at in the morning." She pointed at Mina, returning with a tray of coffee cups and some donuts.

Tony shook his head. "Her wife is the other agent. Nash Running Bear. We haven't heard anything yet."

The man stood and grabbed the cup of coffee. "Thanks. I'll go check on the other surgeries." He turned and strode back into the hall.

Tony waved his finger around. "Mina, this is Katie. She's the surgeon who worked on Muna."

The redhead shook her hand and then pointed at the door. "Todd is a skilled surgeon… but his people skills…"

Mina cocked her head up. "But no word on my wife?"

"We only have two operatories here. I don't know who is where, but he'll track them down and get back to us."

Tony frowned. "How many…"

The woman bit into the apple fritter, and her eyes slid closed as she chewed. She held it out toward Mina. "Thank you." She sipped on the coffee. "It was a real rodeo this morning when they came in. I know one. They airlifted straight to Providence. The other four came here. Two never left the emergency center. I think they were concussed but also had severe burns. So they'll be in the ICU for the burns, but they didn't need surgery. We got the other two in surgery."

Mina hunched forward. "There was a dog…?"

The surgeon looked tiredly back over her shoulder. "If it was part of the cluster fuck of this morning, it's being taken care of somewhere. Dogs aren't throwaway around here."

Mina thinned her eyes. "My daughter is more than a dog. She saved my wife's life…"

Tony laid his hand on her arm. "I'm sure they will find Powder, and wherever she is, we'll find her being pampered. We just landed, and they just got out of one surgery. These things take time, and nobody has used the words dead or dying."

The surgeon raised her paper cup. "Here's to a day when everyone gets to go home… eventually."

Tony raised his cup as he moved Mina's hand toward her cup. "Hear, hear. People and dogs."

"Dog?"

They looked up at the returning surgeon. Mina squinted one eye. "My daughter. Powder."

The man sat as a small smile tugged at one side of his mouth. "She's up at the prison. Knut Magnusson is their doc. When we were in the sandbox, he was the K-9 doc. But after a surge, they found most of the trauma stuff was the same as a nasty dogfight. Broken bones, puncture wounds, stop the bleeding, and don't let it get infected. When he came back, the job at the prison paid better. Same shit with the same shitty hours, but more retirement and benefits. One of the smart responders scooped the dog up and drove it straight there. We can call out if you need to know now..."

Tony rested his hand on her arm again. "We can go out later. What about the other surgeries?"

"The Asian gentleman, Wanaka, or something, he went to Providence. He's in their ICU. He's critical, but they will probably downgrade him to guarded but stable by morning. The explosion crushed his rib cage. His left lung got nicked, but the concussion also hit his abdomen hard. They spliced nine ribs, but they might have to go into the abdominal cavity later. One of his legs is iffy, but they'll reassess him in the morning."

"And Nash Running Bear?"

"She's here. They're still pulling shrapnel out of her. They thought something had nicked her spleen, but it was a leaker from behind. Whatever they threw her against was hard. Five of the ribs cracked on her right side but not broken. The bad news/good news of it is that it will hurt a lot longer, but none of them did secondary damage. Evidently, her body armor saved her life. Some shards were stuck in the ceramic plates. What stuck through only gave her superficial cuts."

"She's a firm believer in being prepared for battle." Mina patted

Tony's hand on her arm and snuck a peek. She smiled at the surgeon. "Any word on the other two? The burns?"

He nodded and looked at his empty coffee cup. Thought for a moment and then placed it on the table. "They have the one guy sedated. But the other guy said whenever anyone showed up, he wanted to talk to them."

"Did you catch a name?"

The guy's face screwed up on one side. "Maybe. Or maybe they were talking football…"

Mina snorted. "Thomas fucking Brady."

The surgeon's eyebrows raised.

Mina nodded once. "Sheriff of Harkin County in California. He grew up with my wife."

"Kind of out of his jurisdiction, isn't he?"

Tony wagged his head. "Provisional consultant to the FBI, DEA, ATF, and Homeland. He's a valuable team member of her wife's gang."

The redhead rolled her eyes. "Not a smart gang to be blowing up."

Tony yawned and rubbed his one eye and face. "Several criminals would agree with you."

Mina reversed the hands and laid her hand on Tony's arm. The squeeze was gentle but insistent. "When can I see my wife?"

The surgeon, with a thicker than just a five o'clock shadow, shook his head. "If they were close to wrapping up, they would have said so." His eyes were bloodshot and glazed. "But if you need it… I'll go get changed and scrub in. But it would just be another cook in the small kitchen. I watched from the observatory… I would take you up there, but unless you've been in a battle MASH, it would just be upsetting."

He rubbed his face with his hands as he leaned forward. "The best thing I can tell you for right now is to go home. They'll call you when they know more. But my gut tells me she won't even know you're here until at least tomorrow night. She was comatose when they brought her in, so she may be the same after the surgery. It's always a wait-and-see."

Mina's voice had an edge. "We're two thousand miles from home."

"Then see the nurse in the surgical center. They have relationships with the local hotels. She'll set you up close by. You're probably going to be there for a while. This isn't a slap a band-aid on it and release. This kind of injury is a stay until they move her to a rehab facility. We're talking weeks for her and al-Faragi. The guy over at Providence might be out sooner, but I doubt it. You don't get blown up on Thursday and go play golf the next Wednesday."

Mina took a deep breath and let it out slowly. She closed her eyes and sat back in her chair. She studied the man as she chewed on her lower lip. "Yeah, this isn't our first rodeo." Her eyes narrowed to slits as she glanced at Tony. "It seems to go with the job."

Tony put up his hands. "I think even Nash will tell you nobody could have known. It's not her fault, my fault, or even the FBI... It's the fault of whoever set the bomb. And we'll get them."

"Look, I'm just a knife jockey. My people skills..." He glanced at his fellow surgeon. "As she can tell you, it ends when they stop the anesthesia. I did better in cutting on the troops in the sand. It's why I stayed for four tours. In my med school class, I got voted most likely to never find a bedside manner that worked. And I'm still looking. But I do know what works and what doesn't. My father used to call it walking like a deer. When a deer walks through the forest, every step is silent. It's so no other animal knows they are there. If you walk like a deer when you come to visit your wife, the charge nurses will forget you're there past visiting hours."

The redhead smirked and nodded. "Or you showed up before breakfast."

The man rocked in agreement. "Or you're the lump under the extra blanket on the other bed. The lump who was there all night. But you must walk like a deer."

Mina recognized the wisdom of the man and the saying.

She turned to place her hand on Tony's shoulder and stood. "Time for us to go find an extended stay hotel. And then we can go up to this prison."

Todd and Katie stood and stuck out their hands. Mina thanked them for their work and for spending so much time with her, as well as for the information. "The nurse can also get you Knut's information you'll need at the prison. He's a good guy. And the K-9s are his first love. Even the prison dogs like him. And they don't like anyone."

19
WHY?

THE MIST HUNG THICKER and heavier than she remembered. The dark limbs and trunks of the dead black locus trees didn't remind her of nightmares or look like they were trying to grab her. They were softer and quieter somehow. The dead grass on the edge of the creek was forgiving instead of prickly. The creek still smelled like dirty gym socks—musty, but reassuringly comfortable.

She looked down. Her feet hid in the warm waters of Bone Creek. She put her hands behind her and leaned back. She looked up at the sky. Gray, only gray.

She closed her eyes and thought about lying back. Taking the afternoon off... but from what?

There was something she was supposed to be doing. A need. She had responsibilities. Didn't she?

She laid back. Her hands smoothed out the grass to her sides.

"Sometimes you need to just get away and soak your toes in the lifeblood of Mother Earth."

A slow smile formed on Nash's face. She didn't open her eyes. The grass felt even softer. "It's what you always told me."

"You were cute, but you never mind good, little rabbit."

Her forehead wrinkled in a shrug. "When was a daughter supposed to mind everything her father told her to do?"

"Not everything. But the important things. Life things. Those you needed to learn."

She sat up. "But you never told me they were the important lessons. You just threw them in with how to stuff some trout with huckleberries and mint. How was I supposed to know soaking my feet in Bone Creek was more important?" She looked over at the man.

His hair was the same. Black as night, with only one wave just behind the front. She knew that by the end of the month, the wave would be two, and his hair would brush the tops of his ears. After dinner, he would drag the red stepstool out onto the front porch. Her mother would follow with the comb and scissors. The poncho came from Korea. While the two talked and cut his hair, they expected her sister and her to do their homework. They all knew a haircut in town only took a handful of minutes, but they would be out there until it was too dark to see.

She smiled at the memory and looked down the bank and across to the other side of the creek. The old tracker shed was barely visible in the mist.

She smiled at the memory. "Nice haircut.".

He ran his hand through it and shrugged. "End of the month."

She nodded and wiped her eyes with her sleeve again before replying. "Fire season is coming soon. Are you going to still work the northern rail routes?"

He coughed. "They don't run here."

Her head ground around. "Then where do they run?"

He gazed at her, an odd mix of emotions in his eyes. Half of him seemed to plead with her to ask something else, while the other half seemed almost scared of her response. "Is that really what you want to know?"

"She doesn't know how to ask. She never wanted to learn." The woman kept looking at the surrounding water. "There's no fish here."

He looked over at his wife standing in the creek up to her thighs. The dress was her buckskin dress. Nash had only seen her wear it a few times—only when there was a special ceremony or funeral up at the VFW hall.

Nash frowned. "Ask what?"

Her father ran his fingers through his hair and hung his head. After a moment, he swung his head up to the side to look at his daughter. "Maybe… why you're here?"

Nash frowned harder and cocked her head. "Here?"

The bright light washed out the mist and people. She took a breath, but it hurt. The new gray wasn't mist. It was darker. She fell in.

"No… It's gone now. For a moment there, her heartbeat and respiration spiked."

"Would she have felt the scalpel?"

The anesthesiologist shrugged. "Hard to say. By all indications, she's still in a coma. But… she twitched."

"Well, watch her. I have one more to chase down in this leg…" The surgeon glanced up at the clock. "And we're on the backside of the seventh hour…"

The woman looked at her monitors. "I've got twenty more minutes. After that, I need to flush her and up her oxygen."

The surgeon bent over. "Let's roast this pepper." He held out his hand. "Clamp."

The woman in the creek ran her hand through the water as if searching for something. Her voice was sad. "There were never any fish," Her eyes turned to meet her husband's. She shook her head. "Nash never asked because she wanted nothing of our world. She was always reaching for the white man's world and nothing else."

The man paused in his whittling small curls off a stick with his pocketknife. "Little rabbit liked our world, but she had her place in their world as well. But all she ever did was run between them both so fast that she couldn't find balance."

"Balance is where you can find it," the woman said breathlessly, throwing her arms wide before letting herself fall back into the creek. There was no splash, only the water embracing the woman as if joining.

Nash ran her hand along the grass, feeling a strange mixture of emotions. The soft blades were so green and lush, so different from the dry, browned grass she remembered blanketing their land. She thought about her father's words—words talking about balance, but he never seemed to practice what he preached. She whispered like she didn't want him to really hear her. "What balance? You never talked about balance. You only worked until you came home and then stuffed the heads of deer you never shot. They were trophies of someone else's killings. But you hung them on our walls like they were yours."

Suddenly, Nash felt a presence behind her and turned to see her mother standing there. Her moccasins showed an intricate unfamiliar beading—Navajo or Ute, not Paiute—and the blue dress clashed with the beading's colors. There was something off-putting about it all, yet comforting at the same time. Her mother opened her hand and offered a stick of meat to Nash. "Roadkill jerky? It's fresh. Your father picked it up just last Saturday. You were playing basketball with the white boy."

Nash took a deep breath as conflicting emotions flooded through her body.

Nash looked at the jerky. *Which animal?* "I play well so I can get scholarships. Nobody will give a Paiute girl an academic scholarship. The white world doesn't think we can think. I must prove them wrong by showing them at being best."

The woman was back in the water in her buckskin dress. "But you try to be the best in their world." The water was up to her waist. "There is no balance in their world. You can only find parity. Parity is not balanced. The coyote is a dog, the wolf is a dog, and so is a Chihuahua. But the Chihuahua and coyote are not wolves. The wolf is powerful alone because he is with his family. The coyote is only as powerful as his own jaw. He is alone. No family." Nash snickered as she looked at the ink markings on her moccasins. She had only worn them in the sixth grade. The year that they couldn't afford new shoes for her growing feet. Her father had made them out of a doe he had found on the highway. The meat was cold and already buzzed with flies. But he skinned the carcass and continued to work. He had a barrel of water and battery acid he used to tan hides. He made copies of her feet out of boards and used them to form the moccasins. They had no beads, so she drew the symbol of bear claws on the toes.

She looked up at her mother in the creek. "But I always had bears."

Her mother wagged her head in a sad sweep. "They're not your spirit animal."

"Then why am I Running Bear?"

Her father grumped from behind her. She looked back at his battered steel-toed boots and bib overalls. "Because it is my name. And I married your mother, and she birthed you two girls, so it is our name." He looked at the eagle floating in the gray sky. "But it is not a spirit guide."

"She never wanted her guide." The woman was in the water up to her neck now. *When did the creek get so deep here?*

"I thought only the boys went on spirit walks..."

Her mother, sitting on the grass next to her, straightens out her gingham dress as she clucks her tongue. "Boys walk. Yes." She reached over, and Nash could feel the warmth of a hand on her arm. "But you are not a boy, Nash. You are my daughter."

"So is my sister…"

The eyes seemed to look more through Nash than at her. "She is your sister. But you are your fathers and my daughter. You are not like your sister."

Nash looked across the creek to the mixing grays of the mists. "How can that be? I mean… In what way?" She looked to her left at the air. The woman was gone.

Turning to her right, her father braced his thumb as he pulled another small chip off the stick with his knife. He turned to look at her. "How can what be?"

"How can I be…?" She stopped and couldn't remember what she was thinking of.

THE MORNING LIGHT FILTERED THROUGH THE HOSPITAL room's sheer curtains. Gently, it illuminated the sterile space. The slightly raised head of the bed helped with breathing and allowed the soft light to caress Nash's face. Lying in the other bed, Mina pushed on her pillow, shifting it out of her way to get a better view of her wife's finger twitching. She pressed the button again but knew it wouldn't work until the nurse arrived. The room was quiet except for the sound of machines beeping and whirring in the background. Outside, birds chirped, and cars honked as life continued on. Mina waited anxiously, hoping for any sign that her wife would recover. The soft rubber of the clogs squeaked as the nurse turned the corner into the room. "Wha…?"

Mina pointed. "Watch her middle finger."

The nurse stood, hugging her arms. Finally, there was a twitch. She turned to the Asian woman on the other bed and nodded. "They do that. If we watch her feet, she will also curl her toes or draw the toes back. It's called myoclonic twitching. We watch it to see if it gets more pronounced. But other than that, it's normal. Mostly, it shows the brain is still working. Her breathing on her own is another good sign of that. But for now… It's just a wait-and-watch game. But I'm guessing you need some breakfast." She closed one eye and raised the other eyebrow.

Mina froze but finally nodded. "And pee." She sat up.

"Do you want it here or go down to the cafeteria?"

Mina smirked as she stood on the cool linoleum floor. "I don't think they'd want me peeing down in the cafeteria."

The nurse breathed through her nose at the humor. "What would you like for food?"

Mina stopped at the bathroom door and looked back. "Are you a vegan?"

The woman barked a laugh. "No. I'm a Colorado native. If it stops moving long enough, I'll eat it."

Mina nodded and gave her a thumbs up. "Whatever looks good to you is good enough for me. As long as there's a large carafe of coffee attached." She closed the door.

<hr>

NASH LOOKED UP AT HER FATHER AND THEN LOOKED back at the soft moccasins. There was something important about her footwear.

Her father set the small carving in her hands. "This is a rabbit. It runs here and there. They are fast when they run. But they don't know where they are running to or from. They just run because it's what they do. You need to know where you're from to know where you are running. Or you're just another rabbit among the bushes. Running."

Nash held up the carved rabbit with long ears. "Is this my spirit guide?"

He gently shook his head. "You don't have to ask if something is your guide. You will just know." He stroked the knife along the stick. Bark peeled off.

"Where are your feet?"

Nash looked at the woman standing on the other bank. The woman stood dressed in... or she was the dry grasses of the bank. Or she was naked. Nash narrowed her eyes to see better. Then she looked down at her knees. Straightening her legs, the wet feet rose from the creek. She cocked her head. "There are no fish here."

She frowned at her words. She looked down, and her small feet were in moccasins with a diamond pattern drawn with ink from the pens she found in the teacher's desk.

The young Nash looked up and then around. She was alone. The mist blanketed everything. It hung like peanut butter from the roof of her mouth—thick... and heavy.

20

NO. I WON'T

"You were incredibly lucky. You didn't catch much of the blast. Relatively speaking, you got away unscathed. The blast just nudged you around a bit."

Muna winced and touched her side, and frowned. And then tapped the intubation tubing taped into her mouth.

The surgeon nodded in agreement. "Yes. We had to go in through your right side to get the shrapnel stuck behind your lung —it gave us quite a scare. We thought we were through, and you could rest easily in the ICU until your lung suddenly collapsed, and we had to find out what was going on with it. So, we took a CT scan to see if you were filling up with either fluid or blood, and that's when we found out about the shrapnel. You may feel some soreness on that same side of your body, so we're going to keep you on this intubation for a few more days as a safety measure. If you would rather, we can sedate you to make sure you get plenty of rest for the next several days."

Muna's face froze and then shook. She waved her hand as if wiping off a whiteboard.

"Sedated or not, the best thing for you to do right now is just sleep. If you can't sleep, just ask the nurse for sedation. I've put it in your chart so you can just be a rag doll and sleep. You're getting all your nutrition through the IV, so we don't even have to wake you up to eat or do the other. Okay?"

Muna nodded. She acted like she was writing in her palm.

He patted his pocket for a pen, but there was none. She pointed at his pants and then acted like she was texting on the phone. He laughed. "Yeah. That'll work." He pulled out his phone. Opening it, he handed it to her.

She opened text messages and typed.

He looked. "Agent Running Bear is still in a coma. The Asian fella is over at Providence, but he's doing fine. Unlike you, he caught most of the blast. The two other fellas are down the hall, here in the ICU, because it's the best care for their burns. And I understand the dog is being spoiled out at the prison in Cañon City. If you behave yourself, we'll move you up to a room in recovery. But you must behave. The others told me you're the troublemaker of the bunch."

She typed.

He read the text and shook his head. "No. But your uncle is here and wants a few minutes with you. But the nurse is going to send in the armed guards after five minutes. I'm serious about sleeping. If you don't sleep on your own, I'll take you out myself." He took his phone back and held up his hand with the fingers spread. "Five minutes."

She nodded.

Uncle stood in the door as the surgeon left. He nodded.

Strolling to the side of the bed, Uncle took Muna's hand in his. "They told me about the five minutes." His voice rumbled like rocks tumbling in a waterfall, but it was the sound of home. She nodded.

He handed her a tablet already booted to the memo app. Her face glowed.

Her fingers flew and then adjusted the font size to large. "Got any rinds hiding in your pocket?"

He chuckled. "No. Not yet." He pointed at her mouth. "They tell me you need to keep chewing on the plastic hose for a while. Behave. It's their house, so their rules."

"This will help. I feel useless."

He closed his eyes as he gently wagged his head. "Far from it. This is the universe just telling us all to take a breath. Slow down. Regroup and just think. We are on an important hunt. The hunter who runs through the forest is hungry and tired at the end of the hunt. It is only when he walks gently on the sticks and leaves that he finds the prey unafraid and unaware. Then he sleeps with a full belly."

"My belly is empty."

He smirked, pointing to the two bags hanging on the IV pole. "Your body doesn't know that. For now, you need to just sleep and dream of hunting. Soon enough, you will step silently through the great forest of the internet."

She looked at the tablet and pointed at the one icon with a yellow lock overlapping it. She glowered at the old man and typed a question mark. Her fingers pinched the screen and made it larger.

He chuckled in a deep rumble. "Oh yes. The internet thing. You only get to use this app to write things. If you think of something, you can save the memos. But the internet? I locked the door with a code word. And before you try to crack it..." He smirked. "I used a phrase in Athabaskan. It is an old Hopi saying about the forming of the world. I think what you are wondering is how many characters I have to use in trying to break this old man's code. Well, the Japanese were good, but Uncle Sam was gooder. He asked the Navajo to talk on the radios. The Japanese never could crack the Wind talkers code because they were just talking to each other in everyday Navajo." He reached into his jacket pocket and pulled out the charging cord. He placed it on the counter with the small sink and an electrical outlet.

Uncle looked at the nurse standing in the doorway. Rocking with understanding, he stepped to the bed and patted Muna on the hand. "Time to sleep, little one. Dream of hunting. I'll be back in a few days."

She frowned in confusion. She didn't need the tablet.

He pointed south. "I need to go home." He shook his head. "No. Not California. South, where I grew up. I need to go have a conversation. And for that, I need an old friend of mine—a shaman. But I'm taking Thomas, so I'll be back."

He turned to walk out. He stopped beside the nurse. The man looked at him and nodded as he held up a syringe. Uncle patted him once on the shoulder. "Then I'll leave you to it."

Uncle poked his head into the next room. Felix was sitting next to the bed, talking to Alex. He looked over and smiled. "We can't speak ill of the man as he still walks above the dirt."

Alex's chuckle was muted. "It must be Uncle."

Felix looked down at the mirror on the floor, reflecting Alex's face. "Thomas was grabbing the nurse's asses, so they knocked him back out."

Alex chuckled some more. "Yeah, those male nurses have no sense of humor."

The tall blonde, who could have played noseguard for Thomas in his heyday, turned from the dry-erase board on the wall. "You do know I'm still here, don't you? Or do I need to stir the martini with your rectal thermometer to remind you?"

Felix laughed. "Ooh… someone just got burned."

The man turned with one hand on his hip and the other palm held out toward the charred and blistered back. "And from the look of things, it's not his first time." He looked over at the door. "Oh Daddy. Who is this tall drink of aged whiskey?"

Felix rocked back in the chair. "No Daddy, just Uncle. And no, he doesn't play for your team, Roger."

The nurse snapped the cap back on the dry marker. "Shame. Him coming with a rein and whip all in one." He pointed at Felix. "No fair passing him any moonshine while I'm gone and can't share." He excused himself past Uncle. His voice was deeper and more in keeping with his looks. "Watch the little one. I think he's a troublemaker."

Uncle nodded. "In more ways than you can imagine." He pulled up a second chair and turned it around backward as he sat. "What did I miss?"

"Felix was just telling me he thinks someone followed him from the massage parlor."

The kid winced. "I was distracted... I almost missed the GMC one ton."

"Did you catch anything?"

He passed over his phone. "I'll go back and see if there is more with a better shot of their faces, but at least I captured a side view of them when I turned into the motel."

Uncle watched the video from the rear-view dash camera in the truck. The one truck stayed a couple of cars back. "It's not his first time tailing someone. Don't beat yourself up over this. Most people would have never..." He watched the angle change, and the truck drove past. He tapped the screen and backed it up. Pinching the screen, he made the truck larger.

Felix nudged his chin. "Let it run out. I grabbed the best shot and cleaned it up. It's come up next."

Uncle let it play. The video turned black. A still image replaced it. The full-screen image was the side of the truck, and the driver turned to look at the truck entering the hotel. The driver's face was slightly fuzzy, but maybe doable. "Muna can clean this up." He looked up at the deadpan face of the kid. "When they let her play with her computer again."

Felix rolled his eyes as he held his hand out for the phone. "I might be retired by then."

Uncle held it away from him. "You kids. Always in a hurry. Rushing here, rushing there. Nobody just sits and watches anymore."

Alex chuckled. "Says the man who made a career out of sitting in a bar."

Uncle huffed. "We put away several criminals by my sitting and watching. Besides, the wooden seat is hard on these sittin' bones."

They watched Alex's head roll back and forth. "True story. Been thinking about retiring?"

The fire glinted in Uncle's eyes. "I've been thinking about the lucrative move to consulting for the FBI. I hear they let you just lie around on your tummy all day."

Uncle passed the phone back, and Felix shoved it in his pocket. He looked down at the face in the mirror. The eyes were closed. Felix lowered his voice and turned to the older man. "Tell me, mister consultant to the FBI, have you heard anything from the agent we met before?"

"I was going to call him or go call on him. I would have thought he would at least call or drop by each day to check on everyone. It's not like it was some obscure event nobody heard of."

Felix nodded. "I wonder if they have all the windows in the motor lodge replaced yet. I'll bet they have a ton of crime-scene crazies wanting to rent a room."

Uncle grumbled. "A crazy world." He glanced up. "Who got the Max fella's business card?"

Felix turned in his chair and crossed his legs. Resting his crossed arms on his knee, he leaned toward Uncle and away from Alex. "I'm fairly sure it was Nash. She was the FBI agent in charge. So, the ICS would have her on the top. What are you thinking?"

The man vibrated his head as he blinked, looking at the floor. "Just how strange it is. Four days since the bombing, and still no contact from the local office. None of the local offices." He looked up at the kid. "Have you heard anything from Homeland?"

He eased his head back and forth. "I hardly ever hear from them. It's like they deposit a check each month, and that's enough. But then, it's my job. Hang out in Harkin with the big kids, keep my nose clean, and mature as an agent."

"You don't check in? Do they even know you're here?"

The kid stretched his face in a shrug. "I didn't think anything

21
WHO?

THE NURSE GLANCED at the monitor by the bed as it beeped softly. Almost as if it was counting time. The minutes, the hours, the days. Passing gently in the dim room. The woman lay motionless on the bed. Her black hair, brushed and shiny, splayed to one side of her head and, like a waterfall, cascaded down over her chest.

The sunshine felt soft as it filtered through the light gray of the low clouds. A few trees in the distance looked squat and stunted. Gray mist played through their limbs and trunks like worms in the garden soil.

The panorama was a study in gray. Nash slowly turned around in a circle. *I don't remember everything being so gray—no color, no life.*

She stopped turning. An older woman bent over a large bush. The once darker buckskin had faded to a soft sand color. Colorful beads glowed from the softer background. The reds looked like fire ants, pushing drops of blue sky and green bits of plants as they marched their way around the patterns.

Nash's mother straightened. The spring cuttings of blue-green sage hung from her younger hands. There were no wrinkles on the face as she squinted against the light to see Nash. The beaded pattern of a bear claw was only half finished. "You have to harvest the soft, fresh growth of the blue sage if you're going to use it for your hair."

Nash looked around the dense carpet of sage. "Where is this?"

The young man, dressed only in dungarees, walked past Nash. The muscles rippled with the soft sheen of sweat. He peeked back at her. "Our home." He stopped and looked about. "Our forever home."

Nash frowned. "Dad?"

The young buck smiled and nodded as he continued to walk to the woman. He picked up a large tarp by the corners and wound it into a carry bag. Hoisting it onto his shoulder, the youth became an older man in bib overalls. He glanced back at Nash, and the mist became the man and bundle as the bundle and man became the mist.

The older woman in the beaded buckskin bent back to the sage. "If your hands don't touch the spirit, the spirit can't talk to your hands."

"What spirit? All I see are brush, brush, and more bushes of brush. Why do you always have to talk in riddles like some Eastern mystic?"

As the old woman straightened, the beading fell from the dress. The youth squinted at Nash. "How do you know when a storm is coming?"

Nash cocked her head as she grimaced at the non-sequitur. "The wind picks up and blows like hell."

Her father stood from behind a larger sage bush. Stalks of cuttings and his pocketknife hung from his hands. His face looked tired. "When does the wind blow hard, but there is no storm, little rabbit?"

"When? Every spring. The storm is over the volcano. We only get the wind."

His face smiled and was young. The sweat glistened off his naked body and darkened the waistband of his weathered jeans.

"How do you know the storm has stopped to give Withassa a drink?"

"The radio."

Her mother smiles and snickers. "You always listen to a radio? Which radio is that?"

The young father laughs and bends back to the bush. "We never had a radio." Nash smells the fresh, astringent tang in the air of the cut rabbitbrush sage. *Chrysothamnus.* Yellow and white flowers heaped the tarp beside him—*field asters.*

Her mother straightened and snapped the small branch. Nash smiled. The smell was camphor, but she thought of Christmas and remembered the fresh-cut sprigs laid on the mantlepiece to be thrown occasionally into the fire. "Giant sagebrush." *Artemisia tridentata. Why would I remember the Latin name?* "It stops bleeding. You used to make a tea for my cramps."

Her mother smiled and looked at the youthful version of her husband. "Maybe the rabbit doesn't run so fast anymore."

The older man in the worn bib overalls squinted back. "Maybe little rabbit is tired? She sleeps a lot. Maybe she is dying." He winced and looked behind him into the distance. "A storm is coming." He turned back to Nash. "Little rabbit needs to hide or run."

"No. I don't hide anymore. Let the storm come. But why do you keep changing your ages? One second, you're young, and the next, you're old. Stop it. It's giving me a headache."

Her mother stepped forward in her blue and white checked gingham dress. She held out a small leather bag. "Here. Smell this. Open the bag and just breathe."

Nash hadn't seen the small leather bag since she was small. She knew it was lavender, spearmint, and peppermint. Nash laid the bag against the side of her nose. She didn't need to open it for more. As she held it to her face, she glanced down. Her feet were small, and the white moccasins didn't have any symbols drawn on them.

It was in the spring when she turned six. Her father had taken her up to the summer camp. The high-altitude meadow had called to her in the gray of the morning. She had walked out into the tall grass. A doe and her small fawn grazed a few feet away. Nash stood silently still. The doe's ear twitched as she watched her curious fawn approach the small girl. Gently sniffing, the fawn relaxed and stood in front of the girl.

As Nash gently raised one hand, the fawn sniffed.

She touched under the jaw, and then along the cheek, and finally the ears. Stepping into the embrace, the fawn leaned against her hand.

Shifting, the doe turned and walked away. The fawn looked back at its mother and then sniffed one more time at the waist of the naked girl. Turning, it stepped and then bounded after its mother. Nash stood watching until her father stepped beside her. He rested his hand down on her shoulder and hugged her to his hip. "Breakfast is ready, little rabbit."

The man in blue scrubs erased the numbers on the dry-erase board and wrote the new ones. He glanced back at the numbers on the machine. They were higher. Stepping to the bed, he felt a pulse on the wrist. The beats were stronger and closer together. He watched the small mounds at the end of the bed. The toes weren't moving. "If you're not running, why is your pulse up?" He watched the face. There was no movement except the eyes under the eyelids. *REM.*

"It goes up and down. But she doesn't move."

He had forgotten about the tall Asian woman sitting in the corner. Always there and always reading. "I'm sorry... What?"

Mina closed the cover on her pad. "You noticed the change on the monitor. Her blood pressure raises... well, for her, it's up. But the pulse speeds up. I don't know what it is, but give it a few minutes, and it goes back to..." She waved her hand at the dry-erase board. "... <u>What</u> you just erased."

He smiled and cocked his head. "I'm sorry, but you are...?"

Mina stood. "I'm Mina, like the bird but spelled like the hole in a mountain. I'm her wife."

He shook her hand and relaxed, slumping his weight on one hip. "It all makes sense now. There is no second patient in here, but I've seen you in the other bed. But you're always here."

Mina rocked as she watched Nash. "We live in Washington D.C." She looked back at the man. "I didn't even take the time to find a room." She frowned and looked at the floor. "Oh. Yes, I did. Extended Stay, I stayed there the first night..." She rolled her eyes. "My bag is probably still in the middle of the table in the room. I hope they don't just throw it out."

"It can't be restful sleeping here."

She snorted softly as she brushed her hand over her short, fuzzy head of hair. "Between the operations, chemo, and radiation, I've spent half my time in hospitals these last few years. Hospitals are old friends for me. Nobody wants to come hunt me down in a hospital, so I got a lot of work done." She pointed at Nash. "The last serious time I was in, I woke up to her face. I want to be there for her."

"Because it's the least you can do?"

"No. That's the martyr's creed. Because it is the least I want to do for her."

He rolled his lips and took a deep breath through his nose. "We never see enough of that around here. We have people who nobody ever comes to see."

Mina thought about it. "Give me their room numbers. I can be the friendly face."

He pointed. "Three doors down. She was in a crash or something. She's as torn up as your wife, maybe even more, but at least she's awake. But all she has is a pad to play with. I don't think it's even Wi-Fi enabled."

Mina snorted with an enormous smile. "They just took her off the ventilator yesterday. What she needs right now is you. Her throat must be trashed. Maybe a little sherbet? And her name is

Muna." She pointed at Nash. "They work together for the FBI. Who else you got?"

He blushed. "I'll make a list."

"I want names and room numbers so I can have flowers delivered."

"Some are guys."

She smiled and rested her hand on the man's shoulder. "Trust me, everyone likes flowers. It means someone is paying attention to them."

He turned at the door. "I'll make you the list. You want the pediatrics, too?"

Mina scowled. "If kids aren't getting visitors, I especially want their names and rooms." She snapped her fingers in memory as he disappeared. "Hey...?"

He stepped back. "Nathan. Nurse Nathan."

"Nathan. Thank you. You said Muna isn't on the Wi-Fi?"

He crunched his face and shook his head. "I think the pad was just so she could communicate. I've never seen someone type so fast on a pad before."

Mina growled. "Wait until you see her on a laptop. Where's the nearest tech store?"

He winked. "I'll get you some names and addresses." He pointed at her. "As well as the patients. Kids first."

She walked back to her wife lying on the bed. Bending, she stroked the hair and kissed her lightly on the forehead. "I'll be back. I need to go get Muna her drug of choice."

* * *

MINA STOOD LOOKING AT THE LONG TABLE OF LAPTOPS. All were open. All were running the same screen saver. Some were the size she liked—compact and discreetly portable. Others were large to accommodate the screen and the ten-key calculator, like a regular keyboard. Her eyes glazed over.

"Maybe I can help you."

She turned to look at the older man with more salt mixed with his pepper. The face was gentle but showed marks of work outside of four walls. She glanced at the nametag. "Maybe you can, Phillip. Maybe you can. They all look the same to me." She waved her hand over the table.

He chuckled. "Far from them being all the same. And it's just Phil, like gas in your car."

Mina leaned her hip against the table and thought about her cousin and her own car. "So, you know about cars?"

He glowed. "Mostly older muscle cars. I was a mechanic for twenty-eight years—until I broke my back in an accident. Rehab taught me about computers."

"I have a Mustang with a positraction rear-end off a custom six-speed manual. I wanted alpine and airport gearing. Still with me?"

He smirked. "That's funny. Most people only brag about how their V8 is big and sucks gas like an alcoholic at an open bar." He chuckled at her smiling face. "Okay. I'm in. You have a road racing car. What kind of mill?"

Her eyes narrowed in mirth. "We started with a two-eighty-nine, and then blue printed it at twenty over. She's balanced, ported, and polished to accept the dual quads. She runs out on the dyno at just over six hundred horses."

He leaned against the table as he thought. "Did you ever consider a turbo and only a single carburetor?"

She shook her head softly. "No. A turbo negates all the advantage of gears and back-pressure."

"What's the shell?"

"Seventies B-body fastback. I live in Washington D.C., not enough sunshine to consider a convertible."

Phil laughed. "And she's your daily runner. I like your style. Did you build it?"

"My cousin did. He made me learn everything about it and why before he gave me the key. I took a few courses on driving down in Daytona. I didn't want to be a menace to society."

He pointed at the computers. "So, how can I help you here?"

"I need a Chevelle, radio-delete, with a four fifty-four, turbo double pumper, with nitro. Ostensibly, I need an eight-second car I can take to Indie. Looks aren't the major concern here, but power and ability to dance in the dark spaces are."

He nodded. "A super gamer with the ability to pick up and go. Funny, I didn't peg you for a fast car and faster computer type."

She laughed. "Yeah, I get the little ol' granny thing all the time."

He nodded and bumped off the table. He looked around. "Hey, John. Where's Selena?"

The kid looked toward the back and then smiled. "Chips is on her break. What do you need?"

"A massively overclocked mega-gamer, stripped to the essentials. She'll load her own. Something she can go head-to-head with a water-cooled tower in competitions."

The kid laughed a bubble out of his nose. "This I gotta see. I'll go get her."

Phil jerked his thumb over his shoulder. "She's a mega-gamer who makes almost as much building battle machines for other gamers."

Mina harrumphed. "I know of a company in southern California who would pay her top dollar to scratch her itch on company time. In fact, they would encourage it."

"Talk to her. She's wasted here in the badlands."

2 2

WE NEED A BREAK

ONLY THE EDGES of the corrugated metal roof showed signs of rust. Thin brown lines traced in waves along the length of the vast building. Two gigantic doors stood rolled back in deference to the chilly morning air. The static of arc and other welding on the manufacturing floor punctuated the sounds of steel on steel. If it was custom-fabricated steel, G&G Fabrication produced it. The owners liked to brag if they were near big water, they'd be building ships and barges.

The truck nosed into the large yard and swung into one of the three parking spots between the large barn doors and the smaller office doors. Only five vehicles ever parked in the parking spots. The two owners, the secretary, and their wives. A buyer had once parked his Mercedes in one spot. A worker forklifted the offender into the middle of the lot and turned the cutting crew loose. Betting ran heavily toward the ten-minute mark, but the plasma torches made shorter work of the non-Detroit car.

A new employee with a Japanese car had taken the hint and sold his car that night. By the weekend, he drove a ten-year-old Chevy truck with a double gun rack in the back window.

Even with the windows up, the welder in the barn door could

155

hear the two men arguing. The driver opened his door and swung his legs out. "Just hush, Grady. Ain't nothing going to happen. Now, let's get this contract hammered out." He kicked the door closed.

As they turned the corner of the large door, Jayson looked across the shop toward the expansive wall of hanging plastic strips. The twelve-inch heavy plastic strips overlapped to create a solid barrier between the welding floor and the wet cutting area. The strips allowed a person to walk through the barrier or any extensive project to be moved to or from the large cutter.

"How's the new cutter head working out?"

Grady winced with one eye and looked elsewhere. "I haven't had time to check on it…"

Jayson growled as he changed course from the office to the wet room. "Lazy fuck."

"Hey. We've been busy."

Jayson closed one eye in disgust as he turned to the operator poking information into the machine's computer interface. "Hey, Juan?"

The man glanced over. His shirt, under the company logo, read Palo. "Yeah, boss?"

Jayson scratched at his graying beard as he watched the machine's arm and head move into position over the plate of steel. Water bubbled up around the steel, and then a jet streamed from the cutting head. The tone changed as the operator touched the screen to add the micro garnet into the water stream.

He talked loudly over the sound of the machine, water striking the steel, and the garnet cutting the metal at a speed faster than the speed of sound. "I see the new cutting head fixed the problem?"

The man watched the stream cut through the one-inch-thick armor-plating steel. Satisfied with the sound and speed of the cut, he turned. He shook his head. "Same cutting head. The new one they sent was the wrong one, so I rebuilt this one."

Jayson's face darkened. "We lost over a month of production. What was wrong with it?"

The man looked back at the computer screen. "Same as before. Someone keeps using it to cut up their deer or something. But instead of having the water flush into the sewer, they use the recycle function, and the biological gets in the flow tube and gums it up. As heavy-duty as these machines are, they aren't meant to be a butcher shop. Even I know that if the steel has a lot of surface rust or scale, don't use the recycle function on the water. Flush it. But as for meat and bone, the shit is nasty and gums it all up."

Jayson glowered at his partner. "Alright. Well, good to see it's back up and running."

"Yes, sir. I can cut a lot of the backlog with eighty percent garnet to speed up the cutting. It leaves a lot of cut mark, but it's a heck of a lot faster than when I need cutting at twenty for the super smooth finish."

Jayson scratched at the side of his beard as he nodded and turned. "Just get 'er done. We need those parts." He gave his partner wide eyes as they walked through the wet wall.

Grady whimpered quietly on the other side. "They aren't meant to be a butcher shop..."

Jayson stopped and slowly ground his head around. "I told you to use the flush. It doesn't use that much water to cut up a body."

"But I was—"

"Shut up Grady. When I tell you to do something, you do it. Do you hear me?" The man bristled and then nodded as his shoulders slumped. "Good. Now go ask Jose..." He pointed back through the wet wall. "... to work overtime. And then come back here later and cut him up and burn him in the heat treat furnace. It shouldn't take more than a half hour if you crank it up into the red zone. He knows too much about what we've been doing. So make sure you get rid of him tonight."

"But he's our best operator on the cutter."

"I don't care. He's a Mexican. Just go find another Mexican. How hard can it be?"

The man's face froze behind his massive mustache and goatee.

Jayson's growl was primal. "What?"

"Nothing."

He turned toward the office. "Good. Get-er-done. It's Midge's and my twenty-fifth anniversary, and I don't want anything to screw it up tonight."

———

"HOW'S MY DAUGHTER?"

The man smiled. "Come on back. She's kind of groggy. I aced her to do a dental. I don't think she'd ever had a dental cleaning before."

Mina chuckled. "Any cavities? She is kind of sweet, you know."

The man laughed. "Sweet? Yes. Cavities? No. Just a little plaque. Most of these blue heelers have great teeth. Get her a dental every year, and she should have all her teeth until she dies."

Mina had expected a kennel area, but the room was more like a small bedroom. Powder lay on a low twin-sized mattress. She looked up and moved, so Mina quickly kneeled to sit on the bed and hug her. "How's my hero daughter?" She snuggled her face into the neck of the dog. "Your other mommy is still in a coma, so you need to stay here until we can take you home."

"I've been having her walk with me when I make my rounds. She's not afraid of the prisoners, but she spooks the inmates a bit. She sits where they might hide some contraband. So I was wondering what she usually does."

Mina snorted as she rested her head on top of Powder's. "She's a sniffer. Well, she finds things. Dead bodies, skeletons, treats, drugs, weapons, or anything you ask her to find."

The man squinted one eye and cocked his head. "I've trained and dealt with K-9s for years. No one dog does all of those."

"In the words of my Paiute wife, that's because you trained them to do only one thing instead of just asking." She kissed Powder's head. "You were military, right?"

He nodded. "Army."

"They spent weeks teaching you how to walk. Right?"

He frowned and rubbed at the silver creeping into his hair. "They call it marching."

She stood. "And you've been walking the same way ever since. Right?"

He sighed. "Yeah."

She waved her hand along Powder's head, leaning against her thigh. "I'll bet when you take her for a walk, you put a leash on her. Because that's the way you've always done it."

He squinted.

"What area can I go into where there are people? The more the merrier."

He glanced at his watch. "It's lunch. So there would be several people in the commissary."

She snorted. "Perfect. Lots of people, lots of smells, and plenty of distractions."

Mina scowled as he reached for the leash hanging on the wall. "Let's just do it her way this time."

Small clusters of people filled over half the tables. Mina smirked in surprise at the food plate trays, which were the same stainless steel she expected for the inmates.

Turning to the man, she held out her hand and counted off her fingers. "Noise, smells, and confusion. Perfect."

"So, what is she going to find?"

Mina smirked evilly. "I know edibles are legal in Colorado…"

He shook his head. "But not at work."

"So let's not embarrass anybody." She kneeled and hugged Powder as she whispered. Ruffling her head one last time, she turned her loose.

They watched Powder sashay around the tables. The nose came

close to people but didn't show the usual seriousness associated with the working dogs. Finally, she sat with her back to a woman guard.

Mina chuckled. "Ten bucks says the candy is life savers or lemon drops because she's trying to quit smoking."

They walked over, and the woman looked up. "What?"

Mina smiled. "The candy is in your pocket."

The woman frowned and pulled out the half roll of hard candy. "I'm trying to quit smoking."

"I've heard lemon drops are better. And those tiny licorice drops are even better. And it's good for you to quit the habit. When did you quit?"

"Three weeks ago. But it's getting better."

Mina shook her hand. "Switch to the lemon drops. It's not as sweet. Trust me. I had to push through some congressional bills, and it wasn't easy. Hypnosis also helps."

The woman frowned. "You're in Congress?"

She pointed at Powder. "Nope. Just her mother. She's the hard worker these days."

A horrified look crossed the woman's face. "She sniffs out candy?"

"Among other things." She glanced at the doctor. "I've got other places I need to be, but you're doing a great job. So you can keep her around for a while?"

"Do you think she can find shanks?"

Mina shrugged. "Show her what you want found and let her go."

The woman rolled her eyes. "If she can find shanks and drugs, we ain't ever letting her go."

Mina snorted. "Her other mother might have something to say about her being kept here. And she's FBI."

The doctor rested her hand on Mina's shoulder. "We'll be happy to take care of her. With or without the shanks."

Tony leaned against the doorjamb. "I might be all rubbed out, but personally, I don't know. Maybe I'll know tomorrow."

Matt glanced up from his computer and laughed at the visiting Deputy Director. "Oh, the suffering one has to put up with for the job."

Tony snickered. "Who knew field work was so stressful?"

Matt leaned back. "How many massages today?"

"Two and a half."

"How do you get only a half?"

Tony stepped into the small office and sat. "Just a shoulder massage to work out the stress from the hard work."

They both laughed. Matt reached out and grabbed the squishy that looked like a Mickey Mantle signed hardball. He squeezed it a few times. "Any luck?"

Tony frowned. "Happy ending?" He shook his head. "It was offered, or hinted at, every time. But I just told them my wife had a nose for those things."

Matt opened his mouth in the traditional ah-ha sign. "Oh yes. The old, hen-pecked husband routine. Works every time."

"But I found Sarah. And I think I even found the two Japanese girls."

Matt waved his hand at the computer screen filled with documents filled with numbers. "And I think I've found some owners and their other businesses. Some of them are already financially ahead of the usual game. Even a local politician and another who is still with the local sheriff's department. Even more interesting was they belong to the same country club."

Tony rolled his eyes. "Oh yeah, that's not suspicious at all." He growled. "But lately, it's becoming more and more and too many times. But great work."

The agent's lips rolled into a hard grimace as he glanced back at the computer. "It was the least I could do, given the circumstances. Like I told Running Bear, my background is a forensic CPA. But I've felt awful about the bomb." His face winced. "I haven't slept much…"

Tony leaned forward and reached out. "Don't. There was nothing anyone could have done. Even buried in the building in Washington, I felt it, too. But we can't go back. Only forward. As Nash would probably say, the bombs have dropped. All we can do now is lay on our bellies and probe with a knife until we get through this, or it goes boom."

Matt shivered. "Now, there's a scary thought."

Tony leaned back in his chair. "Try doing it on frozen sand a zillion miles from anywhere."

Matt pointed at the deputy director with a question on his face.

Tony nodded softly. "Last fall. In California. I'm not going to say it was fun, but doing it with Nash and her dog? I wouldn't have that time spent in any other way. Even the old dog can learn new tricks."

The agent nodded. "I get the impression I could learn a lot of tricks from her and the little black gal."

Tony nodded and pointed at the computer screen. "We all can. The computer. That's her battlefield. And she's a terrifying juggernaut in the cyber arena."

FINDING ANSWERS

The white hallway was sterile white, but at least they had dimmed the lights. Felix knew if he pulled the wheelchair with one leg, the nurses wouldn't be alerted to the movement. He would just be another patient out for a late-night stroll of sleeplessness.

He reached forward and grabbed the doorjamb. Pulling hard, he whipped forward and turned into the doorway. Muna looked up, scared from the laptop at the fast movement. And then laughed as Alex turned his head to look at her. At the movement in the door, he had dropped his head behind her raised knee under the blanket.

Muna laughed in a hushed voice. "You two are going to get us all thrown out of here."

Felix snorted. "Speak for yourselves. Only you two are here. I'm all alone with Uncle on the bus." He frowned at the large laptop. "Where... did you...?" He put his face in his hands. "Do I even want to know?"

Muna chuckled evilly. "Mina. The first one is free... the rest I pay for."

"Anyone heard about Nash's condition?"

"Still in a coma."

They turned to the voice at the door.

Thomas pushed a wheelchair in. Piled in the seat were small tubs of orange sherbet and a bag of pork rinds. "Sorry for being late, but I stopped for the beers."

Muna laughed and clapped her hands quietly. "Yay. Orange beers."

Felix looked at the pork rinds and curled his lip in a sneer. "Better take those back. They're just the white bread and mayonnaise kind."

Thomas winked at Muna. "Kids..." He passed the open bag to the small hand, grabbing air.

She peeked inside and smiled. Hugging the bag to her chest. She turned the bag to show Alex in his wheelchair. The man laughed and gave Thomas a thumbs up.

Muna pulled the smaller bag out of the large bag. The nuclear mushroom cloud was immediately obvious. She fell back into her stack of pillows, hugging the contraband in a death grip.

Pulling the bag open, she popped one into her mouth and closed her eyes as the morsel melted and burned her tongue. She drew in a slow breath through her nose as the men watched the cathartic transformation.

Alex watched Thomas clear the wheelchair and sit. "Still in a coma..."

Thomas nodded as he peeled open a tub of sherbet. The small wooden spoon flickered between his middle fingers. "The nurse who has been spending the most time with her says her blood pressure has stabilized at a hundred over sixty. Low for you and me, but good for a coma, I guess."

"But still no signs of coming out?"

Thomas looked at Felix and shook his head.

Muna opened her eyes. "I wouldn't either. She wakes up, and all of you guys would gang up on her, asking questions. You're like the worst Senate Hearing Committee. Bark, bark, bark."

Nash looked around at how the gray mist had cleared. Overhead, the sky was an intense blue. Raising the stalks of sage in her hand, she nibbled on the small, bitter flower. She knew the larger yellow flower on the rabbit brush was less bitter, but even the rabbits didn't eat them. The starving animals would only graze on the evergreen leaves in the winter when the oil wasn't so bitter. She smiled; it wasn't candy, but it was a connection to this memory.

The sagebrush tumbled across the high desert toward the mountain the white men called Shasta. The summers all started here in this valley of the desert. The edges didn't rise high but were enough to shelter the sage from the harshest winter storms. The flowers were always strong here. And every year, they came to collect the yellow flowers by the gallon. It was a young Nash and her sister's job to strip the yellow flowers from the stalks. Then, carefully stack the stalks in the burlap bags. Throughout the year, they used the flowers for several medicines. The gray-green leaves of the stalk were boiled for tea or cooked for an astringent poultice. The remaining stalks started fires or added to a barbecue for the aroma.

Nash stripped the flowers into the plastic bag held open by a ring of sage she had woven when she first arrived. Then the stalk, she set on the stack she would put in the burlap bag later. The burlap bag would hang in the pantry. No weevils or ants would invade the smelly room. She smiled at the childhood memory of sitting in a chair in the dark pantry, reading by the light of a candle made from bee's wax, peppermint, and lavender. The aromas would clear her lungs and sinuses. An evening studying in the pantry would guarantee a healing, restful night.

She snipped the stalk from the bush. The knife could shave her father's arm where he had hair but would only come to seat against her thumb. Every fifth stalk. Four fingers and harvest the thumb. Leave the rest for the animals who need the food for next winter. Only take your share. And make your share light, or share with others who cannot come to harvest. Be a part of the earth, and the earth will be a part of you.

Standing, she nibbled on the yellow flower. Nash looked around the expanse. She would take only a small harvest. It was only her now. Her sister didn't understand the old ways. She bought her medicines from the white man. Her eyes were blind. Nash could feel her sitting in the morning dark at her table, reading the white man's story. She would teach the same story. She would never see.

Nash packed the small burlap bag. The wet nose sniffed at the back of her naked legs. Nash smiled and reached back for the floppy ears. They would see for the others—the ones who didn't see. Didn't want to see. Couldn't see.

———

"CAN I HELP YOU FIND SOMETHING?"

Mina looked around the small shop. The posters pinned to the walls ran from reproductions of former bands in the 1960s in San Francisco to mystic posters from other lands and cultures. Shelves contained figurines of superheroes to cartoon characters to Buddha, and cartoon dogs in yoga poses. Mina burped a chuckle as she recognized the small statue of Ganesh sitting between an H.P. Lovecraft's Cthulhu and a Star Wars AT-AT walking fortress.

She turned at the small, strident voice. But saw no one. "Maybe... well, I hope you can." She continued to look around the displays and life-sized monsters and superheroes.

A voice from a backroom behind a split curtain assured her they would be right there.

The small parakeet in the large cage bobbed its head. "Can I help you find something?"

Mina snorted and then wiped the back of her hand across her nose. It transported her to her youth and discovering magical places. The music store was where *those* kinds of kids spent time together. Not a good girl, a dutiful daughter from an excellent family in the right neighborhood. Anything could happen. It didn't. But the potential was there.

The woman in the long dreadlocks woven with colored yarns came out of the back, licking her fingers. "Sorry, I was mixing some…" She spotted the woman who wasn't her usual clientele. She frowned for a second. "Can I help you find something?"

Mina laughed as she recognized where the bird had learned the words. She pointed at the bird. "They already asked me that. I'm still waiting for your assistant to fill my request."

The woman's face distorted. "I'm confused."

Mina laughed harder. She stuck her hand out. "I doubt your mother named you confused. And if she did, it would have been a cruel thing to do. But I've already met your bird. My name is Mina. It's pronounced the same as the bird, but spelled like the hole in a mountain."

The woman gently shook her hand as she worked out what was being said. Suddenly, she smiled and pointed at the bird. "Oh. Robbie. Yes, he asks that, doesn't he? I'm so used to him, I forget." She stopped and frowned. "Your mother named you after a bird?"

Mina shook her head. "No. After my great-great grandmother in Taiwan. It's a shortening of her much longer name. None of us took the time to learn how to pronounce it correctly. And neither did her family, so they just used the Chinese for the shorter name. My parents pragmatically followed family protocol."

The woman slowly blinked her eyes and then made them large to clear them. "So how can I help?"

"My wife is in the hospital."

"I'm sorry."

Mina nodded, acknowledging the sentiment. "She's in a coma." Holding up her hand to stop the woman from jumping in. "She's Paiute Indian. A while back, she brought home and then had more shipped to us, a handmade shampoo. I know it had some kind of sage in it… We like the earthy smell…" She grimaced. "The hospital keeps using an antiseptic shampoo, and it smells like it, too. So there is nothing for my wife to smell but the hospital."

The woman smiled with a large grill of white teeth. "Maybe if she smells home, she'll come back."

Mina slumped with a wan smile. "Does that sound crazy? I mean, if I were the one in the coma, she'd only have to fan a bunch of money under my nose. But she said her dog wouldn't come close to her until she started rubbing sage in her hair and stopped using the shampoo her sister had."

The woman frowned. "Her dog? But isn't she your wife?"

Mina rolled her eyes. "It's complicated, but it was when they first met. I should say, our dog. Our daughter. Powder. Oh shit... see? It's complicated."

"Honey." The woman shook her head back and forth. "It ain't." She jerked her head at the bird. "Try sharing your business with a twenty-year-old smartass."

The small bird rumbled. "Smartass. Yeah, three o'clock. Judge Wapner. Smartass."

The woman rolled her eyes. "Okay. Sage. But I don't have any shampoo. What kind of sage?"

Mina's eyes went from slits to round. "There are kinds of sage?"

"Sure. Giant sagebrush, rabbit sagebrush, and even squaw tea sagebrush. They say it makes a powerful, strong medicine tea, but I never made it to the second sip. That shit be nasty."

Mina leaned against the counter with her hip as she pulled gently at her lower lip. "What if I got some baby shampoo? When I was in the hospital with my chemo, the smelly shampoo made me throw up. So they used a baby shampoo with no scent."

"I could infuse the concentrated essential oils into the shampoo... That might work."

Mina smiled. "It's worth a shot..." She held her finger out at the woman.

"Dorothy. It is the same as the wizard, lion, scarecrow, tin guy, and the dog. Except I have AreToo, as in Star Wars. Give him fresh millet, and all he does is chirp, tweet, and beep for hours."

"Thanks, Dorothy. I'll get some shampoo and be right back."

"I'll start working up some essential oils and even press some fresh as well. Let's bring your girl home."

THE SWEAT LODGE WAS SMALLER THAN HE REMEMBERED. But the intense smells were the same. Generations had burned small twigs of sage, mesquite, cactus, and other hallucinogens under the wraps of the layers of skins. Each generation added their own hunts and journeys to those of the men who had gone before.

He had washed in the clear waters of the small pool below. The warm spring started the heat and opened the pores. He understood the mechanics, but it was the otherworldliness he sought today. The guidance of the shaman. The man he had been talking with, sitting in the desert's stillness with, and sharing his innermost concerns and needs with for the last few weeks.

This wasn't the usual sweat lodge experience. This was Uncle's first conscious walk into the spirit world since he was a young buck bursting from his best hunt. The pig had fed the tribe, not just his family. He was a man, and it was time for him to meet his spirit guide.

But this time, it wasn't about him. He needed to walk into someone else's spirit world. A place his guide couldn't go.

He took the small morsel of herbs and meat from the shaman. The boy next to them would tend the small fire. He was a shaman in training and could walk the spirit world the important herbs and spiritual twigs would induce.

The small morsel of food seemed to dissolve on his tongue. Uncle dipped the rag into the bucket of cool water and wiped his brow—already beading with sweat.

He took another bite of spiritual food from the shaman. It was a long journey, and he would need energy. They fused the small wad of ground aromatic plant in a pad of crystalized honey and sap from the sacred cactus.

Somewhere, the mean cavity of the lodge grew. The sky overhead was clear and blue. But the heat of the lodge wasn't the air. Uncle looked around at the shallow desert valley. In the distance stood a volcano, long silenced into just a mountain. Overhead, the eagle soared, but Uncle knew he could not come lower. The sage was in bloom. It would be spring in the high desert.

The woman straightened. She smiled like a child as she nibbled on the bitter yellow flower. "You're far from your home."

Uncle grunted. He stepped toward her. Her buckskin dress was the white of the inside of a deerskin. It was new. There was no beading or designs. "Have you found what you sought?"

The woman was far away. "I am home." Her voice raised, so he could hear her.

Uncle crossed his legs and sat among the sage bushes. "I can't chase you. You must help me."

She stood on the other side of the bush. "Why have you come to my home?"

Uncle thought of the song the shaman had taught him. In his mind, he sang it, but his voice was soft. "This is not your home, Secret Squirrel. This is your spirit home. You will bring it with you, but you must wake up and come back to your world home."

"I live here now."

The small moccasins brought a soft chuckle to his lips. "Those were the moccasins I made you when you started school. You needed shoes to go into the outside world. You drew protective designs on the toes. They helped you that year, but then you grew. You need to grow now as well."

The woman was young. Her hand passed over the tips of the sage. "I can grow no more."

Uncle raised and lowered his hand in the air. "You have grown so much more than the shell. You have gone to war and become a great warrior. You have a wife and a daughter who need you. There is so much more than sitting here in your sage valley. You need to come home. I need you to come home. Your wife needs you. Your daughter waits where she is until you come to bring her home."

She was three bushes away. "But this is what I have always needed. I need nothing more."

Uncle could feel the weakness starting. He knew, soon, he would be nothing more than smoke in a small hovel.

Holding out his one hand. "You came here to find your spirit guide. But you don't have a spirit guide. The power has always been in you. Same as your mother and father. You are a shaman and draw your strength and knowing from Mother Earth. This sage: the smell and taste, it is your touchstone. You will carry this forward. It will always be with you because it is you. But you must wake up to understand."

She was standing next to him. The beadwork was just lines of green, but it was a start. "Will you be there, Uncle?"

"Always, Secret Squirrel." He raised his hand. "Help me stand. I am old now."

He was standing and younger. Her hand was warm on his shoulder. He looked at the white shirt and black leather pants. The long braid hung over her shoulder and down her chest. Uncle lifted the brooch at the end. The many-colored lines made the diamond of a wise one. "You will do well, Secret Squirrel."

The small swirl of smoke disappeared into the giant sagebrush. Nash smiled and went home.

The shaman's warm hand rested on Uncle's chest. "Rest. You had a long journey. You can sleep now. In the morning, we will bathe in the pool."

24

FINDING A WAY HOME

NASH LOOKED at the several stalks of rabbit brush in her hand. The flowers were half nibbled away. The burlap bag's label was from an Idaho potato farm. Not her favorite, but it's good with the right meal.

She looked across the high desert. The ground beneath her feet was the warmth of home. Without looking, she felt the dark clouds full of rain pushed against the west face of Withassa. Shasta Lake needed water. It was time for the dry years to end.

Nash felt her mother next to her elbow. The presence was warm and comforting. The smaller hand gripped the back of her hand and raised the sage. Together, they gently shook the bunch toward the north for the winter storms and to the west for the spring and summer winds to cool the evenings. Finally, across the desert from which their strength and bounty came.

"Little rabbit stands tall like the giant sage."

She turned to the young warrior in only a breechcloth and leggings. He'd woven his chest plate from porcupine quills and elk antler beads. She knew he had found them in the forest. Their life purpose was at an end, but they needed a purpose for the next life. It was his way.

Taking his hand, she gently squeezed. "I understand now."

"Listening is more important than saying."

Nash closed her eyes and felt the swirl of warmth as they dissolved. A soft beep replaced the quiet of the desert. Something tugged gently at her hair.

Her hand fumbled and found some hair. She drew it to her nose. *Sage*.

Mina stopped brushing the almost dry hair. As Nash rolled over onto her side, Mina climbed into the bed and gathered on Nash's back. She buried her nose in the long, damp hair. She could smell the desert. *Her wife was home*.

Rushing into the room, the nurse stopped, watched the monitor, and then turned off the lights as she quietly closed the door. Glowing as she walked back to the nurse's station. The other nurse laughed and reached for the phone.

The first nurse shook her head. "They're sleeping. Let them have some peace alone for a while. The doctor can have his time tomorrow."

<hr>

THE DEPUTY DIRECTOR HELD UP HIS CREDENTIALS. "I'M here to see Niko Wakana."

The nurse barely looked up. Her right arm rose, and she pointed down the hall. "Three fifty-four."

He found the man sitting in the sunshine, falling through the windows. In his hands was a large book. The single leg explained the wheelchair.

The chair scraped on the floor as Tony turned it around. Pulling it over, the man was startled. He looked up with bloodshot eyes. Tony held up his identification. "Nash sent me."

The Asian man's eyes narrow to pencil lines. "Nash is in a coma."

Tony shrugged. "Okay, Muna sent me."

"She didn't mention you. We talk every day."

Tony sat back, thinking. "Uncle?"

The man laughed. "You're giving up so easily? You had three more names to try."

Tony smirked as he held up four fingers. "You forgot Powder."

The man shook his head patronizingly slow. "She would have come alone and brought me some scotch."

Tony laughed. "I knew I liked her best."

Niko closed the book on the small, flat wooden spoon bookmark and set it on the bed. Tony glanced over at the cover. "Hell's Angeles?"

"Bikers, but no. Undercover cops in Los Angeles running girls across the border for abortions. A reminder of where we're back to today."

Tony picked at a piece of imaginary lint on his slacks as he crossed his legs. "Abortions or sex trafficking?"

Niko grimaced as he peered into the sunshine. "Probably all the above."

Tony stared at the large white wrap where a leg should have been. "Sorry about the leg."

The man looked over. "It could have been worse. I understand that the fancy legs carry a certain cache these days. I'm only glad I caught it instead of Muna." He pointed at his thigh. "This high up would have struck her in the chest." His smirk was small.

Tony rolled his eyes. "I'm forbidden from talking about the physical attributes, or lack thereof, of our agents. But it surprised me to hear she wasn't wearing a tactical vest."

"I understood the new tactical gear was in the boxes in the rear of the SUV. They're being there saved our lives. And the only thing that saved Nash was she was on the other side of the parking lot. And even then…"

Tony winced and nodded. "I understand. But there was plenty of damage to go around."

Niko turned the chair so his back was to the sunshine. "There was another guy. A big footballer..."

The deputy director nudged his chin out. "Thomas Brady. He's the sheriff in Harkin County. It's in northern California."

"He seemed to have disappeared..."

"He went south with Uncle. I'm not sure what they were doing but with everyone in the hospital here..."

"So, what are you doing here?"

Tony's smile crept onto his face. "Getting massages. Burning my mouth on local food with what's called Christmas peppers. Being a tourist..."

Niko reached to the small roll-around table for the large tumbler of water. He paused the straw at his mouth. "Learn anything?" He bit on the rubbery tube and sucked.

Tony chuffed a breathy laugh. "Now you're sounding like Nash?"

He took a long pull on the water. Gently putting it back on the table, he looked back. "I got the impression if you hang out much with her, you're going to learn things."

Tony bounced his head and glanced out the window. The intense light reminded him of the winter desert and a large knife in the sand, looking for bombs. "She seems to affect people that way."

FELIX RUBBED HIS BARE FOOT ALONG THE OTHER SHIN. The afternoon sun reflecting off the side of the RV created a warm pocket. The new campsite was quiet, but he guessed it was popular in the summer. With Thomas and Uncle gone, he had the whole bus to himself. And it wasn't comforting.

He liked the earbuds to talk on the phone. He could hear her breathing. "I haven't heard from them since they went down to New Mexico. It's weird having the bus to myself. But if I only feel like some jerky for dinner, I have some jerky."

"I could fly up and make some noise and demands. Maybe bang a frying pan with a wooden spoon or something."

He laughed at the image. "Have you ever used a frying pan?"

She laughed. "By the time we gave up nuking pop-tarts and popcorn in the tiny microwave at school, we had hired a cook. And then we built this place. Next, we hired Chef to cook for the construction crew, and well... But I know how to nuke a mean s'more. Oopsie..." He could hear her bending. "Well, so much for the pink. I guess we're going fuchsia this week."

"What happened?"

"I knocked over the last of the pearlescent pink nail polish. It's not the first blessing of the gravel. This roof is looking like the artist who threw paint at the canvas."

Felix smiled. He remembered the view from the roof. "Are you planning on a magnificent sunset?"

"Kind of. The boys brought home another trophy this last weekend, and we signed another long-term contract in France and Germany. So we're catering a sunset dinner on the roof. Just an intimate dinner for forty-nine. Frank and Tinker Bell are coming up. We think they might have some news they want to share."

Felix frowned. "Tinker Bell?"

"Yeah. We're not sure who he's bringing. His longtime girlfriend's nickname is Tink, but he's also friends with two girls who used to work as Tinker Bell at Disney. You know, the zip-line at night thing?"

"Yeah, with the fireworks. Never been there, but I've seen things on the television."

Tree gasped. "You've never been to the greatest place... Holy buckets. Another reason to drag you back down here."

Felix glowed as he tipped the chair back against the bus. "Yeah, but then work gets in the way, and we both know what workaholics we are..."

"Hey! I can be corrupted..." He could hear her bending again. Probably applying nail polish.

"And the research you were doing for us...?"

"Doesn't Muna have access to her computer?"

He rubbed his finger behind his right ear. "She didn't—for a week or more. Uncle gave her a restricted pad to talk with while they had her intubated because of her collapsed lung... But then, she broke it trying to hack around the lockouts. She was silent for a couple of days and finally pulled the tube out of her throat herself while the doctor was there. Scared the hell out of them. But they got the picture: she wasn't going to just lie around and watch stupid TV."

Tree grumbled a muted laugh. "She sounds like she's related to Frank Pounds. Pulling out her own intubation is shit Frank would do... If Tink would let him. So what is she doing for a computer now? Do I need to overnight her a megaton lappie?"

"Mina already took care of it. She got some gamer freak to build her a monster."

"Wait. You're in Pueblo, Colorado?"

"Yeah...?"

"Was the gamer a chick nicknamed Chips?"

Felix screwed up one eye. "Sounds familiar."

"I spoke to her for about five minutes and then had to turn her over to Slug. I think she's joining the boy's team in a few days. They geeked out for a couple of hours while she told her boss to grab his ankles and sit on it... or something. Anyway, she had called from her work on her break and let him know she was quitting."

Felix laughed. "Score one for the home team."

"Oh, shit." Tree cleared her throat. "The team is coming up. Tell Muna all our stuff is in her nasty room. We got the shit on everyone we could. And just so you know... There's a guy in Syria who has connections there. So let Nash know as well."

"She's still in a coma."

"Well, whisper Sergei Romanov's name in her ear. She'll wake up. But you take care. All of you. Gotta go."

Jazz and Ming burst out of the door, laughing. Ming stopped and spread her arms at the beginning of sunset. Jazz folded over the arm in her gut. The dainty Asian laughed. "Stop screwing around and look at this sky."

Jazz smiled and then saw Tree. She muttered out of the side of her mouth. "Rut row. The boss isn't having a fun time."

Ming jabbed a soft elbow into her side. "Hey, sis. Did someone sink a dredge?"

Tree vibrated her head. "I just talked to Felix."

"Did Muna get our package?"

"He didn't know. He'll ask in the morning. Muna's still in the ICU so they can watch her. They had her intubated for a couple of weeks because one of her lungs collapsed. But she got pissed when she couldn't hack around the lockdowns on the pad she had to communicate with. She pulled the tubes out of her throat herself in front of the doctor."

Jazz flexed back with wide eyes. "Whoa. One tough bitch. That sounds more like Pound's kind of tantrum. But those little packages can always surprise you." She raised her arm and playfully rested her armpit on Ming's head.

Tree nodded. "Yeah. I guess as a reward, Nash's wife went out and hired a gaming builder to slap together a competitive monster lappie for her. The builder's name is Chips. Slug hired her after a two-hour geek call. She's driving down and should be here next week."

Ming narrowed her eyes and turned her head to one side, still playfully under Jazz's armpit. "So team testosterone gets a hormone injection... My twin has the super dreadnaught of all laptops. And you got some Felix time. Why am I sensing a *but* in there..."

Tree took a deep breath and sighed. "Thomas and Uncle have been MIA for two weeks. And Nash is still in a coma."

"*Shit.*"

25

JUST A WALK

THOMAS HAD NEVER FELT SO ALONE. EVEN the desert was strange and unwelcoming. The brush stood squat and burned as it dotted the surrounding land and hillside in random polka dots. Even the morning scent was wrong. The light pine scent back home was now more of an astringent creosote smell burning his nose.

The old man slowly bent. His cane was little more than a stick for a large dog. His butt in the weathered bib overalls searched for the scat on the log. As Thomas watched the man sit, he wondered where the moderate-sized log had come from.

The man sat and slowly wheezed as his body seemed to deflate onto the log. "Uncle is still resting. His spirit walk was heroic. Few warriors could have done what he did and survived. I'm talking about very courageous men. But where he walked, it is not about courage, or strength, or even know-how."

Thomas glanced at the unmoving body. "Then what?"

The old man rocked forward and poked at Thomas's chest. "It is what is in here. It is the power in you after you got shot up, blown up, and you got up, picked up your comrade, and carried him on your bleeding back for miles and help. There is no name for it. You can't name it. It just is."

Thomas frowned at the old man with trenches for wrinkles and a black glint in the folds of his eyes. "How did you know about...?"

The man reached into a leather pouch and pulled out a couple of gnarled sticks of jerky. Offering the young man a stick, he explained. "It drapes over you like a heavy buffalo robe. It wears you down. The one you couldn't save. You did not shoot him. Nor did you blow him up. But your guilt festers in your wounds, and it is rotting. I could smell you before you got out of the truck. You need to take your own spirit walk. Talk to that man. He is waiting for you so he can help you move on. So he can move on. Your guilt is his guilt because you do not move on yet."

"In the sweat lodge?"

The shaman bounced his finger on Thomas's chest. "No. This" —he poked the chest one last time—"is a white man thing. You need to do it *within yourself*. We don't know about your worlds— only that they stink up the place."

Thomas tore off a chunk of jerky with his teeth, gazing across the desert as he chewed. There were a few scrub bushes scattered across the dirt to the smooth rock formations in the distance. He blinked a few times. He hadn't thought about his door gunner in... He wanted to lie to himself and say years, but he knew it was days.

Thomas turned back toward the old man shuffling about in his tiny outdoor kitchen. "How did you know where Uncle went?"

Shuffling back across the worn floorboards of his open-air Hogan, his cane, a soft thump by his moccasin's foot. The man bent. His nose was close to Uncle's chest. He breathed in noisily. "White man. Come. What do you smell?"

Thomas smirked as he stood and walked over to where Uncle lay on the rickety table. The shaman and he had been introduced days before. Yet the man had only called him White Man.

He bent and sniffed. Uncle smelled like Harkin County. Home. When the heat of the day caused the oil in the sage to sweat and pungently scent the air in the days before hunting season. He smelled like late summer.

Straightening, he looked at the shaman and then across the desert. "He smells like the sage in the late summer. When we know it is getting close to hunting season. The deer are still up the mountain but will soon come down to eat."

"Which sage?"

Thomas shrugged his one shoulder and wound his face up around his wide eyes. "I don't know. Giant sage, bitterbrush, squaw tea, maybe even rabbit brush. You know… sagebrush. Whatever you were burning in the sweat lodge the other day."

The hunched man turned on his cane and lifted it to point across the desert. "Mesquite. Not sage."

THE TWO MEN WALKED DOWN THE HOSPITAL HALL SIDE by side. Their hard-heeled cowboy boots made a harsh sound in the quiet hall. The puffier vest stopped, and the arm swung out to stop the other. They looked to the left as one. The woman lay on the bed. Black hair and long in the bed.

Jayson elbowed Grady in the gut. It wasn't hard, but the usual alpha dominance over his wingman.

Grady hissed as Jayson crossed into the room as he drew his folding hunting knife out of his back left pocket. "Jayson. No."

The man ignored him, as was his nature. He pushed his black felt Storm Chaser hat back on his head a tad. Just enough to get his face close to the sleeping woman's in the bed. He laid the knife against the woman's chest. His whispered growl was feral. "I should gut you here where you lie. You need to go back to where you came from."

The woman stirred. She rolled slightly to face the man. Mina's eyes opened to wide slits and were angry. "My wife might have a problem with that."

The bathroom door had been silent, and the cold steel cocking of the heavy pistol was immediately behind Grady's left ear. Nash's growl wasn't as soft as the man's. "One more move, and I'll paint your friend's brains all over the wall."

Mina closed her hand on the man's hand. "I'll take the knife, thank you."

Jayson growled. "You have no idea who you're messing with."

Mina smiled. "Oh, I'm sure we know more about you and your business than you know about us. Now, stand up slowly. You forgot to brush your teeth this week."

He turned to look at his mistake. Nash stood in her hospital gown—tied around the neck but flared below. Her naked legs and feet were long below the bottom edge.

"Your attempt at a warning didn't work out so well. All you did was piss us off. Then you came in here hoping to scare me. But now… you've only kicked it up a few notches more. So I'm going to tell you just once. Go home and get your house in order because I'm coming for you and your entire business. You thought you could put on a red ball cap and own the Rockies as your own little fiefdom. Well, I'm here to take it back." She waved the black pistol in the air. "Now get the hell out."

Nash followed them as far as the door and watched them scurry down the hall. She turned back to her wife. She walked over to where Mina's hand was hovering over the knife on her chest.

"I didn't touch it. I knew you'd want his fingerprints."

Nash could read the white-hot patch just in front of Mina's temple. She knew the woman had resisted all her nature to not grab the knife and use it on the man. And it would have been self-defense.

Nash reached back to the wall with the rack of purple nitrile gloves. She picked up the knife by the blade as she fumbled in the wadded sheets and blankets. Finally, she carried the knife back out into the hall.

She looked at the nurse's station, and the three nurses bent to their computer screens. "I need a one-gallon plastic bag and a cleanup in room three-fourteen. Someone shit in my house."

The nurses looked up, but the older one stood. She was halfway to Nash before the other two could react. "I've got some large bags in the crash cart."

Nash dropped the knife in the bag, and the nurse sealed the bag.

"I'm so sorry we didn't catch the intruders. We should have known."

Nash shook her head. "You didn't do anything wrong. They did. And if they hadn't screwed up before, they certainly did so now." She took the bag from the nurse. "Start the paperwork. We're checking out."

"But…"

Nash glared back at her. "No. All of us. It's not safe for us here, which makes it not safe for you if we're here. So we're going."

"But… where…?"

Nash stopped and turned back. She stepped close to the woman. "First, if I tell you where we're going, it puts you in danger. So, second. How much medical does Muna al-Faragi need?"

"She's on steroids and antibiotics for her lung. Other than the monitoring…"

"And the guys are down to just topical lotions any of us can apply. So, does Muna need a private nurse?"

The woman pursed her mouth as she thought.

Nash faced her closer. "I'm not trying to put your license in jeopardy. But you've got the most real-life medical experience on this floor. So in your gut…?"

The gray at the temples shook slightly. "From what I've seen of you four. I think you could dribble blood and think you were fine walking out of here. Slap a dirty rag on it and call it good." He lowered one eyelid. "Kind of like my son in the Marines."

Nash gave a soft snort as her smile grew warmly. "The term we used was to rub some dirt on it. Everything stops bleeding some time."

The woman laughed. "I should have known you were one of

them. And just so you know, you only have eight pints of blood in you."

Nash slapped her hip as she raised her leg. "I pack an extra couple, but Muna is on the shortlist. So we have to watch out for her."

The older nurse rolled her eyes. "Yeah. I've seen how fragile she is. She gives me the chills at two in the morning on that computer of hers." Her palm flew up between them. "No. I don't want to know what she does in the dead of night."

Nash rocked her head. "She's more than just deadly with any kind of handgun. In the service, she would tip over from the oak leaf clusters on the marksman medal. But her computer…? That is where she defends this country. If our enemies knew about her and her abilities, we could retire the entire ICBM missile program."

"Like I said. I don't want to know."

Nash swung her head. "Trust me, you don't want to know. But because of the tiny woman on her computer… you can sleep soundly at night. Muna, has you covered."

"I'll remember it tonight."

Nash turned and then turned back. "Speaking of watching Muna, we could use a private nurse."

Mina stepped into the doorway. "We pay above the prevailing wage."

The nurse turned. "I'm a traveling nurse. They pay me double what they pay the usual nurses around here."

Mina smiled. "My point exactly. We'll pay double that. Cash—if you want it. We only hire talent."

The nurse stuck her hand out. "I have a couple of weeks' personal time coming, and the extra cash can fix my camper bus. My name is Alida, but Lele works too."

THE DESERT HEAT SEARED THE WHITE WALLS OF THE building as it had for over two hundred years. Five men stood next to the Mercedes truck with the bonnet up. One bent into the engine compartment. His hand reached back as he asked for a fifteen-millimeter socket wrench. The conversation was in soft Arabic.

Inside the building, the cool marble floors reflected the soft tone of the aged walls. The building didn't date back to the crusades. But it replaced the building the Ottoman Empire destroyed when they destroyed as they drove the Turks out of the ancient city of Aleppo.

The young girl sat on the soft sheepskins stacked on the floor. She leaned against the couch she would never sit on. Her hand lazily stroked the man's penis as he scrolled through his computer mail.

Slowly, Sergei sat up. He batted the small hand away. Reaching over to the low table, he picked up the cell phone and dialed a number he knew by heart.

"Da, how can I help?"

"Why wasn't I informed the FBI was in Colorado?"

"We emailed you three weeks ago."

"Don't talk back to me, you prissy little cunt."

The man backpedaled. "No disrespect, sir, but we just assumed you knew and didn't care. The agent in Colorado was supposed to be handling them."

Sergei roughly grabbed the young girl's hair and jerked her head over to where her hand had been before. "Find out and call me personally."

His thumb pushed on the red phone icon as he heard the small "Da."

26

DOES THIS WORK?

THE TWO MEN walked down the hallway of the hospital. The deputy director's new cowboy boots gave a dull thump with the heels, but the agent's crepe soles were silent. As they approached the nurses' station, the armed security guard pulled his pistol and held it out in front of him as he bent his legs. "Hold it right there. Put your hands up."

The two raised their hands as they slowly turned around. Tony studied the man's stance and the slight quiver of the gun. He leaned toward the agent and muttered. "Should I tell him, or do you want to do the honors?"

Matt rolled his eyes. "You're the deputy director; go ahead."

The uniformed guard almost sounded like he had a mouthful of chewing tobacco. "Wha?"

Tony stretched the crick out of his neck. "You left the safety on. But even if you had remembered, you light up a nine-millimeter with that stance, and you'll poke a hole in the ceiling right before it knocks you on your ass."

The nurse stepped out from the station with her hands on her hips. "Asshole. Where were you yesterday? Do you think they're going to come two days in a row? Lester, put that fool thing away and go back to sleeping at your post."

"But... but..."

She shooed at him with her one hand as she approached. "Go on now before I tell your mother. And don't think I won't."

Three stabs at the holster, and he had success. He glowered back at the two men and the nurse as he turned and left.

"Sorry about Lester. He means well, but beyond being a poster in a chair downstairs, he's as useless as he is harmless."

"Until he takes the safety off and punches a round through a patient or nurse."

She smiled at the deputy director. "I'm not sure they've been stupid enough to actually give him bullets. But either way, you're about half a day late."

The men frowned.

She shook her head. "They were quiet about it, but your entire team cleared out in the middle of the night. Took our best nurse with them."

Matt's face wrinkled and twisted. "But how did..."

"Two EMTs said they saw an old Winnebago bus thing pull up, and they got on. Staff went into the rooms, and the beds appeared made like nobody had ever been in there. I haven't checked the records, but I wouldn't be surprised if they were scrubbed clean as well. I don't know what happened yesterday, but the administration said for us to forget they were here. The life flights, the surgeries, the ICU... all of it. Especially the attack."

Tony stepped back as he pulled his phone out of his pocket. He scrolled through the shortlist and pushed the contact.

"Why Tony, how are you?"

"Excuse the call, Mina, but is there something I should know about your wife? And where you are?"

He could hear Mina's phone being passed. The voice was deeper. "Hey Tony, where are you?"

"At the hospital."

Nash chuckled. "Did you fall down and go boom?"

He turned toward the wall as his one eyelid fluttered closed. "I have practice sticking a KABAR into frozen sand, but I'm not beyond learning how to use it for questioning unruly children."

"We didn't feel welcome anymore. So, we moved to a ranch. Muna just sent coordinates to your phone. Come on out, but stop at the gate. It's well within long gun range."

"I have Matt with me."

"Bring him. Muna has questions."

Tony glanced over his shoulder at the man talking to the nurse. "So does he. That's why we're here. But you're not. So now I have questions."

Someone muttered something in the background. Nash chuckled. "Mina says the scotch is out here. But if you stop, make sure it's only for gas. We have plenty of roadkill."

The ranch was more of a hacienda perched on the top of a small bluff. Optics for defense were optimum. Local FBI and US Marshals had used the small compound for secure protection in the past, but it was now passed over because of budget constraints. Matt had read about it in a few files, but Lele's uncle had worked security for the US Marshals. She even knew the current owners and reached out.

Nash walked down to the bottom gate. It may have seemed like a small power play, but she also wanted to take a slow look at the approach to the bluff. The rise behind her she couldn't control, but the road and any hiding holes along the way, she wanted to know about. The Marine in her demanded it. And she knew she needed exercise and to get the legs used to moving again.

Tony and Matt leaned against the nose of the black SUV. Nash chuckled as she spotted the new point-toed cowboy boots. Tony even had one heel cocked up onto the front bumper as if it was a fence rail. She could imagine him rolling a cigarette with his black cowboy hat tipped back.

"Going native, I see."

He smirked. "They don't see this brand east of the big muddy. I let the opportunity slide by the last time, and I had time for a fitting this time. So, I took it. After all, you weren't exactly in a talkative mood."

She stopped in front of him. "No. I get it. Hello Matt." She glanced over as the man tipped his air hat from his brow. She turned back to the deputy director. "Did you allow enough room for the lifts?"

The man smiled and started laughing through his nose. "I'm wearing two thick socks. There will be plenty of room. I might even give Mina a run for her money."

"I'll warn her. She hates being left short." She turned and pointed across the bottom of the cliff. "We have a blind spot along there. Felix and Alex are working up some solar-powered spotters." She turned and pointed at the hump of a hill the bluff backed up to. "We're going to run some drones over the hill to see what problems might be on the other side. There was a reason they stopped using this as a secure, safe house, but even the owners don't know why."

Tony rocked his upper body as he nodded. "Jarhead logic. Works for me. I'll reach out to some of the old guys and see if we can dig up the stop. Anything else? I saw you survey the road down. But Powder didn't want to come for the walk?"

"We need to go get her at the prison."

Tony stretched his neck. "We can use the SUV. It's not armored, but Matt says it's plenty fast."

Nash snorted and glowered at the other agent. "I'll be the judge of that."

The man smiled and jerked his head at the driver's side. "Keys are in it."

Once inside the main lodge, Nash turned to Matt. "Are you staying or going home at night?"

"Home for now… I guess."

She pointed at the hall leading off between the kitchen area and the dining room. "When you need to stay, that breezeway leads to the first bunk house. I don't know the arrangement the boys..."

Felix stood and turned as he closed the large refrigerator door. "You have the second room on the right. Alex and I have the defense side overlooking the approach." He scratched at his bare stomach above the tiny running shorts.

Tony coughed into his hand. "Isn't it a bit chilly to run around naked?"

Alex walked out of the hallway in only his jeans and boots. "It is for me. But mister radiator just went for a run." Felix smiled as they exchanged places, and Alex opened the refrigerator—disclosing the healing scab on most of his back.

Felix blushed and ducked into the hallway. "I'll go get a shirt on."

Tony turned from watching the epitome of youth. "And where do you want me?"

Nash pointed up. "Top of the stairs to the left. Take your pick, but the one with the deer antlers over the door has its own bathroom."

Mina looked up from the couch in the pool of sunlight. "We're in the front. But Nash is still recovering, so we'll keep it quiet." She watched for the slight blush on the man's neck.

She wasn't disappointed.

Matt coughed into his hand to hide the smile. "And agent al-Faragi?"

"She and the nurse are on the bus. That way, she has all the gear and magical cyber powers she needs. And it's protected." She pointed at another hall next to the giant fireplace. "Down this way, Matt. The end door leads into the garage. Mind the heavy-duty power cords on the floor."

The man nodded, picked up his computer bag, and disappeared.

Tony watched Nash watching the young man. "You'll warm up to him. He's just quiet until he gets to know you."

Nash turned with one eyebrow arched.

The deputy director shrugged. "We've spent most of the last two weeks together. He's not in Muna's league, but he's better than most. And he doesn't go to sleep looking at financial spreadsheets. I might have to poach him for my office."

Nash shrugged her face. "You know what they say about taking the kid out of the country…"

"You didn't turn out so bad…"

Mina snorted and then laughed from the great room. She pointed her pencil over her shoulder. "I don't think that's Pennsylvania Avenue out there." She frowned. "Are those new Blass slippers on your feet?"

The blush reached his ears this time.

Nash smirked as she turned toward the kitchen area. "Coffee? I'm making up for lost time."

Matt stepped out into the gigantic five-car garage. The RV bus stood catawampus in the far corner. Thick black electrical cables snaked across the floor to several connection ports on the vehicle. His mind called up scenes from movies with an almost dead body in a hospital bed with tubes running in and out of many places, trying to keep them alive. He had seen RVs and trailers parked in homeless camps in better condition.

He knocked on the open door. "Anybody home?"

The snicker was soft. "If I need to defend myself with a pistol, you'll have to come back later. Better yet, call for an appointment."

An older blonde woman stepped backward to the doorway. "Oh God. He looks like another nerd. He must be here for you, Muna. I'm never getting a date for Friday night in this one-cow town." She waved her hand.

As he stepped up onto the bus, he held out his hand. "Hi. Matt. And guilty as cyber charged. And I'll second the Friday night crap. Well, at least for the last… um… oh shit. And then there was the pandemic…" His eyes got large and rolled over in a death drop.

She nodded and shook. "Yeah, it too. Try being forty-four in a town filled with twenty-something. Alida, but everyone calls me Ali."

Muna, wrapped in a blanket, looked up from her laptop. "Welcome to Purgatory, Matt."

He frowned. "Why Purgatory?"

Lele leaned in. "We won't let her have any coffee, go shoot her gun, or chase anything faster than a slow walk and only a block or two."

He nodded. "Oh yeah, the lung thing." He grew his eyes and twisted his smile at the nurse. "I heard about extracting the tubes."

He sat down at the small table as he studied the famous Japanese kitten sprinkled over her pajama top, showing out of the top of the fuzzy blanket. "Wow. If I'd known it was pajama Wednesday, I would have broken out my T-Rex jammies."

Her left hand pulled something orange from a crinkling bag and popped it into her mouth. Her eyes rolled at his comment. "I got your brain dump. Decent work on the usual tracking."

He cringed. "Why do I feel like I just got a midlevel grade?"

She smiled. "Hey, at least you didn't flunk, which is what most of the brain trust back in D.C. usually did. If you keep thinking the US Government is the end-all-be-all of background snooping, you're always going to fail. You can't stay with Encyclopedia Britannica when there is Google on steroids just across the black line."

"Black line?"

She reached out and patted his hand with her scabbed right hand. The scabs matched two more on her arm. "Welcome to Dark Web one-oh-one. I'll be your guide and savior. Let's start with your research and see where you didn't go."

27

BY THE NUMBERS

Lele leaned in. "Matt? Before I go take a shower, can I get you some coffee? If you promise not to share it with Muna."

"No thanks. I don't want you to put yourself out."

She narrowed her eyes and cocked her head. "Where are you from?"

"Cañon City originally. But here in Pueblo since I was thirty-two. Why?"

She turned and leaned next to Muna's head. Her whisper was dull. "Keep your eye on this one. I might have finally found someone worth dating on Friday night."

Muna rolled her eyes. "I hear ya, girlfriend. Go grab your opportunity at the water locker. We've got this." She watched the woman step out of the bus. Muna's left arm snuck out of the blanket. Matt squinted at the Hello Kitty pajamas, and her hand paused on the edge of the laptop.

Hearing the heavy fire door from the garage to the house slam, Muna turned the computer around. The screen was a grid. Down the left side were names and businesses in a column titled County. She'd titled the next column, State. It held fewer names and businesses. In the federal column, there were only a handful of names. In the fourth column, titled Interpol, only one name remained.

The last three columns had the same symbol in the title cell: a closed lock.

She clicked a key, and the first two columns were highlighted in yellow, except for three names and businesses. "This is your research. I'm guessing you used the standard background formula they taught you at Quantico."

Matt nodded. "It's the same protocol used in forensic auditing of financials of any company. Generally, it's the standard for performing a forensic analysis of domestic or international holdings." His head leaned over into his raised hand. "But by the other columns, I'm guessing it's great for the junior high research paper, but we're past college now."

Muna guided the curser to a business name and clicked. It highlighted only a single business. "Let's take this one." She turned around and clicked a remote. The large flat-screen monitor swung down from the ceiling. The display was a much larger version of what was on her laptop.

"How did you sort for this level?"

Matt sat up as he turned toward the large screen and moved back against the outside wall of the booth—mirroring Muna. He could imagine this to be the standard configuration for settling in and watching a movie on the bus.

"I sorted by businesses accepting more cash than credit cards." He looked at Muna with one eye drooping. "Of course, then I had to screen out all the bars and restaurants. Although you might buy a couple of drinks with cash, if your tab includes dinner and drinks, they are more likely to bend a credit card. Then there are laundromats. food truck businesses, street vendors, neighborhood handymen, babysitters, and the farm stand vendors."

She nodded like a professor. "And we knew we were looking for businesses using predominately females engaged in activities of a nature to illicit add-on cash bonuses..."

He nodded with a hardened mouth. "So we're looking for businesses which pose as legitimate, but in reality, are covers for prostitution."

She pointed at the screen. "Which brings us to chicken ranching."

"Right." He jerked and frowned. Leaning over to the laptop, he studied the screen. "What…? Where?"

Muna leaned back. "Oh gawd, I need coffee." She looked hard at him. "Do me a favor. I'm going to teach you how to make a milkshake."

He gave her a hard look.

She sighed. "Who do you work for?"

Heaving an even more dramatic sigh, he stood.

Muna pointed at the far end of the counter. "Open the counter cabinet in the corner. The door that's hitting the counter."

He opened the door and turned. His eyes rolled. "I don't know how to work this kind of machine."

She smirked. "That's the beauty. You don't have to. See the cabinet trim there at the corner? Push on it."

He pushed and felt a slight give. When he released, the hidden draw sprung out gently. He looked at Muna with wild eyes.

"It only needs two of those cups to make a quad shot. And the chocolate mix is in the cabinet above. The guys like their hot cocoa before bedtime."

When Nurse Lele, trying to be Nurse Ratched, returned, she narrowed her eyes at the large, clear tumbler. Muna held it up for her to taste. The woman held it up and could see the traces of chocolate syrup on the inside of the glass. "Wouldn't a blender do a better job?"

Muna squinted a shrug. "We don't have a blender at the office, so I've gotten used to just whipping it up with the spoon. Matt did a good job, don't you think?"

The older woman growled. "I won't check your blood pressure if you promise not to blow a heart attack or something. I can smell the espresso in there."

Matt held up his mug. "That would be my coffee."

She grabbed the mug and sniffed. Putting it down, she leaned in. "I could have had kids older than you. You might have had a shot at it if you had stuck some of her espresso in that NOSM. But you didn't, and then you tried to lie to me. I'm losing faith in the FBI by the second here. I need a nap." She rolled her eyes at Muna. "Try to behave. Nanny's watching you. And by the way, the ladies went to go get their dog."

Muna smiled and snuggled down into her blanket. "Mmm. My sister is coming home."

Lele stood. "You're a weird child."

Muna called after her. "You have no idea." She snickered and looked at Matt. "Back to the next level of research."

Matt frowned. "What is NOSM?"

Muna snorted long and hard. "What you're drinking. Nasty Old Supermarket Manure."

He moved the mug from his mouth, set it on the table, and pushed it away.

Muna shrugged. "I told you the espresso was better, but you didn't listen." She turned back to the large screen. "So this lemonade stand does substantial business in the mall, but that is the extent of it. The owner must make cash deposits every day and hold a butt-load of cash over the weekend." She glanced over. "Makes you glad you chose the bureau, doesn't it?"

"Mmm."

Muna swung her head back. "Also, the mall isn't where you want to be running a hot prostitution center. I don't think the mall rats will spring for anything beyond the five-buck cookies and expensive lemonade. So..." She hit the delete button. "Moving on..."

"Easy there, tiger."

"I'm hungry."

Thomas adjusted the wooden chase lounge so the man could sit up. "I get that. But you've been asleep for two weeks. The medical people would say you should be dead. But your shaman says you're doing fine. Personally, I think you look like death warmed lightly in a burn pit."

"I think I need to pee. Help me up."

Thomas stood. The shaman drew the curtain back from the Hogan's doorway. "Don't let him get up. He'll think he needs to urinate, but it's only because we always urinate when we wake up." He approached with a bowl of something. "But at our age, we don't have the pleasure of also a wooden spear to go with it."

He sat on the edge of the lounge. "Here, eat this."

Uncle took what looked like the light green fruit of a melon. His face soured at the taste. "Your melons aren't ripe."

The shaman chuckled. "Good. Because this is cactus, not melon. Not enough water to grow melons. This will help replace your electrolytes." He turned toward the obvious white man. "Your medicine men learned about electrolytes from our people. In the nineteen twenties, they tasked General Pershing with paving a lot of the trails. He made the interstate highways. Many of his men fell ill in our deserts from the heat. We taught them to eat more cactus." He looked at Uncle chewing on another piece. "Many thought we should have let them die. Something Geronimo couldn't do."

Thomas scratched at the short, patchy beard he hadn't shaved in weeks. "Then we wouldn't have the interstate highways."

The man burped a snorted laugh. "Hundreds of people died building the railroad. But we still have railroads. The federal government tried to kill all of us Indians. But when they found they were dying instead, they put a two-dollar bounty on a pair of buffalo ears. Almost overnight, there were mountains of dead, rotting buffalo stinking up the prairies. And then some smart guy in Washington D.C. read C. C. Curtis's journal and found out only a few tribes lived off the bison. Most of us were more gatherers and smaller game eaters. But by then, the settlers were waging their own wars of farming, building small towns, and drilling for oil."

Uncle grumped. "This tastes better."

The shaman smiled. "Good." He offered out a mug of liquid. "Drink this. It is an old friend of yours. It will thin your blood and let it move again."

Uncle sniffed. "Squaw tea."

The shaman nodded. "In the sweat lodge, you told me to ask about a young woman warrior…"

Uncle nodded as he drank more tea. "Nash." He looked at Thomas.

Thomas wagged his head. "No cell service."

The shaman thought. "Take my truck. Drive over there. About two miles, the road straightens. The first house on the right is my niece. She has a phone. She will see my truck and know you are coming from me. Also, ask her if she has any nut fry bread. I'm out."

Thomas held out his hand.

The man snorted and rolled his eyes down and to the side. "The key rusted into the column. Don't try to take it out. It will only break like the last time. And don't turn it hard."

Thomas stood and looked at Uncle. "I'll be back."

The two older men watched the young man leave. As the dust cloud from the road grew smaller, the shaman turned to Uncle. "That is not what you meant about the warrior."

Uncle moved his head back and forth tiredly. "He's a good man, but he's too close to Nash. As a kid, he was like the brother she needed."

"So, what did you want to know?"

Uncle told the man about the dream like he was awake. The man listened and thought. "I have walked with this kind of warrior before. None of them came home. They carry everything they need with them inside. Nothing ties them to their home or family. Only their obligations to duty to keep them breathing. This is dangerous for her and for those who stand close to her."

Uncle sipped the last of the tea. "I know the valley we were in. It's about an hour west of where she grew up and I live. There is no hunting there. It is where you go to harvest the sage, sleep under the stars, and sit in the silence."

The old man thought. "That is powerful medicine. She must be a powerful shaman to walk there in her spirit dreams with the power to draw you in."

Uncle blinked as his face twitched, trying to wrinkle into a frown. "I don't think she knows she's a shaman. But I wouldn't be surprised. Her mother was known for seeing things. And her father had an uncanny habit of being places at the right time."

The old man shuffled across the lanai to the small cupboard. He brought out a large bowl of cactus and began peeling it with an old knife. "Define the right time." He glanced back at Uncle.

"None of us had any meat for at least a week or more. He got off work a little late, but the big truck had just hit a doe and two fawns. We made a lot of jerky, but we also had some back strap in the stew for a while." Uncle took the bowl of peeled cactus. He chewed as he thought. "I remember Secret Squirrel was sick. Enough to keep her out of school. She begged me to take her down to Chico to take her SAT exams for college. Nash didn't want Harkin schools anywhere near her future. She slept curled to the door both ways. I think she was one of the top scores in the region."

The old man leaned on his cane. "If she reaches out for guidance about her being a shaman. Send her down." He turned and looked back at his oldest friend. "Maybe it's time for a woman to be in the sweat lodge. It smells too much like men."

PAINTED DESERT

ALEX SHADED his eyes as he studied the tablet. The scene repeated what he was seeing. "If you angle it a smidge more to the left...?"

Felix bent and reached into the small cave under the flat rock. His fingers applied pressure without really moving the camera. "Better?"

Alex winced. "Nah. Go back. I guess it was as good as we'll get. The rock next to it is in the way."

Felix studied the angle and the rock next to the small hole, shading the lens from becoming a telegraphing mirror. He kicked at the rock with the heel of his running shoe. The rock popped out of the cluster of rocks and rolled down the hill along with some gravel. "How about now?"

Alex laughed. "Yeah. That'll work." *Just kick a hole in the mountain. Why didn't I think of it?* "Let's find another hole around the knee."

Felix moved some smaller rocks and handfuls of gravel as he buried the wire. "Give me a second. I want a better shelf for the solar collector." Pounding a fist-sized rock on a few others, he flattened a small shelf. He squinted at the sun and glanced at his watch. Nodding, he brought the solar cell up to the ledge as he fed the wire in among the rocks. He flipped down the long spike and wiggled it down into the rocks until he felt the cell sitting securely on the shelf.

He turned and looked down across the desert. "It reminds me of the area where Nash destroyed the Hellcat."

Alex snorted softly and shook his head. "Same state. Different playground."

Felix dusted off his hands on his jeans as he jumped down from the last boulder. "What did ATF have to say about the bombing?"

Alex glanced back over his shoulder with a smirk. "They wanted to know how I knew there was going to be dangerous activity."

"They didn't ask why you were out of territory?"

He shook his head as he picked his way through the boulders and rocks. "I told them it was just a follow-up for the previous extended case."

Felix changed the shoulder strap to up and over his head and across his chest. "And the bomb?"

Alex stopped and looked along the front wall of the cliff. He pointed out across the desert. "That's the way I'd come." He looked back at Felix. "I told them I hung out with the people who attracted radical activities. Destroying cars, blowing up government SUVs, and getting shot at. The boss just told me to keep up the excellent work. What about Homeland?"

"Yeah. Pretty much the same attitude. Excellent job. Keep us posted, and when are you going to take a vacation?"

Alex looked into the sky and around the desert. "Vacation. Vacation." He looked back with a humorous snarl. "What the hell is a vacation?" He looked back at the desert and then snapped his head back around. "Are you setting them up for a sortie to Disneyland, maybe?"

Felix blushed. "May... be...?"

"I approve. She's cute. A little young... but cute."

Felix busied his hands and face down into the large bag of equipment. "And smart..."

"She sounds tired. But they're up and out of the hospital. She said she needs to talk to you when you're up to traveling."

Uncle rolled back over. "That's good. Get some rest. We'll leave in the morning."

Thomas looked at the shaman. The man shrugged. "He's a grown man. If he thinks it is not his day to die, who are we to tell him to stay in bed? Did my niece give you a package for me?"

Thomas snapped his fingers and walked back to the truck. He gave up trying to open the passenger door and leaned across from the driver's door. The bag was large and heavy.

"She said she'd send over some more jerky tomorrow. It just wasn't ready yet." Thomas leaned into the shaman and lowered his voice. "Are you sure he'll be okay to travel? I mean, I'll do all the driving, but it is a long drive to Pueblo. And if we were going home, I damn sure wouldn't be going this week."

Uncle barked softly from his bed. "I'm right here, you know. I'm old, but I'm not deaf."

The shaman rolled his eyes. "Now you did it. Bring the bag. We might need one of the plastic ones for his head."

Thomas chuckled. "You sure you two aren't related?"

The shaman glanced back. "Not by blood. But we are blood brothers." He held up a scarred thumb with many pinkish lines running along the pad.

Nash handed the keys to Tony. "You've got this. My wife and I need to bond with our daughter in the back."

Tony looked down at the dog leaning against her leg. He doubted there would be any separation for several days.

As the government black SUV approached the bottom of the

mesa, Nash leaned forward. She gripped the deputy director's shoulder. He pulled to the side of the road.

"Something's wrong."

Tony scanned the cliff. "What do you see?"

"Nothing. It's… shit. I can't explain it. It's just a gut thing. Just a minute." She pulled out her phone and scrolled through her brief list. She thought a moment and then scrolled back.

"Go for Felix."

"Felix. Nash. We're at the bottom of the mesa, heading up. You two need anything?"

She could hear some panting and grunting. "Just a second…" More panting. "Ah. Yes. There you are. Whoa, the black gets dirty fast."

Nash looked out the window and then rolled it down. At the far end of the cliff stood a half-naked man waving his arm in the air. Nash waved back. "You guys, okay?"

"Sure. We're just installing some perimeter security. We'll be up in a few. The local boy is out on the bus getting schooled by Muna. The nurse is riding mother-hen over her, so I'd guess she's out there as well."

Nash waved at Tony to proceed. "Okay. I was just checking if everything was okay or if you needed anything."

"Nope. We're good. Plenty of water and some munchies if we're out longer."

She rolled up the window as they drove up the long driveway to the top of the small mesa. Mina leaned over, her head resting on her warrior's shoulder.

Mina's voice was more of a murmur than a whisper. "What did you see?"

Nash's head vibrated slightly. "Nothing. It was more of a feeling than seeing. But Powder also stiffened." They looked at their daughter standing with her front paws on the console between the front seats. Her head swung from left to right and back. The scan was deliberate and comprehensive. Not a single rock or bush was missed.

The sun beat softly against the cliff face as Alex picked up the almost empty bag. "What do you think?"

Felix flexed his neck and head as he scanned the desert. "The cameras, or Nash calling out of the blue?"

Alex stopped walking and turned. "Okay... both."

Felix pointed at the far outcropping of tumbled boulders. "If they do come from out there, the decoy is the only one they can spot from the ground. But then, that was the idea. If they use a drone, the solar chargers are small and will be almost impossible to see. And even if they use a hi-res camera, it will take them time to find them."

"I concur. And Nash?"

The young man sighed heavily. "Sometimes..." His lips rolled into hard ridges as his face stretched in thought. "It's like she sees things. Things we can't. Things we only wish we could see. She's like Muna... but the pocket rocket has to use a computer. Nash... It's like she smells the air or feels it through her feet from the ground. She's like Powder that way." He glanced up at the cliff. "In a lot of ways." He shouldered his bag and pushed past his older partner. But after a few steps, he stopped and turned back toward the desert. "This is the kind of question I wish Uncle were around to ask about. I think he would at least have something to make it okay to sleep at night."

———

LELE HAD HEARD MUNA GET UP EARLY. THE TOILET WAS obvious. But when she heard the water running in the kitchen sink, she worried her charge would try to sneak some caffeine. She stood in the dark, at the edge of the doorway, as she watched Muna remove her Hello Kitty pajama top. Next came the body armor Lele had not known about. But it made sense.

Muna stood at the sink, slowly washing her hands and arms up to her T-shirt sleeves—just above her elbows. Lele wasn't sure if she was hearing her talk or just the sound of the water on the stainless-steel sink. Next, she put a large shallow bowl under the water flow.

Setting the bowl on the floor, she sat in the booth and slowly washed each foot. In the quiet, Lele could hear the recited ritual. Although it wasn't in English, Lele could guess the meaning.

Having dried both feet, Muna took up the bowl and quietly poured it into the sink.

Standing to face the front of the bus, she held her hands and forearms out in front of her. The ritual continued.

As she knelt and then bent forward, Lele realized for the first time why the bus sat parked strangely in the garage. They aligned the front to face east. Mecca. Whoever parked the bus knew and respected the very private young woman.

Feeling ashamed for watching such a private ritual, Lele quietly closed the thin door, turned, and went back to bed. She pulled the covers over her head. She felt as dirty as the time she had walked in on her parents when she was only fifteen and realized what they were doing.

Muna had heard the small click. She knew what it was. She had heard it enough before. She ignored it and continued her prayers.

As she rested with her head resting on the small rug for the last time, she heard the one roll-up door open. She didn't have to hear the size ten cross-trainers squeaking on the smooth concrete of the garage floor. Just the hour was enough to identify Felix. The red and black shoes, white socks, powder blue nylon running shorts, and the recent addition of the belt, Beretta, and four extra clips for balance.

His run for the mesa location would be a seven-mile swing. Also, surveying the panoramic desert surrounding the face of the cliff. And then a heartbreaking last climb up the half-mile approach to the gate. He would walk from the gate to cool down.

She would have his coffee ready for him. His blackout-insulated thermos filled with a six-shot Americano, with just enough half-and-half to match her skin. The two teaspoons of honey took the edge off the bitter nature of the automatic coffeemaker's commercial coffee.

She tapped the timer on her new heavy dive watch. Flipped the armored vest over her head and pulled on the Hello Kitty pajama top as she opened the bus door.

Only Lele and she used the shower in the main floor bathroom. Felix would wait until he had cooled down to use the bunkhouse showers. He was Alex's alarm clock.

Nash and Mina would wait out the congestion in the kitchen, but then there was Powder to deal with.

Muna opened the door to the house and was greeted with the urgent tapping of claws on the slate floor. She backed out. "Okay. But make it snappy. I'm already…" She glanced at her stopwatch. "Forty seconds behind. And you know how Felix is about his coffee."

She found herself talking to the empty garage. But it felt right.

29

SCHOOLING CONTINUES

MUNA SAT, sneaking sips from Felix's coffee. She chuckled as she had misjudged his obvious need for a longer run.

"What's so funny?" The small Chinese woman was wearing a matching set of Hello Kitty pajamas. But the sisterhood ended there. Ming almost never braided her hair but preferred it to hang in all its glistening black glory.

Muna sipped on the black thermos and then held her finger to her pursed lips. "Nurse Ratched has me on a strict, no-caffeine diet. Not even those nasty gummies."

The eyes on the computer screen were enormous and mimicked the mouth. "How the hell do you stay awake?"

"She hasn't figured out my Beyond Scoville Pork Rinds yet. I don't think she's a snacker."

"How's the lung?"

Muna made a face. "I'm getting better, but I'm still not up to walking a mile. Just shuffling around this big place can get me a little winded. But the nurse says I should be ready for walks again in another week or four."

Ming looked up and over. Muna knew she was sitting at one of the consoles with six or eight screens. They both liked to multi-task when it came to doing research. "What did you think about the package I sent?"

"I think your new girl is coming along."

Ming laughed. "No silly. The research Bunny honked out."

Muna lowered her eyelids and growled. "I'd be happier if it had a solid address for Romanov. The world will be a better place when they till his ashes into the desert and pack it down with salt."

Ming looked to the left and keyed in some typing. She clicked the mouse a few times and looked to her right. "Any idea when you guys might wrap up the case?"

Muna sipped on the thermos. "Soon, I hope. I'm missing my San Francisco food fixes."

"Maybe you'll swing down here for a few days. I'm sure your toenails could use some paint."

Muna frowned. "Are you asking me out on a Mani-Pedi date?"

Ming snorted and looked back at Muna. She grabbed her pink sequined mug and took a long sip. "Kind of. But I also know Tree already offered to show Felix around Disneyland." She bounced her eyebrows as she smiled evilly.

Muna started at the sound of the roll-down door closing. She snuck another long sip. "Speaking of the devil."

Lele called from the back bedroom. "Muna, time to quit sneaking sips of Felix's coffee."

Breathless, the young man stepped onto the bus and swung around to the booth. "Thanks." He lifted the thermos and then shook it.

Muna rolled her eyes coyly. "Have a good long run?"

He opened the top and stared at the empty bottom with a shocked and hurt look on his face.

"Hi, Felix."

He turned to the laptop as Muna turned it. "Hey Ming. How ya hangin'?"

"Living the dream, baby. Living the dream."

He closed the thermos and gave Muna a glare. "Aren't you up early?"

The tiny Chinese tinkled musically. "Didn't you mean up late? I've been pulling an all-nighter. We have four dredges in the Missouri River. They got caught in the mud when they closed a dam. We're trying to float them in half the amount of water they usually need. I can do magic, but it doesn't work when the mud is sucking the underbelly of a two-hundred-ton barge and backhoe."

He glowered at the thermos again and then waved at Ming. "Well, gotta jet. I have drones to wrangle at oh-ten hundred." He glared at Muna and hissed. "Behave yourself."

Muna swung the laptop back to face her. "Now I need a nap." The two laughed.

"I'll bet. One of the guys kicked around your other question."

Muna scrunched her eyes in thought. "Which question?"

"Cutting without leaving marks."

Muna reached down under the table and brought up a couple of orangish red pork rinds. "Any luck?"

Ming looked up and clicked. The screen filled with a video of a large industrial machine. From the movements, Muna guessed it was computer-driven.

"What am I watching?"

"It's called a water cannon. Or water gun, or just a water jet. Maybe it's a water cutter. Anyway, when you need a precision-cut chunk of steel two inches thick, you don't use a blowtorch. This is super high-pressure water, and in the cutting head, they also inject a cutting agent. It's a micro-fine garnet. The water is the carrier, and the cut speed is determined by how much garnet to water you're using. But the more garnet, the faster the cut. But then you leave tracks. So at only twenty percent garnet, the surface left is almost polished smooth."

Muna leaned in as she watched the video.

Ming had obviously watched the video more than twice and seemed ready to sell the machine on its features and benefits.

"They use the garnet because it isn't hygroscopic or absorbs any of the water. So it stays the same size, and they easily separated it from the water and metal fines at the other end."

The video showed the polished surface of the thick steel. It reminded Muna of the body parts lying in the lab in San Francisco. "Who would use something like this, and are you selling them yet?"

Ming laughed. "It would be a large metal fabrication company. But they must be making some large stuff to justify the quarter-million-dollar machine—but for you, only two twenty-nine." She sat back as her one knee came up. She had cocked the foot in the chair. "I have a couple of clients who could put such a machine to effective use. If they haven't already."

Muna leaned back as the video disappeared. "Do I sense another division of Deep Six?"

"No, but Slug sends his regards and did your research." The new video was not as polished but was just as much an advertisement for services. The two men invited the viewer into their enormous metal fabrication shop. Passing through a wall of plastic strips, the same model machine was cutting some even thicker steel. There was a close-up of the cutting as the men talked. Finally, they lifted the piece of metal out of the larger steel plate. It was the logo of GnG. Muna reached for her mouse before she remembered the computer wasn't her wall of screens in San Francisco. "Shit."

A laughing Ming replaced the video. "You just tried to go look up the company on one of your other screens. Didn't you?"

Muna growled.

"Don't worry sister. The company is there in Pueblo. And yes, the owners also own the massage parlors and have connections to Romanov."

Muna pumped her fist in the air.

Ming held up her palm. "But... and the but is huge here... one owner is the head of the sheriff's volunteer posse. They both are enormous whales with political contributions and, therefore, connections."

Lele walked past Muna, grumbling. "Language young lady."

Ming paused as she sipped. Her voice was quiet. "Is she gone?"

Muna nodded. "Heading over to the feed bag."

Ming laughed. "Oh, my gawd… she's done gone native."

Muna rolled her eyes. "The jargon from being in the country isn't as bad as the dad jokes at the office."

Ming held her mug near her face. The black between her eyelids shifted only slightly. "But you miss it." Muna nodded sadly. "Well, here is the big headline I buried. Your FBI agent… the local guy…"

"Yeah? Matt Keeton? What about him?"

"Unique name and spelling—that double vowel." The screen fluttered, and several documents filled the area.

Muna dragged them over one by one and made them large enough to read. "Interesting. Which would explain his incompetence at research. Or what seemed like incompetence… but was just maneuvers."

Ming's head snapped toward something over her left shoulder. "Hey. Gotta run. I just dumped all this in your nasty room. Keep your head down and your weapon close." The screen blinked black and then returned to Muna's regular screen.

Muna sat thinking about what she had seen. She pulled her phone up and pushed the icon of the bear's paw.

The voice was gravel in the mud. "Thanks for letting Powder out. Let me know when the sun is up."

Muna thought about what to say and who needed to know. "Black alert."

The voice cleared. Muna could hear the blankets thrown back and a groan from Mina or Powder. "I'll be right there."

"In the bus. Armor and sidearm from now on."

"Always." The phone clinked.

She scrolled through her contacts and pushed the number.

"I hear you're up early but not allowed to go shoot."

"Where are you at, sir?"

"Just finished breakfast. Headed for my room… Or not."

"Are Felix and Alex still eating?"

"Alex. He's with the nurse. Felix headed for a shower."

Muna thought about the sleeping arrangements. "Make some kind of excuse to find Felix… and then come the back way out and around to the garage, please. Are you armed?"

"Um…"

"Just make sure Felix knows to strap up from now on."

She could hear him pounding down the large, open-log stairs. "What's going on?"

"Black alert, sir."

The man stopped and chuckled loudly. His voice took on the college sophomore doing evil in the night sort of giggle. "Oh. Sure. I'll get him. This is going to be good."

He hung up and turned to Alex. "Has Felix come back out yet?"

The man shook his head. "He was going to grab a shower and then probably call Tree. We'll be lucky to see him before lunch."

Tony chuckled. "Hopefully, I can catch him between the water and him climbing back into bed."

Alex started to rise. "What did you need?"

Tony swung around the log newel post. "Just Felix. Carry on." He sauntered down the long hallway. "Oh, lover boy…"

The young man looked out his door. The phone was up to his ear.

Tony waited until he was within arm's reach of Felix. "You need to call her back. Are you armed?"

He rotated the phone. "Hey, Tree…?"

"I heard. Stay safe." The metallic click was loud.

"Give me a second." Felix turned back into his room.

Tony cleared his throat. "Pants and shoes might be good as well. Muna called Code Black."

Felix looked up, frowning. "What's Code Black?"

Nash paused at the door. "It's the code for hurry your ass. Are the rest of the body armor still on the bus?"

He blinked at the word armor. *Shit.* "Yeah." He pulled up his pants, grabbing his socks, T-shirt, and shoes. "So are my better weapons." He twitched his head at the back door of the bunkhouse.

They kept to the walls of the hacienda as they skirted the backyard, such as it was. There was no grand patio, barbecue, or swimming pool. Just pebbly sand to the back cliff. Nowhere to hide.

At the back door, Nash slipped a thin knife out of her boot. Four seconds later, the door swung open. Tony and Nash slipped in. Nash glanced back at Felix, looking up but hiding under the overhang. He waved for them to go on.

Moments later, he joined them on the bus. "Surveillance drones. Not ours."

Nash frowned. "How many?"

He held up his fingers. "I only saw two. The way they were twitching around up there, my guess is a single controller. And probably near the bottom of the front cliff. Absolutely within a mile."

Nash pointed at the computer. "Show him."

Muna turned the laptop. The document was a juvenile arrest record.

Felix leaned in. "Hah. Just like mine, except he used dynamite instead of computers." He straightened. "How do you want to play this game?"

Muna smiled, pulled her Desert Eagle out of her blanket, and laid it on the table. "The fucker set the bomb. He doesn't get a chance with the tiny three-eighty. Mess with my family, and you face the full fifty."

Nash rested her hand on Muna's and calmed the vibration. "Let's see if he shows up for school first." She looked up at Felix. "I don't think he'll come alone. Where do you want to set up with the Barrett?"

"I'll want high ground. There's a shaded small cave about sixty feet up the back cliff. Someone dug it just for a sniper perch. The overhang would protect it from anything coming from above. I'll set up there and take a go-bag. Alex knows where it is."

Muna looked at Nash. "What do you want to do with the nurse?"

"Is there any reason she would be out here if Matt shows up?"

Muna grimaced. "Just to run all nanny over my coffee habit."

"How are you feeling?"

Muna wavered her hand in the air. "Don't ask me to run a mile, but I can shoot just fine."

Nash nodded. "Let's just hope it doesn't come to that. Let me get Alex and Lele out here. I'll deal with Mina later."

30

WELCOME

ALEX READ the text and stood. "They need us out on the bus."

"But..."

A growl edged his voice. "No buts. Now. And from here on out, just do. Your life will depend on it."

"What's going on?"

Alex grabbed her hand. "Unless you have a concealed weapon and are expert at it, then we are protecting you."

Muna sat with a large mug of coffee next to her laptop. Lele scowled. "For today, there are no patients. Only agents and it's a workday. Alex, Felix is pulling the Barrett and gear. My guess is you're best utilized joining him up the hill in the hidey-hole."

He gave her a two-finger salute. "What are we expecting?"

She looked back up from her computer. "My guess is Matt will show up. He's one of them. He set the bomb in the SUV. And... Felix spotted a couple of drones doing surveillance earlier. So maybe they'll make a frontal assault, thinking their man on the inside is still good. Or they come over the top from behind. Either way, the Barrett is the best we have. I think he's also packing up some mini-drones and some vipers. He can fill in the rest."

He saluted again and spun on his heel. As he left, Muna looked up at Ali. "How are your acting skills?"

"I take it we're going to be attacked…?"

Muna nodded at the other side of the booth. "I think it's more of a small invasion than an attack. But when Matt left here yesterday, he thought his cover was still intact. So I'm thinking he's coming back. Your job, along with Nash and Mina, is to make him think everything is still chill. I want him back here to myself."

"How do I…?"

"What would you normally be doing at, say, ten this morning?"

"With this job? Either beating you for having coffee or sitting in the kitchen reading or doing the crossword puzzle."

Muna nodded as she sipped on her mug and then tucked her hand back into the blanket. "Perfect. And when Matt shows up?"

The woman shrugged. "Tell him you're up and waiting."

"What else?" She raised the mug in a prompt.

"Oh yeah. Ask him if he wants some coffee."

Muna fluttered one eye half closed. "As long as he doesn't…?"

"Share it with you."

Muna sat back against the wall and the thick window. "By gum, I think she's got it."

Nash pulled open the bedroom door and strode out. In the kitchen area, she stopped and slowly pivoted with her hands out. "What do you think?"

The oversized sweatshirt was old and washed hard until the Chico State had all but faded and chipped off. The black leggings hit her mid-calf.

Muna giggled. As she half-covered her mouth, a tear squeezed out of her left eye. "Are those my leggings I left in here from Orange County?"

Nash looked down at her legs. "And if this isn't all over and done in the next few hours, I won't be able to feel my feet." She looked up. "Viva las spandex."

Lele coughed in her fist. "Girls' best friend for all month. But they're a lot more comfortable when they fit right."

Powder came out of the bedroom. Stopped to look up at the leggings and then continued to the booth. She crawled up and snuggled against Muna and the blanket.

Muna's eyebrows were raised. "Hmm. Looks like my sister likes the binkie more than spandex."

Nash narrowed her eyes. "She's just giving me a tough time for leaving her up at the prison for so long. But I think she made a friend."

Muna smiled. "I might get a brother?"

"This dog is retired. An ugly German shepherd and mastiff mix. He's so old he would be your uncle."

Muna shook her head with a sour curl on her upper lip. "Nope. One Uncle is enough." She waved her hand at Nash. "What about your nine? Will Alex's sweatshirt hide it?"

Nash pulled up the sweatshirt. The tactical belt hung along the lower edge of the body armor.

Lele's eyes opened wide. "I didn't even notice you had gained… what do those weigh? Twenty pounds?"

"Nah. I just ate too much dinner last night. This is one of Alex's old hard plate models, and it's only about ten pounds. Muna's soft armor is only about five pounds. The vests that blew up in the bombing were the lighter stuff like hers."

Muna nodded. "Good thing I never wait for Christmas morning. The shrapnel that hit me tore me up a bunch, but at least it stopped instead of going through me. I'll settle for the few scars and the weakened lung."

Lele grinned. "The lung gets better. Just keep using it. Before you know it, you'll be playing the piano like nothing ever happened."

"I never played the piano."

The nurse shoved out her two hands. "And there you go. My job here is done. Just ease up on the coffee for a couple of more weeks. We need to keep your blood pressure lower."

Nash glanced at her orange-faced dive watch. "Time to go to work."

The three women hanging out in the dining room could hear the SUV pull up. Nash watched out the window as the man approached the front door.

Lele erased a part on the page. "Twelve letters for qualification to protect harem?"

Mina snickered. Nash gave her a hard look. "It's her profession in Washington—emasculation."

They looked up at the knock on the open front door. Nash smirked. "Come on in, Matt. Leave the door open. We can still smell last night's dinner."

He crossed into the dining area. "What is that? Broccoli?"

Ming looked up. "My grandmother's recipe. Twice barbecued beef, broccoli stir-fry. I forgot you don't barbecue the broccoli."

Lele looked up. "Fifth letter of the Greek alphabet? Seven letters?"

His right fingers twitched. "Epsilon."

"Thanks." She buried her face back in the newspaper. "Muna's been awake for a couple of hours."

He turned toward the garage.

Nash cleared her throat. "The coffee is still hot. The mugs are in the cabinet above the maker. Cream is in the refrigerator."

He turned right into the kitchen. "Thanks. I overslept, so I only had time for a cup. And then I couldn't find my insulated flask."

He quietly fixed his coffee and quietly left the three women to their newspaper.

As the sound of the door, Nash growled softly. "Just another peaceful day in paradise."

Muna looked up at the sound of the door from the house. She changed from her research to the lesser research she was using to teach Matt with. She grabbed a game of solitaire off the taskbar at the bottom of the screen.

Matt stepped up onto the bus. The sounds from the laptop were ubiquitously recognizable. "Are you winning?"

Muna lazed an eye at him. "Sometimes. Did you bring me any coffee?"

He snorted. "The nurse was watching."

She waved her hand at the end of the kitchen counter. "Can you fetch me the painkillers? It's the larger bottle." She knew they were only vitamins. But also knew he would read the bottle.

"How many?"

"Three. I had a coughing fit a while ago. The pain isn't going away."

He held it up in front of him. "It says only one every four hours. But you aren't driving or operating heavy equipment…"

Muna wobbled her head. "Yeah, yeah, yeah. And my mother told me never to go swimming right after eating. But I'm still alive. They just make me groggy. It helps me take a nap later." She gripped her hand in the air.

He shook out the three and brought them over. "Against my better judgment." He set them on the table.

She wiped them off the table and swallowed them with a sip of water from the clear glass. "Thanks." She pointed across from her. "Take a seat."

She clicked on the two apps to call up where they had stopped the day before and to share the screen on the large remote screen. "Where were we?"

Up the cliff, Alex scanned the desert with his binoculars. "What makes you think today is the day?"

The young man took a sip from his water bottle. "Muna."

Alex lowered the binoculars and looked over.

The Homeland Security agent was smirking. "You ever play poker?"

"Not as much as I used to…"

"She's been schooling Matt on how shitty his research was. To hear her talk last night, the joker did little more than ask Alexa to…"

"Don't use that name."

Felix laughed. "Asked Siri to Google massage parlors making illegal cash. But she showed him a spreadsheet. His work was in the first column with a couple of hits in the second."

"So…?"

Felix snorted. "There are seven columns."

Alex frowned. "What's that got to do with poker?"

"You play draw or hold-em?"

Alex nodded.

"So yesterday, she showed him the top card and the river."

"Okay…"

Felix looked out across the desert and pointed at a distant truck. "This morning is the flop."

Alex squinted at the truck and now the one behind it. "Okay…?"

Felix inserted the large clip into the belly of the big rifle and struck it with the heel of his hand. The click had a metallic click of finality to it. "So he either folds or doubles down." He glances at his partner with a smile. "If he folds, we zip-tie him and throw him in the barrel until it's all over."

Alex raised the binoculars to his eyes. "And if he doubles down?"

"Muna cleaned her Desert Eagle last night. She's got four speed-loaders full of fifty caliber semi-wadcutters on her belt. She also has six clips for her nine-millimeter."

Alex lowered the binoculars a half-inch as he thought about the explosion and what it had done to her, the Japanese man, and Powder. "Yeah. She's pissed."

Felix shrugged. "It beats the heck out of thirty years of therapy." He raised the rifle and looked through the scope. "That's not a front bumper you see every day."

Alex studied the large shield on the front of the heavy truck. "How thick do you think they got away with?"

"Weight is everything when it comes to armor and a vehicle you want to still move. My guess is it is about an inch of armor plate."

"Can you get it through those view slits?"

Felix pulled back his rifle and took out the clip. "Not when it's moving. I'd need it to stop at the gate. And my guess is, it wasn't designed to stop for a gate." He pulled a fresh clip of bullets out of his large bag. The black tip of the tungsten-carbide penetrator was obvious on the large bullet. "I don't know if these will get through, but at least there's a chance." He jammed the clip in and rammed it into the seat with a loud click. He snapped the bolt and slid the round into the barrel.

Laying the long rifle back on the rest, he eased into the scope. "Let's see what we have now..."

Alex, always the spotter, started feeding him information. "The second truck doesn't have a crazy shield. My guess is it will stay below the crest. The wind is null to nothing but out of the north by northwest. The range to the gatepost is one hundred seventy-four yards. You have a sixty-eight-foot drop." He stopped as they both watched the trucks start and stop at a distance.

Felix kept in position. "What time is it?"

Alex glanced at his dive watch. "Eleven seventeen."

Felix relaxed and looked over. "They have a set time. Which would you choose, eleven-thirty, eleven forty-five, or high noon?"

Alex looked out across the desert. "I'd go with eleven forty-five."

"Because..."

Alex rolled over on his shoulder. "Element of surprise. It's not at the bottom of the hour, nor is it at the top. So if they're expecting a noon assault, it's early. And you?"

Felix sat up. He softly whistled the theme song from a classic spaghetti western.

Alex scrunched his face up. "The good or the bad?"

"No. Just classic Western. I forget who the guy was, but it was a classic black-and-white Western. And if Colorado is anything, it's the Wild West."

"So when's the assault?"

He pointed out toward the truck with the driver standing next to it. They watched as the other truck pulled up next to it.

Alex frowned. "What are they waiting for?"

Felix smiled and turned. "High noon."

31

ALMOST HIGH NOON

MUNA CLICKED on the header of the second column. "This is where you would need to start your cross-referencing with business owners, banking, and associates."

"Associates?"

Muna nodded as she sipped her water. "Guys you bowl with, golf buddies, old school chums, and other connections that aren't in your business." She twisted her head to stretch her neck. "We have a lot of connections about which we don't think. Church, dentist, doctor, recreation, sports, and bar, where we buy our food consistently. All those habits and connections can lead us to a bigger picture of who a person is."

She clicked on a cell. The business popped up in a larger dialog box as she noticed Matt checking his watch for the third time in ten minutes. "I'm sorry. Am I boring you, or do you have somewhere more important to be?"

He fumbled. "No, I'm fine. I'm just not seeing the point."

She moved the cursor down the grid and clicked on another cell. "Okay, let's make this relevant. This is a large metal fabrication company. On the second layer, we see the owners..." She clicked on the second cell, and a large list box populated. "They have their fingers in a lot of pies. Massage parlors, barbershops, and gun stores. Including the random pot shop, gambling, whores, armed terrorist camp, and my all-time favorite: white slavery."

"Who the hell…"

"Stick with me." She clicked on the next layer of cells. "Known associates. Local kids. Grew up in Cañon City. Dads were prison guards together. Went to the same schools. Moved to Pueblo together and still attended the same church. Well… to be fair, it's more of a tent revival in an actual building now. But you get the picture." She glanced over at the face, turning redder. "Moving on to their so-called gun club. They got the land in two thousand… Looks like some shenanigans by the county, taking the land from a family trust under eminent domain. They granted it to them to set up a supposed training camp for the police and sheriff's departments. But… hmm, it seems by invite only."

"What's your point?" His voice was feral.

She turned in the seat to face him. "It doesn't say anything about the FBI. Or about one of their other silent partners… Mister Keeton. Unique spelling and friends since the second grade in Cañon City primary school. Mrs. Wonacott's class. If I remember right, but then it would explain a lot about why you fumbled the research so badly. And how you forgot to mention learning how to make the bomb you loaded into the SUV and so conveniently left for us to use it."

He ground his teeth together with pure rage as he pulled his right hand above the table. The Beretta looked more like a shadow in his large hand. "You miserable little black flea."

His body bent as he tried to stand in the booth. Muscles tense, he tried to lunge across the table toward Muna. Swinging his gun backhanded, the pistol and hand struck her face.

Muna turned her head, but was too late. The end of the pistol struck her jaw as she angled her own gun under the table and pulled the trigger. The explosive boom of the large barrel shook the contents of the bus.

Alex and Felix could hear the concussion in the air, as well as their earbuds.

Alex glanced at his watch. Two minutes until high noon. The OK Corral had started early.

Nash could hear Muna being hit again as the man howled in a full rage at being shot. "I'm on my way, Muna."

As Nash burst from the table, Mina pushed at Ali. "Time for us to get back to the safe room."

Lele's eyes exploded with surprise. "There's actually a safe room?"

As they stood, Mina shrugged. "It's the well pump house. But Nash thinks it's the last place anyone would look."

Lele looked out the window. "Fuck that, get me a gun."

Mina frowned. "You shoot?"

"All the time. It's an old Browning that was my uncle's… but…"

Mina pulled the small gun out of her bathrobe pocket. "I hardly ever shoot. And when I do, it's everything but the target."

Lele pulled the clip out of the PPK as they rushed down the hall. Slapping it back in, she pulled the slide to check the load. "Good to go."

They both turned to the sound of three shots.

Mina grabbed her arm. "Hurry. It's not our fight."

Lele looked back. "But Nash just…"

Mina gritted her teeth as her face hardened. "It's Nash's fight. Not ours." She kept pulling.

Nash yanked the door open just in time to catch Matt pushing the button for the large overhead door. She threw her hand behind her back for her gun, but her sweatshirt was too loose and long and fouled her hand.

Matt turned with the Beretta in his hand. The first bullet ricocheted off Nash's armor, causing her to spin around to her right side. The second stood her up, where the third knocked her over in the middle of the large doorway.

Gripping his wound, he limped out of the building, leaving a trail of his own blood behind him. He glanced toward the front of the house where he had parked his SUV, noticing an armored truck cresting over the top of the mesa. It careened down the driveway, skidding as it curved and raced for the gate. Its dual rear tires threw gravel with every fishtail around the curve as it approached the gate. He raised his arm and started hobbling forward to meet the truck.

Muna crashed into the bus door and attempted to maneuver herself down the two steps onto the garage floor. She stumbled, landing face-first on the cement. A voice echoed in her ears from Quantico: "Get up, agent. Do the course or go home to your mommy". But she knew that the genuine tests were in the field, not during training.

She struggled to stand up, her leg slipping beneath her. Desperate, she resorted to crawling instead. Ahead of her, the man left while a body lay on the ground; she picked up speed as she headed for it. Her chin and nose collided with the hard pavement as she moved too quickly. Re-adjusting her weight, Muna continued toward the body; it was Nash.

Nash moaned, trying to form words. "He's getting away."

Muna lay down behind Nash. "Shut up and don't move." She thought about the large Desert Eagle in her holster. Instead, she pulled up Nash's sweatshirt and pulled out the nine-millimeter SIG Sauer and gripped it with both hands. Muna felt her pulse quicken as she took a slow, deep breath, focusing on the limping target through her iron sights.

Dip, and then a smooth pull. Dip and smooth pull. The dip was his limp; the pull was him dragging the leg Muna had put a slug through. Dip and smooth pull. She watched through the iron sights at the end of the pistol. She could hear every instructor's voice echoing in her head—screaming about body mass. Take the sure shot. Go for body mass. Aim for the heart!

Taking a deep breath, Muna stretched her neck to adjust her hard body armor. It was the same kind of armor that had saved

Nash's life. The same armor that left a nine-millimeter slug on the outside and a large bruise on the inside. The armor she wasn't taking a chance of him wearing as she lined up her shot.

His ears dipped below the sides of the iron sights and then were alongside. Then they dipped... All Muna could see was the small white paper target clipped to the trolley as it ran away down the firing alley. Its vertical and horizontal lines intersect at a dark brown circle of dark brown hair in the sunshine. The ears dipped, rose, and then were alongside the sights. The lines crossed at the base of the skull. Muna gently squeezed the trigger with deadly precision.

The ears froze. The target bulged into a misshapen water balloon, its skin drawn taut against the bone beneath—and then deflated out of sight.

Muna blinked twice, and the iron sights looked farther. The space between the metal slats was black. The blacked-out windows glared back without a hint of light behind them. There was no way of knowing if the glass behind was armored or just tempered. She squeezed the trigger lightly. The gun jumped as an explosive roar doubled the volume of noise from overhead. The truck slewed drunkenly to the right and jerked violently to a stop.

Muna smirked. "Good to hear you guys are working today."

Alex's voice oozed into her left ear. "It looks like both bullets penetrated."

Muna kept her gun trained on the truck as she glanced over at Nash's shoulder. "Are you still with us, chica?"

Nash groaned. "You told me not to move." She rolled over onto her back, moaning softly as she struggled to lift her arms above chest level. "What the fuck was he using? After the mule kicked me, it felt like red-hot needles under my skin."

Muna watched as Nash winced every time she tried to sit up straight again and then stopped trying entirely.

Muna rose slightly and looked at Nash's sweatshirt. Lifting the edge, she peeked into the baggy shirt. She reached in and wrestled with something and then brought it out. With a low whistle, she held up the slug. "Full metal jacket. You got lucky. I don't think the soft class four would have stopped this bad boy or his brothers."

They flinched at the sound of a rifle. The sound of a couple of fully automatic gunfire followed it. "Guys, I can't see anything. Where's the gunfire coming from?"

The deputy director's voice cut in. "I could use a little help at the edge of the cliff. Their truck is about fifty feet down the driveway from the edge. One man had snuck to the edge. His body is just west of the driveway. The other three are at their truck."

Nash, gritting her teeth and wincing in pain, extended her hand out to Muna. "Help me up."

Muna gave Nash a hard look and growled back. "Right after you help me up."

Two powerful hands reached around Muna's middle and stood her up. "How about I make myself useful around here? It's past lunchtime, and Mina's getting hangry."

Muna rolled her eyes but smiled at the comment. Looking back toward the nurse, she asked, "Did someone call for Florence Nightingale?"

Four more shots rippled through the air. Nash held her hand up. "I'd settle for Jack the Ripper about now. Where's Mina?"

The nurse pulled Nash up. "I hope she's making lunch. I'm getting hungrier by the second. And before you ask, we couldn't find a pump room."

Nash held her hand out for her pistol as she nodded her head toward the edge of the mesa. "I think we contained the invasion over there."

The deputy director's voice sounded winded or anxious in their earbuds. "Are you guys coming or not?"

Muna rolled her eyes at Nash. Pulling her Hello Kitty pajama top off, she exposed her armor and utility belt. "Weez comin' boss." She pulled her Desert Eagle out and replaced the two spent shells.

Lele lightly touched and examined the side of Muna's face. The red scrape mark was already swelling.

Muna jerked her head. "Later." The muffling of the words told Nash and Lele everything they needed to know about the woman behind the broken jaw.

At the cliff, Muna carefully edged her way to the right of the cliff, praying she was beyond where the bad guys and their truck were. She got down on all fours and crawled to the edge before rolling onto her side, bringing her arms with the large pistol over the edge of the cliff. Muna didn't try for finesse; she could see the dark sweat down the middle of the man's back.

The man was only thirty feet away, standing rigidly with a gun in his hand. Muna offered the man an out. "If you want to live, drop the gun now."

Before she could blink, he spun around and fired in her direction with no hesitation. Dirt flew from the edge of the cliff ten feet to Muna's left. In an instant, she retaliated by taking him out with one round that pierced through his body and then his truck door.

Without skipping a beat, she aimed at another man who had been nearby and repeated her offer of escape. "Same offer."

The man hesitated and then spun, searching for the shooter. The soft slug flattened his shattered jaw against the spine as it took the man's head from his shoulders.

Muna heard the soft pop of a sandwich bag off to the distant cliff wall. The voice coughed in her ear. "Sorry, Muna. The jerk was sneaking around the back of the truck."

She watched as the two hands rose from the bed of the truck. "No problem, deputy director, I've got the last one corralled. Nash, can you mosey on down and hogtie this guy in the truck's bed?"

Nash snorted. "You betchem, Red Ryder."

Alex groaned as he watched from their vantage point. "Oh great. Bad TV from the ancient age."

Nash chuckled. "Hey, Red Rider was on television before it was on the ShowMe app."

Muna coughed muted, her words becoming more mumbled. "The last century had some interesting technology and magnificent shows. Now, can we wrap up here? My face is starting to hurt."

They could all hear the huffing and puffing from the lower cliff. "Hey guys?"

"Yeah, Tony."

"I know I'm kind of new to all this field stuff... but if the sheriff's department is corrupt..."

Nash pulled the zip-tie snug. "I think I might know a guy who wants answers."

32

WHAT THE HEY

THE TALL BLOND giant looked down at the six bodies. It was one body more than his former record of seeing five body parts to make a single body. He sucked at his tongue as he swallowed his spit. Closing his eyes, he rolled them and turned. "Well, at least these bodies have all their parts connected. But I still don't think I have any authority here."

Nash turned. "Let's talk out here where it's warmer."

The large butcher shop was known for processing wild game, at least according to the sign out front. Of all their services, freeze-drying whole carcasses had been the most popular one. This shop was the only facility within a thousand miles that offered such a service. An old employee even mentioned that some of these carcasses didn't always come with four legs. In what had been the front lobby, they took seats.

The man looked like an adult having tea with his daughter and sitting on a tiny seat for children. "You have my sympathy here, but there are local..."

Nash cut him off as she drew her flat hand across her throat. "Look, Connie, we've—"

He cut her off. "It's Kani. Half the length of your Connie. Americans don't hear the difference, but I do. Please, my American name is Thumper. Neh-noose?" Nash could hear his years of speaking the Ute language.

She hung her head and thought. "I rarely heard my Paiute language spoken at home when I was growing up. I speak enough Spanish to maybe eat, get into trouble, and, on a good day, find the bathroom. My Japanese is better but rusty. My Mandarin is what my wife tells me is good enough. But never to speak anything but English when we're around her parents, and I haven't spoken any of the three dialects of Urdu or Pashto in years. So, I'm not going to try to match you tribal for tribal. I'm just going to figure you said something like asking to be called Thumper, and I'll leave it at that."

He bobbed his head slowly. "My wife is the chief. Her mother is his wife, and she's also on the council. But on the way up here, we were both scratching our heads, wondering how we get roped back into the body parts on the monument, and this here?"

Nash stretched her neck as she pulled down on the neckline of the body armor. "The body parts all belonged to men trying to find a relative. Specifically, a young girl. One was only sixteen." She held up her index finger. "Remember that fact. It plays an important part here."

"Okay, underaged... White or tribal? Because all I saw of the body parts, they were white."

Nash shifted. "One was Japanese. We'll get back to him. But yes, the girl was white and Muskogee. And a member of the tribe."

He smiled. "Okay... tribal. But the uncle or whoever was white?"

Nash shoved her chin up. "Yeah. Not enough Muskogee to get in, but her favorite uncle. Or at least, she was his favorite niece. Enough to come looking for her."

"Uff-dah." He crossed his legs and turned on the chair. "So, body, or parts, found on the reservation but split into multiple states, which is why I called you. But you come out, and umm...

clean up the mess. But you need me to do what? And how do I get jurisdiction in the middle of white man's land? And I do mean white. Pueblo is more than half Latino, but the sheriff..."

Nash looked over at the little black girl with shiny new braces. Muna smiled. Thumper couldn't tell if the braces were braces or some heavy-duty grillwork.

Muna lifted her computer pad. "According to Duro versus Reina, in nineteen ninety-nine. The jurisdiction of trial and punishment of an offender may rest outside the tribal territory, but the tribal officers can exercise their power to detain the offender and then transport him to the proper authorities."

She glanced up. "The United States versus Cooley affirmed this with its accord in twenty-nineteen. They cited that the federally endowed power to exclude persons from the reservation gives tribal law-enforcement officers the power to deliver non-Indians who have committed crimes to state or federal authorities." She coughed softly into her hand and looked up. "Basically, the federal government delegated the power to enforce federal law directly to you, the tribal police. Instead of forcing them to wait for federal authorities to respond." She looked up. "So, simply put, you can detain a criminal and bring them to the proper authorities. And combining with us, the FBI, we supersede any other local law enforcement. Especially once we are showing to be corrupt."

Nash held out her hand as if to say, *there you go*.

Thumper gave a low whistle and looked at his father-in-law. "Don't ever let her near my wife."

Cooter raised his hand. "Nor mine."

Thumper turned back to Nash. "So, how can we help?"

Nash held up her index finger as she pulled the vibrating phone out of her pocket. She snorted softly at the caller's image. "Where the hell have you two been? The party was over four days ago." She punched the speaker.

The voice was tinny, but it sounded good. "I think you know

where I've been, but the quarterback was lazing around in the Hopi sun. We're just coming into Pueblo. You still here?"

"Muna is texting you the address. Don't bring her any nuclear pork rinds. She's on a strict religious diet for a month or more."

Thomas boomed across like he was calling a football play. "We picked up a couple of cases of rinds called Beyond Scoville. Just dump it on the side of the road?"

Muna laughed and, with what sounded like clenched teeth, yelled. "You'd get arrested for toxic dumping, and then I'd take your manhood card away. Bring them. We need to restock the bus."

Thomas laughed. "What's wrong with you? You sound funny."

Nash rolled her eyes. "She broke her jaw. Just get here. We'll tell you about the party over dinner." She thumbed the call closed and looked at Thumper. "Some days, it's like herding cats."

Muna snorted wetly. "With those boys, it's more like most days."

He wobbled his finger at Cooter and him. "And us?"

"Right now, we have about forty-seven businesses to shut down. The first business we're going to do now. It's a massage parlor. We've identified several young girls, including the one who isn't eighteen yet." She glanced at Muna.

Muna nodded. "We have fifty agents from the FBI to the Bureau of Indian Affairs, to ATF, DEA, and Homeland flying in this afternoon and evening. Tomorrow, we will hopefully have everything for you to be up to speed, and we can turn it all over with you at the top of the Incident Command System."

The man rolled his eyes at his partner. "Uff-dah. I knew I should have packed another pair of underwear."

THE BUS SAT PARKED ON THE EDGE OF A REMOTE RV camp. The sight looked south, across a vista of eastern Colorado's rough terrain. Stubby brush dotted the tumbling rolls and folds of the jumbled landscape. The two chairs were at the backend of the bus. Felix had pumped the manager's hand with a hundred-dollar bill folded in his hand as they shook. Not exactly fibbing, but explained how his uncle was old and wanted to sit and look toward the land he grew up on one last time before moving on.

Alex had blown it into a dramatic scene, with a hang-dog face and a quivering lower lip, over dinner. The sunset was spectacular as the collective soaked in the relevance of them all being alive. Battered and beaten but alive.

Uncle paused the mug at his lips. "How are the ribs?" His eyes took in the orange and reds washing the sky. The arid air allowed the micro dust of the storm hundreds of miles to the south to hang for days in the air. The sunrises and sunsets would be brilliant medicine.

Nash reached out and touched his arm. "The sage and squaw tea salve help. Thank you for having Tracy send it." She sipped on her coffee as her bare foot rubbed the furry belly. The rewarding soft moan brought a soft chuckle from both humans. "You still haven't told me how you could come into my dreams."

"I couldn't. But I knew the man who could. And with luck, he could take me along." Uncle looked over and squinted. "You're still thinking your dreams are only in your head. But... they aren't. It is more of you traveling to the dream universe. It's a lot like what science fiction is based on. The multiple universes."

Nash rolled her mug between her two palms. "It's a scary jump for a person to make when everything I've done is here, and I can touch it."

"When you were sitting on the edge of Bone Creek, could you feel your feet in the water? Or the prickle of the dry grass?"

Her head shook in a soft vibration. "Not at first. But the grass was green. Wherever mother stood, the grass under her feet was green and vibrant."

"Her connection to the earth was powerful. Only your father was more powerful. If you could call it that."

Nash glanced over. "But I don't remember him being known for seeing things."

Uncle's head vibrated briefly as his lower lip pooched out. "He didn't. He just knew things." Peeking over, his smile slid onto his right cheek. "We were hunting one year on the backside of Shasta, over near Top Hat. Across a small valley, I could see a deer. As I raised my rifle to collect the meat we needed, he put his hand on the barrel as he told me she was still pregnant. It was late, and she should have fouled long before then, but as she turned, I could see the enormous belly." He sipped on his coffee. "On our way home, he took a detour. A truck had hit an elk and her fawn. They were both still warm. I made you a pair of moccasins the next year out of the fawn's hide."

"I always remembered my father making those moccasins."

Uncle snorted softly. "If he had, they would have come with stuffing in them." He shook his head softly. "He didn't know how to scrap and tan the hide white. When he tried, it would turn yellow or become dark brown. Then it would crack and break. Better to wear bib overalls than a belt that breaks."

Nash rocked at the wisdom of the words. "I took some pens from a teacher's desk and drew the diamonds on the toes." She glanced over. "But I don't think I knew it was the symbol for a shaman."

Uncle patted her hand resting on the arm of the chair. "It isn't. But it also wasn't Paiute. It's Ute, for a wise man. Or wise person. The black line on the outside is what the world sees. But the red diamond is the spirit world the wise person can see and walk in."

Nash chuckled lightly. "But I liked the pattern, so I drew a few inside... I think."

He nodded a single confirming nod. "You showed me. I was the black outside line, but the green was your mother, and the blue was your father. Do you remember the other diamond and the dot?"

She squinted. "A red diamond? But I don't remember the dot..."

He closed his eyes and thought. "The small red diamond was

you. But you promised you would grow as big as my black diamond." He waved his hand at her. "And here you are."

"And there was a dot in the center?"

"It was your sister. You said it was your new sister. But you explained she wasn't a diamond. Even then, you knew who the shaman was and who was not." His eyes narrowed as he peered over. "Do you remember when your sister was born?"

Nash thought, and then her eyes flew open. "The next summer." She looked over in horror at Uncle.

Uncle nodded. "Your mother wasn't even pregnant then. But you knew."

33

HARD EARNED

THE DAMP, cool air felt good. Muna knew the musky smell of a swamp resulted from the cavernous building housing almost seven hundred thousand gallons of water. The two major waterfalls aerated the water. The extremely high humidity gave the impression of dining on a pleasant evening somewhere in the Caribbean. And the ride was fun.

"Compliments of the chef, miss." The server set down the large fountain malt glass filled to the brim. "Orange sherbet, protein shake, with a deadly dose of cayenne pepper."

Muna's smile gleamed in the LED candlelight. "Thank you."

Ming glanced up at an approaching man in a white chef's jacket. The man was slurping on his own shake. "I think you made a convert."

Felix and Tree turned in their seats.

"Good evening. I must admit, it was an unusual order, but it was intriguing. But then, my one guilty indulgence is hot jerk pork rinds." He sucked on the straw. "I'm Chef Ramon. And I couldn't stay in the back and not meet the inventor of such a splendid dinner. And now that I see your smile, I understand."

Muna stuck her hand out. "Muna al-Faragi. And these are my friends, Ming, Tree, and Felix."

"Pleased to meet you all. I understand having to drink all your meals through a straw, but the request for a specific Scoville rating…?"

Muna snorted sloppily as she dabbed at the escaping drool. "Your hot jerk rinds are only a start for me. Recently, I found my new love. It's called Beyond Scoville. Just look for the atomic explosion on the bag. The first one goes in like a puffed cheese reeking of Cajun hot sauce, but then the lips go numb, the throat closes, and your eyes burn like you pulled an all-nighter. Then it gets hot."

He pointed with his shake glass. "But with a broken jaw…"

"It was worth a shot. After all, what else have you got? Run a salad through a blender?"

"I've whipped up instant pudding packed with protein powder before."

Muna flexed her lips together as she vibrated her head. "Nope. If it's chocolate, the chocolate takes the heat out of the pepper."

He lowered one eyelid. "We're talking instant pudding here. I think the only chocolate in the stuff is the name."

Muna sucked on the straw. Her eyes closed as she leaned back in the electric wheelchair in bliss. "Perfect."

The man beamed. "Happy to be of service. Would it be offensive if I ask…?"

Muna smiled. "Dad is Lebanese, and mom is a mix of Sudan and Ethiopian. But I'm all Pittsburg and San Francisco."

He laughed as he pointed at his mouth.

Muna giggled. "Oh, the grill." She shrugged. "Broken. I was pistol-whipped."

His face snapped in horror. "Please tell me you're joking."

Felix shook his head. "Nope. The FBI never jokes about such things. It was the only way she could get a vacation here in Disneyland."

The chef frowned. "You're…"

"Nope. In fact, right after the shootout, I remember her distinctly saying, I'm going to Disneyland. Right after a brief trip back to the hospital."

"Back to the hospital?"

Tree rolled her eyes and grabbed Felix's hand. "You'll need to pull up a chair. He left out the bomb blowing her up, the collapsed lung, and her saving almost a hundred girls being held as sex slaves."

He reached over for the empty chair at a nearby table.

"HEY NASH?"

She jammed the shovel into the pile of compost and turned. "Yeah, Connie?"

The man stood with his arms akimbo at his hips. "Can I trust Uncle with the brisket?"

Nash looked over at her sweating wife leaning on another shovel. Nash laughed. "Why not? You're trusting us two to shovel this shit into your garden. How do you know we won't just kill your plants? After all, our condo is on the fifth floor. The only houseplant we have is a painting of a single yellow rose in a juice glass."

"But he's pulling out the cayenne pepper..."

Nash hung her head. "How hot do you eat your chicken paprikas?"

"So you sweat. Why?"

"Just tell him you have a delicate tummy and hide the paprika. Or better yet, take the pepper away and show him how to use the paprika."

The man was in horror. "On a brisket?"

Nash turned back to the large mound of compost and the shovel. Pulling the shovel out, she glanced back. "Just think of it as dry rub barbecue or something. Do I look like a cook?" She shoveled a load of compost into the wheelbarrow.

Pausing, she leaned over as she removed her glove. Running her hand into the compost, she held up a handful and massaged it with her fingers. Holding it to her nose, she breathed deeply. "This is good stuff." She looked sheepishly at Mina. "Don't worry. I'm not going to turn into a farmer."

Mina sighed as she leaned on the shovel. "No. I was just thinking about the painting. You're right. Maybe we need some houseplants."

Nash snorted. "They'd be dead in a week."

Mina ducked her lower lip. "Plastic ones?"

Nash growled as she turned for more compost. "Talk to Chester."

NASH SET THE WHEELBARROW DOWN AND FISHED THE phone out of her pocket. The number was an international number she didn't recognize, but the call was FaceTime. She thumbed the green icon.

The man was sitting in a sidewalk café. She knew of only one glass pyramid in the world. "Bonjour?"

Nash frowned at the head of sandy red curls. "Hello?"

The man smiled. "You're prettier than I was told. My name is Rusty."

Nash's smile slowly grew. "Is Niko there?"

Niko backed his wheelchair into view. "Certainly. You and Muna send me an address in Paris and arrange for lunch. Did you think I would turn down this chance to come play a bit of Go with an old friend?" The screen dipped enough to show the board game. "And after this, we are going to go watch an international computer gaming match."

Nash chuckled. "I wonder if some friends of mine are playing. I think their team name is Deep Six."

Rusty laughed. "Not this time, but I've played against them. Slug is a worthy adversary."

Niko put his hands together with a small bow. "We just wanted to call and tell you how thankful we are to you two for finding Rusty." He raised his shortened leg. "We now have even more in common."

"Enjoy the games. And keep me posted."

"Until next time."

EVEN WITH THE SUMMER HEAT, THE WARM WATER FELT good on her feet. The brown grass was still prickly but didn't penetrate her leather pants. The sun felt good on her shoulders and face.

Daisy's voice stumbled slightly on the uncomfortable topic. "Your wife seems... nice."

Nash scraped her teeth on her upper lip as she drew it out. Thinking about what she could say to her sister that she had known all her life and yet never known. "She actually is—down deep." She looked over. "I think she was just as afraid of you as you were of her."

"Why would she be afraid of me?"

Nash smirked and closed her eyes as she turned her face back to the sun. "Why would you be afraid of her? You don't even know her."

Daisy flipped her right foot up and out of the water, tossing a few drops out into the creek. "I've never met a... well, not really..."

Nash chuffed. "What? A Chinese person?" She turned her head with a frown. "I know for a fact you teach the two children down in Taylor. The kids of the owners of the Lucky Fortune restaurant."

"No... not that..."

Nash's face lit up in shock. "What? A lesbian? Oh, please tell me you did not mean to say lesbian."

Daisy's face froze as her hand shot out in a stop motion. "No…" Her face suddenly flushed deep red as her eyes slowly closed. Her hand dropped.

Nash laughed. "Oh, my goodness. You just now realized I was one of *them*? All these years and seven years being married to another woman… and it just now dawned on you who I am? What I am?" Nash lightly rested her hand on her sister's shoulder. "Was it easier for you to just think we were roommates? Just friends?"

Her sister shook her hands in the air as if something dirty had touched her. "It's not like that."

Nash scooted over until their hips touched, and she put her arm around the vibrating shoulders. "Yes. Yes, it is like that… But it's okay. It's why I'm here. It's why we are taking. We grew up together in the same house…" Nash reached out and turned the delicate chin to face her. "But we never talked or knew anything about the other sister. As an adult, I kind of gathered you were religious, but I didn't know when you started going to church. I didn't follow our Paiute heritage or ways, and any kind of church was beyond me."

Daisy squinted at her. "Your church was sports. And books. I carried my bible to classes; you carried all of your textbooks everywhere with you. I remember the belt you bound them up with. I snuck your stack once and weighed it. It was twenty-seven pounds. I remember thinking how I could barely pick it all up and marveled at you carrying it over your shoulder every day, all day."

Nash rolled her eyes into her raised eyebrows. "Only twenty-seven? It must have been my sophomore year. I took more extra credit classes in the last two years. They probably added a dozen or more pounds."

"But you got a scholarship for sports…"

Nash nodded. "It helped. ROTC also helped. There were also a few small scholarships from the Bureau of Indian Affairs, the Rotary, and even one from the Masonic Lodge. Some of the hardest research, once I got down to Sacramento, was finding more money. It's why I took so many classes and graduated in three years. There was no more money left for a fourth year. Even the railroad didn't offer a scholarship for any girls, but especially for ones of color." She squinted as she realized how hard it was for her, but probably worse for her less academic sister. "What about you?"

Daisy chewed on her lower lip as she studied her sister's face and then looked across the creek. "I worked as a nanny for a young couple while I was at the junior college. Once I had my associate degree, I got the job with a provisional teaching license at the church school. They just never made me go get a bachelor's or anything."

Nash nodded her head. "They don't ask, so you don't offer."

"It would cost a lot of money to get a real teaching credential. I don't have that kind of money. Besides, I need to work. It would take me four or five years to just become a student teacher... and I'd have to live in Sacramento or somewhere else..." Her face took on a wistful appearance. Nash wasn't sure if it was from want or fear of the unknown.

"There are always courses online..."

Daisy's head snapped around. "I don't use computers. There is evil..." Her voice drifted off.

Nash started to point out an email and then realized her sister only had a phone. The avocado green one plugged into the wall and sitting on the counter in the kitchen—the same phone and number they had grown up with. Her sister had no cell phone, no computers, nothing that might be the workings of something evil. "Maybe things are just best the way they are."

ALSO BY BAER CHARLTON

The Very Littlest Dragon: NEW Editions
(All-new full-color ebook, a paperback with
coloring pages, and a full-color Collector's Edition hardback)

Stoneheart — Pulitzer Nominee 2015
Angel Flights
What About Marsha?
Pirate's Patch
Flat Surf

I Drink Coffee and Make Shit Up
One Writer's Journey Without Signposts

JOLIE "ROCKET" ROBERTS SERIES
Dry Bridge of Vengeance – Book One
Dry Ridge of Redemption – Book Two

THORNY WALLACE SERIES
Death in the Valley – Book One
Light to Light – Book Two

SOUTHSIDE HOOKER SERIES
Death on a Dime – Book One
Night Vision – Book Two
Unbidden Garden – Book Three
Boomtown – Book Four
One Day Under the Grass – Book Five
Southside Hooker Series: Books 1–5 Box Set
(Collector's Edition hardback & ebook available)

BAER CHARLTON

ABOUT THE AUTHOR

Bestselling author Baer Charlton graduated from UC Irvine with a degree in Social Anthropology, monkeyed around for a while, and then proceeded onward with a life of global travel, multi-disciplinary adventure, and meeting the memorable array of characters he would come to describe in his writing. He has ridden things with gears, engines, and sails, and made things with wood, leather, and metal. He has been stitched back together more times than the average hockey team; his long-suffering wife and an assortment of cats and dogs have nursed him back to health after each surgery.

Baer knows a lot about many things in this world. History flows through his veins and pours out of him at the slightest provocation. Do not ask him what you may think is a simple question unless you have the time to hear a fascinating story.

You can find more at
www.mordantmedia.com

www.ingramcontent.com/pod-product-compliance
Lightning Source LLC
Chambersburg PA
CBHW010553170726
48285CB00011B/2888